the Summer Proposal

VI KEELAND

The Summer Proposal
Edited by: Jessica Royer Ocken
Proofreading by: Elaine York, www.allusionpublishing.com, Julia Griffis
Cover Model: Michael Yerger
Photographer: Rodolfo Martinez
Cover designer: Sommer Stein, Perfect Pear Creative

the Summer Proposal

In every girl's life, there's a boy she'll never forget and a summer where it all began.

—One—

Georgia

"What can I get you?" The bartender set a napkin down in front of me.

"Ummm... I'm meeting someone, so maybe I should wait."

He rapped his knuckles against the bar. "Good enough. I'll keep my eye out and stop back over when I see someone join you."

But as he started to walk away, I reconsidered. "Actually!" I raised my hand like I was in school.

He turned around with a smile and arched a brow. "Change your mind?"

I nodded. "I'm about to meet a blind date, so I wanted to be polite, but I think I could use something to take the edge off."

"Probably a good idea. What are you drinking?"

"A pinot grigio would be great. Thank you."

He came back a few minutes later with a hefty pour and leaned his elbow on the bar. "So, blind date, huh?"

I sipped my wine and let out a sigh as I nodded. "I let my mom's seventy-four-year-old friend Frannie set me up with her grandnephew to make my mom happy. She described him as 'a smidge ordinary, but nice'. We're supposed to meet here at five thirty. I'm a few minutes early."

"First time letting someone fix you up?"

"Second, actually. The first was seven years ago. It took me this long to recover from it, if that tells you anything."

The bartender laughed. "That bad?"

"I was told he was a comedian. So I figured, how terrible could it be going out with someone who makes people laugh for a living? The guy showed up *with a puppet*. Apparently his comedy act was as a ventriloquist. He refused to speak to me directly—wanted me to talk only to his dummy. Who, by the way, was named Dirty Dave, and every other comment out of its mouth was obscene. Oh, and my date's mouth moved the entire time, so he wasn't even a very good ventriloquist."

"Damn." The bartender chuckled. "Not sure I'd give another blind date a chance after that, even after a few years."

I sighed. "I'm sort of regretting it already."

"Well, if anyone comes in with a puppet, I got you covered." He gestured toward a hallway behind him. "I know where all the emergency exits are, and I can sneak you out."

I smiled. "Thanks."

A couple sat down on the other end of the bar, so the bartender went to help them while I continued to stare at the entrance. I'd purposely taken a seat in the back corner so I could watch the front door, hoping to get a look at my date before he saw me. Not that I planned to ditch if he wasn't handsome, but I didn't want him to read disappointment on my face if I felt any. I'd always been terrible at masking my feelings.

A few minutes later, the restaurant's door opened and a drop-dead gorgeous guy walked in. He looked like he belonged on a men's cologne ad, probably emerging from crystal blue Caribbean water. I got excited, until I realized he couldn't be my date.

Frannie had described Adam as a computer nerd. And pretty much any question I'd asked her about him, she'd answered, "About average."

How tall is he? About average.

Is he handsome? About average.

Body type? About average.

This guy was tall, with broad shoulders, big, blue bedroom eyes, a chiseled jawline, dark hair that was sort of messy, but totally worked for him, and even though he was wearing a simple dress shirt and slacks, I could tell he was buff underneath. Frannie would have to be crazy to think anything about him was average.

Oh.

Oh!

Well, she was a little...different. Last time I went to Florida to see Mom, we went to lunch with Frannie, and she'd glowed orange from an excessive amount of self-tanner she'd bought on the Home Shopping Network. She also spent all afternoon telling us about her recent road trip to New Mexico to attend a UFO convention in Roswell.

But even with that factored in, this guy didn't look like a computer nerd. Nevertheless, his eyes scanned the room, and when they met mine, he smiled.

Dimples.

Deep ones.

Oh, Lord. My heart did a little pitter-patter.

Could I be this lucky?

Apparently it was possible. Because the guy headed right toward me. I probably should've played it cool and looked away, but it was impossible not to stare.

"Adam?"

He shrugged. "Sure."

I thought that was a bit of an odd response, but his smile widened, and those cavernous dimples seemed to turn my brain to mush.

"Nice to meet you. I'm Frannie. My mom is friends with Georgia." I shook my head. "Sorry. I mean, *I'm* Georgia. My mom is friends with Frannie."

"Nice to meet you, Georgia."

He extended his hand, and when I placed mine in it, mine felt really...small.

"I have to say, you are definitely not what I was expecting. Frannie didn't describe you very accurately."

"Better or worse?"

Was he joking? "She may have described you as a nerd."

He sat down on the stool next to me. "I usually don't admit this when I first meet a woman, but I do have a *Star Wars* action figure collection." He reached into his pocket and pulled something out. "In fact, I almost always have one on me. I'm a bit superstitious, and they bring me luck."

Adam unfolded his big hand to reveal a tiny Yoda. He leaned over and set it on the bar in front of me, and a hint of cologne wafted through the air. *Smells as good as he looks*. There had to be something majorly wrong with him.

"Women tend to not like *Star Wars* for some reason," he said. "Or a grown man carrying around an action figure."

"I actually like *Star Wars*."

He put his hand over his heart. "A beautiful woman who likes *Star Wars*? Should we skip the formalities and just grab a flight to Vegas to get married?"

I laughed. "Maybe, but first promise me you aren't into ventriloquism."

He crossed his heart. "*Star Wars* is as bad as it gets."

The bartender came over to take Adam's drink order. I was surprised when he asked for a Diet Coke.

"You're not going to join me for a cocktail or a glass of wine?"

He shook his head. "Wish I could, but I have to work later."

"Tonight?"

He nodded. "Yeah. I wish I didn't. But I actually need to get out of here in a little while."

I'd thought we were meeting for drinks *and* dinner, but perhaps Frannie had gotten that wrong.

"Oh, okay." I forced a smile.

Apparently Adam saw right through it.

"I swear I'm not making that up. I do have to work. But I definitely would love to stay. Since I can't, is it too early to say I'd love to see you again?"

I sipped my wine. "Hmmm… I'm not sure about that. Normally, I get to know someone on a first date, so I can weed out the serial killers and nutjobs. How am I supposed to know you're not the next Ted Bundy if you're running out of here?"

Adam stroked the scruff on his chin and looked at his watch. "I have about fifteen minutes. Why don't we cut the small talk and you can ask me anything?"

"Anything?"

He shrugged. "I'm an open book. Take your best shot."

I gulped my wine and turned in my seat to face him. "Alright. But I want to watch your face as I grill you. I'm terrible at hiding lies on mine but great at reading others."

He smiled and turned, giving me his full attention. "Go for it."

"Okay. Do you live with your mother?"

"No, ma'am. She doesn't even live in the same state. But I do call home every Sunday."

"Have you ever been arrested?"

"Public indecency in college. I was pledging a fraternity, and me and a bunch of other guys had to walk through the center of town naked. A group of girls stopped us and asked if any of us could hula hoop. Everyone else kept walking. I figured they were all too chicken, so I stopped. Apparently, the guys weren't afraid; I was just the only one who didn't see the cop coming out of a store a couple of doors down."

I laughed. "Can you actually hula hoop?"

He winked. "Only naked. You wanna see?"

The smile on my face widened. "I'll take your word for it."

"Shame."

"When was the last time you had sex?"

For the first time, the smile on his face wilted. "Two weeks ago. Are you gonna hold that against me?"

I shook my head. "Not necessarily. I appreciate the honesty. You could have lied and said a while ago."

"Okay, good. What else you got?"

"Have you ever been in a relationship?"

"Twice. Once in college for a year, and then I dated a woman for eighteen months, and that ended two years ago."

"Why did they end?"

"College, because I was twenty and...it was a crazy time in my life. And the woman I dated a few years back, because she wanted to get married and start a family, and I wasn't ready."

I tapped my pointer to my bottom lip. "Hmm... Yet you just asked me to go to Vegas and marry you."

He grinned. "She didn't like *Star Wars.*"

We were both too busy laughing to notice a guy walk up to us. I figured he must have known Adam, so I politely smiled and looked to him. But the guy spoke to me.

"I'm sorry to interrupt, but are you Georgia Delaney?"

"Yes?"

He smiled. "I'm Adam Foster. Frannie showed me a picture of you, but it was from a costume party." He motioned to the side of his head, twirling his hand around in a circle. "You were dressed as Princess Leia, with your hair all pinned up on the sides, so you looked a little different than you do now."

I furrowed my brow. "You're...Adam?"

The guy seemed just as confused as I was. "Yes."

Now *this man* looked like what I'd been expecting: worn, brown tweed jacket, cropped hair parted to one side—sort of the average Joe that worked in the IT department at your office. But...

If he was Adam, then who was this?

I looked at the guy sitting next to me for an answer. Though that's not what I got.

"Did you really dress as Princess Leia for a Halloween party?"

"Yes, but..."

Adam, or whoever the hell the guy sitting next to me was, put his finger over my lips and turned to the man who was apparently my date. "Can you just give us a minute?" he asked.

"Umm...sure."

As soon as average Adam walked away, I laid into hot Adam. "Who the hell are you?"

"Sorry. My name is Max."

"Do you make a habit of pretending to be someone else?"

He shook his head. "I just...I saw you sitting at the bar through the window when I was passing by, and you had such a pretty smile. I came over to introduce myself, and it was clear you were here to meet someone else. I guess I sort of panicked that you weren't going to talk to me since I wasn't Adam. So I went with it."

"And what if my date hadn't showed up? Would you have pretended to be Adam on a second date?"

Max dragged a hand through his hair. "I didn't think that far ahead."

Normally catching a date in a lie would make me angry, but finding out Max wasn't Adam was more disappointing than anything. We'd had great chemistry, and I couldn't remember the last time I'd laughed so much meeting someone new.

"Was every answer a lie? Do you even like *Star Wars*?"

He held up both hands. "I swear. The only thing that wasn't the truth was my name."

I sighed. "Well, *Max*, thanks for the entertainment. But I don't want to keep my *real date* waiting."

He frowned, but nodded and stood. "It was nice meeting you. I guess asking for your number would be stupid right about now?"

I gave him a look. "Yes, it would. Have a good night, Max."

He looked at me for a few seconds, then slipped a bill out of his wallet and tossed a hundred on the counter. "You, too, Georgia. I really enjoyed meeting you."

Max took a few steps away, but then stopped and walked back. He again took out his billfold, only this time he peeled off what looked like a ticket of some sort and placed it on the bar in front of me. "I'd really love to see you again. If your real date turns out to be a dud or you change your mind, I promise I will never tell you another lie." He pointed to the ticket. "I'll be at the hockey game over at the Garden at seven thirty, if you would consider giving me another shot."

What he said seemed heartfelt, but I was here to meet another man. Not to mention, I was really disappointed. I shook my head. "I don't think so."

With a sullen face, Max nodded one last time before walking away. I didn't have time to process everything, but I felt a strange sense of loss when I watched him walk out the door. Though as soon as he disappeared from sight, my real date was next to me.

I had to force a smile. "Sorry about that. We, um, just had some business to wrap up."

"No problem." He smiled. "I'm just glad that guy wasn't hitting on you, and I didn't have to defend your honor. He was a tank." Real Adam sat down. "Can I order you another wine?"

"That would be great. Thank you."

"So...I take it you're a big *Star Wars* fan?"

"Hmm? Oh, because of the costume."

Adam pointed to the bar. "And the little Yoda."

I looked down. Max had left his Yoda figurine behind. I guess he hadn't been lying about being a *Star Wars* fan, considering he carried an action figure in his pocket. At least I hoped it wasn't just a prop he used when he told strangers tall tales at bars and lied about his name.

• • •

Real Adam talked about artificial intelligence—*a lot.*

I tried to get my head back in the game after the Max letdown, but I knew before my actual date and I had finished a drink at the bar that this would be our only date. Adam was a nice-enough guy; there was just no connection, physical or mental. I wasn't into computers or Bitcoin, which seemed to be a big thing for him, and he wasn't into any of my hobbies, such as hiking, traveling, and watching old black-and-white movies. He didn't even enjoy going to the movies. Who doesn't love bingeing on popcorn and a gallon of soda while watching a big screen? Not to mention, when I told him about my work, he said he was allergic to flowers.

So when the waitress came by with a dessert menu, I politely declined.

"Are you sure you wouldn't like a coffee or something?" Adam asked.

I shook my head. "I have to work in the morning. Having caffeine after noon keeps me up all night. But thank you."

He nodded, though I could tell he was disappointed.

Outside the restaurant, he offered to share a cab, but I only lived eight blocks away. So I extended my hand to set the tone for the end of the evening.

"It was very nice to meet you, Adam."

"You, too. Maybe we can...do this again sometime?"

It was so much easier to be upfront and tell a guy there wouldn't be a second date when he was a jerk. But I always struggled with the nice ones. I shrugged. "Yeah, maybe. Take care, Adam."

It was late April, but the cold weather just wouldn't relent and allow spring to start this year, and a gust of wind blew while I waited at the intersection at the corner of the restaurant. I shoved my hands into my pockets for some warmth, and inside, something pointy pricked at my fingers. I slipped it out to see what it was.

Yoda.

His plastic ears were tapered to points, and there was a tiny chip on the left one. I'd forgotten I'd stuck him in my pocket when Adam and I had moved from the bar to a table. Looking down at him, I sighed. *God, why couldn't your owner have been my actual date tonight?*

It had been a very long time since a man gave me the warm fuzzies in the pit of my belly—not since the day I'd met Gabriel. So maybe finding Yoda in my pocket was a sign? The light changed, and I walked a few more blocks, lost in thought.

Did it really matter that he'd pretended to be Adam? I mean, if he was telling the truth, he only did it so I'd talk to him. Let's face it, if he had walked over and introduced himself as Max, I wouldn't have invited him to sit down. I would have been polite and told him I was waiting for my date, no matter how gorgeous the man was. So, I couldn't really say I blamed him…I guess.

I stopped for another red light at the crosswalk on 29th Street, this time at the corner of 7th as I made my way down to 2nd Avenue where I lived. While I waited, I looked to my right, and the neon lights of a sign hit me. *Madison Square Garden.* Now that was definitely a sign—quite literally. Between Yoda and walking right past the place Fake Adam had said he'd be…perhaps it was more than that.

I checked the time on my phone. Twenty after eight. He'd said he would be there at seven thirty, but I was sure the game took a few hours. *Should I?*

I nibbled on my lip as the light in front of me turned green. People on both sides of me started to walk…but I just stood there, staring down at Yoda.

Screw it.

Why not?

What do I have to lose?

The worst that could happen was that our initial connection fizzled or it turned out lying was one of Fake Adam's hobbies. Or...the spark we'd had might lead to just the distraction I was looking for. I wouldn't know unless I tried.

For the most part, I was pretty conservative with my choices in men. And look where that had gotten me. I was a twenty-eight-year-old workaholic, going on blind dates with my mom's friend's relatives. So screw it—I was going.

Once I made the decision, I couldn't wait to get there. I practically jogged to Madison Square Garden, even in my heels from work. Inside, I showed my ticket to an usher standing at the entrance to the section listed, and he showed me to my seat.

As I walked down the stadium stairs, I looked around and noticed I was pretty overdressed. Most of the people had on jerseys and jeans. There were even a few shirtless guys with their bodies painted, and here I was wearing a cream silk blouse, red pencil skirt, and my favorite Valentino pumps. At least Max had been pretty dressed up.

I hadn't noticed the row number on the ticket before handing it over to the usher, but the seats must've been decent because we just kept walking down toward the ice. When we hit the very first row, the usher extended his hand. "Here you go. Seat two is the second one in."

"Wow, first row, directly in the middle on the fifty-yard line."

The guy smiled. "In hockey we call it center ice."

"Oh...okay." But the seat next to the one he'd shown me to was empty, and Max was nowhere in sight. "Did you happen to see the person sitting in the seat at the end?" I asked.

The usher shrugged. "I'm not positive, but I don't think they've arrived yet. Enjoy the game, miss."

After he walked away, I stood looking down at the two empty seats. This was one outcome I hadn't thought about: I might get stood up. Actually, would it even be considered standing someone up if the other person didn't know you were coming? I wasn't sure. But I was here, so I might as well take a seat and see if Max showed. He'd said he had to work, so perhaps he was running late. Or maybe he was already here, just in the men's room or in line for a beer.

A woman sat on the other side of me. She smiled as I settled in. "Hi. Are you here to watch Yearwood? He's on fire tonight, already slashed two in the net. Too bad they're probably not going to be able to hold onto him for next season."

I shook my head. "Oh. No, I'm actually meeting someone. I've never been to a live hockey game before." Just as I said it, two guys slammed into the glass wall directly in front of me. I jumped, and the woman next to me laughed as they skated away.

"That happens a lot. You'll get used to it." She reached out her hand. "I'm Jenna, by the way. I'm married to Tomasso." She pointed to the rink. "Number twelve."

"Oh, wow. I guess I'm sitting next to the right person for my first game." I put my hand to my chest. "I'm Georgia."

"Anything you want explained, Georgia, you just let me know."

For the next twenty minutes, I tried to watch the game. But I kept looking around to see if Max was coming down the stairs. Unfortunately, he never did. By nine o'clock, it was pretty clear I'd wasted my time. Since I had early meetings tomorrow morning, I decided to call it a night. The game clock showed less than a minute until the end of the second period, so I figured I'd wait until then so I wouldn't be blocking people's views as I climbed the stairs back up to the exit. These hockey fans seemed pretty into the game.

When the clock hit nine seconds, one of the guys scored a goal, and the place went crazy again. Everyone jumped up, so I did the same, only I used it as an opportunity to slip on my jacket. I leaned to the woman next to me and yelled. "I don't think my date's coming, so I'm going to head out. Have a good night."

But as I turned to leave, something caught my attention on the Jumbotron. The player who'd scored held his stick up in the air celebrating, and a bunch of the guys on his team were whacking him on the head. His helmet covered most of his face, but those eyes... *I know those eyes*. The player took out his mouth guard, waved it in the air, and smiled right at the camera.

Dimples.

Big ones.

My eyes went wide.

No...it couldn't be.

I continued to stare at the screen with my mouth hanging open until the guy's face was no longer on it.

The woman next to me finished cheering. "See? I told you he was on fire. If this is your first game, you've picked a good one to watch. You don't see a lot of hat tricks in a single period. Yearwood is having his best season ever. Too bad the rest of his team isn't."

"Yearwood? That's the name of the guy who just scored?"

Jenna laughed at my question. "Yup. Team captain and arguably the best player in the NHL these days. They call him *Pretty Boy* for obvious reasons."

"What's his first name?"

"Max. I figured you knew him, since those are his seats you're sitting in."

• • •

"Hey, *Pretty Boy*. Are you looking for someone?"

Max walked out of the locker room. He'd looked right and then left, but hadn't noticed me sitting on the bench across from the entrance.

He smiled when his eyes landed on me, and his entire face lit up as he walked over. He'd known I was at the game. Right before the second period intermission, he'd skated over to where I was seated and banged on the glass. But he hadn't known the woman sitting next to me had given me her all-access pass so I could come downstairs to the locker room and see him after the game.

"You waited..."

I reached into my pocket and pulled out Yoda, holding it up in my palm. "I had to give this back. You said you were superstitious."

He took it from my hand and slipped it back into my jacket pocket. Then he laced his fingers with mine. "I am. I just had the best game of my career. So guess where Yoda needs to be for every game from now on?"

"Where?"

"In my girl's coat pocket while she sits in my seat."

"Oh, I'm your girl now, am I?"

He swung our joined hands. "Maybe not yet. But the night is young."

"Ummm... It's almost eleven, and I have to work in the morning."

Max stared into my eyes. My insides did a somersault. He raised our joined hands to his lips and kissed the top of mine.

"I'm glad you came," he said. "I wasn't sure if you would."

"Really?" I tilted my head. "Because for some reason, I get the feeling you usually get what you want."

"Is that a bad thing? Maybe it's because I'm not a man easily deterred. I don't mind working for something."

"Tell me, did you have to work hard for the woman you slept with a few weeks ago?"

Max chuckled and shook his head. "You're a handful, aren't you?"

"What if I said I wouldn't sleep with you just because you say sweet things?"

He raised a brow. "Not ever?"

I laughed. "You know what I mean."

"That's fine. I'm not in a rush. Will you at least have a drink with me?"

I smiled. "*One*. Because I do have to get up early tomorrow."

"Deal. I'll take whatever I can get." He put an arm around my shoulder and started us walking. "Though I should warn you. It doesn't matter what exit I walk out of, there are usually a few people hanging around for autographs. It feels wrong to just walk by, so it might take a while to get clear of here."

I liked that he was the type of person to stop for his fans. "Okay."

The minute we exited, people started screaming his name, and there were more than just *a few* of them. Security flanked us on both sides while he scribbled his name over and over. A few asked for selfies, and he leaned over and hammed it up for the camera. Those dimples definitely saw a lot of mileage. Some people professed their undying love, while others asked questions about the game tonight. Max took it all in stride, answering in good spirits. It took almost a half hour for the line to dwindle down. When we got to the last few people, a kid who was probably about eighteen lifted his chin to me as Max scribbled his name.

"Is she your girlfriend? She's hot."

Max stopped mid scrawl and leveled the kid with a warning glare. "Hey, watch it. Have some respect for women. Especially this one. She might be the future Mrs. Yearwood." His eyes flashed to meet mine. "She just doesn't know it yet."

—Two—

Georgia

"So what does my good luck charm do for a living? Wait, let me guess..."

As he spoke, Max reached across the table and wiped the corner of my lip with his thumb. He showed it to me—sugar from the rim of my lemon drop martini—before sucking it off with a devilish smile that caused a tingle between my legs.

I sipped more of my drink to cool off before answering. "This should be interesting. I'm curious to see what it is you think I do."

His eyes dropped down to my outfit. It was now almost one o'clock in the morning. We'd walked across the street from the Garden to the nearest bar and taken the most private booth in the back corner, but I was still dressed in my work clothes, having gone straight from the office to meet my blind date, and then the game.

"Classy, yet sexy," he said. Max leaned to the side and looked down at my feet. "Those hot-as-shit heels don't look like they'd be too comfortable to stand in all day, so

I'm going to guess you work in an office of some kind. You were able to get out pretty early to meet your date, so you're probably the boss and make your own hours. You also dumped your blind date to come meet a guy for a hockey game—a sport you said you know nothing about—without knowing I was a player. So you're either in a profession that takes risks, or one that requires you to be an optimist."

I made a face that said I was impressed. "Go on..."

He rubbed the scruff on his chin, which had definitely gotten darker in the few hours we'd been apart. "I'm gonna say lawyer or advertising exec."

I shook my head. "And here I thought you were doing so well."

"Was I close?"

"Sort of. I do sit for the majority of the day lately. I also make my own hours, and I suppose starting my own company was risky. I own Eternity Roses."

"Eternity Roses? Why does that sound so familiar?"

"Oddly enough, even though I've never been to a hockey game, I have advertised at Madison Square Garden. My company sells roses that last a year or more. Maybe you've seen one of our billboards."

"The ones that have a guy sleeping with his head in the doghouse?"

I smiled. "That's the one. My friend Maggie does all the marketing. She got the idea because her soon-to-be ex-husband was always in the doghouse and coming home with flowers."

"I've sent your flowers to my sister-in-law. Last time I was at her house, my brother and I were goofing around and we broke a chair. She wouldn't let me pay for it, so I sent one of those big, round, hatbox-looking arrangements. Your website is funny, too, right? I remember it had a page with suggested notes for when you were in the doghouse. I used one for the card I sent with the flowers."

I nodded. "I used to pick all of those myself when I first started. It was one of the things I enjoyed doing most. But we update so often now, I don't have the time anymore."

"That's pretty cool. But I gotta say...those things were expensive as shit. I think the big one I sent was something like six-hundred bucks."

"Does your sister-in-law love them?"

"She does."

"Well, regular roses only last about a week. If you buy four-dozen roses, the amount that comes in that large hatbox you sent, you'd have to spend a minimum of two-hundred-and-fifty dollars. In a year, that's thirteen-thousand dollars for weekly roses. So six hundred is actually a bargain."

Max grinned. "Why do I have a feeling you've said that a few hundred times before?"

I laughed. "I definitely have."

"How did you get into that line of work?"

"I always knew I wanted to own my own business. I just didn't know what kind. During college and grad school, I worked at a florist. One of my favorite customers was Mr. Benson, an eighty-year-old man. He came in every single Monday to buy his wife flowers during the first year I worked there. He'd been giving her fresh roses every week for their entire fifty-year marriage. Most of that time, he'd grown the flowers himself in a small greenhouse in their yard. But after his wife had a stroke, they'd moved to a retirement home because she needed more help than he could handle alone. After that, he started buying her weekly flowers at the store. One day he came in and mentioned he was going to have to cut back and only bring her flowers once a month because the co-payments on his wife's new medicines were so expensive. He said it would be the first time in more than half a century that she didn't have fresh roses on her bedside. So I started researching how I could extend the life of cut flowers, hoping I could find a way for Mr. Benson's wife's roses to last longer between his trips to the florist. I wound up learning a lot about the preservation process, and things just sort of took off from there. Eventually I opened an online store and started selling arrangements out of my house. It was a slow start until a celebrity with twelve-million followers on Instagram placed an order and posted about how much she loved them. Things snowballed from there. Within a month, I'd moved production from my living room and kitchen to a small shop, and now, a few years later, we have three production facilities and eight boutique showrooms. We've also just started to franchise the brand in Europe."

"Damn." Max lifted his brows. "You did that all by yourself?"

I nodded proudly. "I did. Well, with my best friend, Maggie. She helped me get it off the ground. Now she owns a piece of the company, too. I couldn't have done it without her."

He looked over his shoulder and glanced around the room. "Beauty and brains? There's got to be a line of guys around here somewhere that want to kick my ass for getting to sit with you right now."

He'd meant it as a compliment and to be funny, yet my smile wilted for the first time. The reality of why I was out on a date tonight hit me smack in the face. I'd gotten caught up in the excitement of the evening and hadn't stopped to think that I'd have to tell Max about Gabriel. Frannie had filled my blind date in on my situation, so I hadn't needed to consider how or when I would bring it up there. But I suppose the how or when with Max had just presented itself to me on a silver platter, so there was no time like the present.

I smiled pensively. "Well...to be completely honest, I am sort of seeing someone."

Max dropped his head and lifted one hand to cover his heart. "And here I thought the arrow through my heart was Cupid's. You've wounded me, Georgia."

I laughed at his dramatics. "Sorry. It feels odd to bring it up, but I thought I should be upfront about my situation."

He sighed. "Lay it on me. What's the deal with this other dude whose heart I'm going to break?"

"Well, I...uh..." Damn, this wasn't easy to explain. "I guess you could say I'm in an open relationship."

Max's brows rose. "You guess?"

"Sorry...no." I nodded. "I am. I'm in an open relationship."

"Why does it sound like there's more to it than just you're dating someone without a commitment?"

I chewed on my bottom lip. "We were actually engaged."

"But you're not now?"

I shook my head. "It's kind of a complicated story, but I feel like I should share it."

"Okay..."

"Gabriel and I met when I was working on my MBA. He was an undergrad English professor at NYU, and I went to Stern Business School there. At the time, he had just begun working on a novel. Gabriel taught to pay the bills, but he wanted to be a writer. Eventually he sold his book to a publisher, along with a deal for a second one he'd write someday, and we got engaged. Everything was going well until about a year ago when his book was published. It didn't do well. In fact, it pretty much flopped—low sales and terrible reviews. Gabriel got pretty down about it. Not long after, he found out that the parents he'd thought were his biological parents were actually his adoptive parents. Then his best friend since childhood died in a car accident." I sighed. "Anyway…long story short, Gabriel felt really lost and decided to take a visiting-professor position in England for sixteen months. He never even discussed it with me before accepting the job. He said he needed to find himself. With everything he'd been through, I understood. But then a few days before he left, I got another surprise: He told me he wanted to have an open relationship while he was gone."

"And everything between the two of you was fine before that?"

"I had thought so. I work a lot—more than I need to or really should—and sometimes Gabriel thought it was too much and complained. That was probably our biggest issue. But we weren't a couple who fought all the time, if that's what you're asking."

Max rubbed his bottom lip with his thumb. "How long's he been gone?"

"Eight months."

"Have you seen each other during that time?"

"Just once. About six weeks ago. My company opened a franchise boutique in Paris. I went for the grand opening, and he met me there for the weekend."

"And you've both been seeing other people since he left?"

I shook my head. "Apparently he has been, but I haven't been too much." I bit my lip again. "Adam was actually only my second date in many years. The first was a guy I met on Tinder two weeks ago, which lasted for coffee only. To be honest, I didn't even want to go out tonight. But I'm trying really hard to make some much-needed changes in my life, now that I'm on my own. So I made a list of things I'd been putting off, and since dating was at the top of that list, I sort of forced myself to show up."

Max's eyes jumped back and forth between mine. "Did you have to force yourself to come to the Garden?"

"No, just the opposite. I was trying to force myself *not* to come."

"Why would you do that?"

I shrugged. "I'm not sure."

He stared at me some more. "When are you seeing him again?"

"We don't have any more plans to reconnect in person until after he's finished in London and moves back to New York. So I guess December, when he gets back."

"Are you just looking to get even with this guy because he's dating? Or are you really looking to see what else is out there for yourself?"

That was a damn good question, and one I didn't really know the answer to. My relationship with Gabriel was a gray area, and I was a black-or-white type person. Lord knows, I'd spent enough time agonizing over decisions about that man, only to wind up now questioning every decision I'd ever made.

I looked Max in the eye. "I'll be honest; I'm not sure what I want." I cocked my head to the side. "Does it matter to you?"

A slow grin spread across his face. "Just want to know what I'm getting myself into." He reached across the table and took my hand, weaving our fingers together. He looked up with a sparkle in his eyes. "But I'm in."

I laughed. "You're a hard sell."

"I can't help it. I want to know everything about you."

I squinted. "Why?"

"I have no damn idea. I just do."

"What do you want to know?"

"Everything. Anything."

"Like what?"

He shrugged. "You said you sometimes work more than you need to. Why do you keep working if you don't need to?"

I smiled sadly. "That's a question I've given a lot of thought, since it was a source of contention in my relationship. I think I work a lot because I've always had to. I'm dyslexic, so ever since elementary school, I've had to put in extra time. A reading assignment that might take my friends twenty minutes could take me an hour or two, so I'm sort of trained to expect to do more. I also have a tendency to overanalyze everything to death, which can be time consuming, and I'm super competitive—at times obnoxiously so. But I love my business, and I enjoy watching it grow from what I put into it. That said, I actually did hire a director of operations four months ago, so I can work less if I want to. My mom is getting older and lives down in Florida, and I want to be able to go visit her more often. And I love to travel. I also thought it would make Gabriel happy, but you already know how that's worked out."

"Nothing wrong with working a lot if you love what you do. You probably wouldn't be where you are if you didn't put in the time. I definitely wouldn't."

"Thanks."

"And being competitive is good. It pushes you to do better."

I shook my head. "My friends won't even play board games with me anymore, and I'm banned from the Easter egg hunt in my mom's retirement community because of..." I raised my hands and made air quotes. "...an *incident* with a super-sensitive nine-year-old I accidentally made cry."

Max grinned. "That bad, huh?"

I rubbed my finger over the condensation on the bottom of my glass. "I'm working on finding the right balance. I even went to a four-day meditation retreat a few months ago to learn how to relax."

"How did that go?"

My lip twitched. "I left a day early."

Max chuckled. "What about family? Lot of siblings?"

"No, I'm an only child. My parents had me late in life. They married at thirty and agreed to not have children beforehand. My dad had a vasectomy shortly after their wedding. Then at forty-two, my mom got pregnant. Turns out, a vasectomy isn't a hundred-percent foolproof. They cut the man's vas deferens, but in rare cases the pieces can grow back and reconnect. It's called recanalization."

"Holy shit." Max shifted in his seat.

I laughed. "Did you just squeeze your legs together?"

"Damn right I did. Mention cutting anything down there and my body jumps into protective mode. How did your parents take that news in their forties?"

"My mom said it was a shock, but when she went to her first appointment and heard the heartbeat, she knew it was meant to be. My dad, on the other hand, wasn't as elated. He had a terrible childhood and had his own reasons for not wanting a family. So he went off and had an affair with a woman who had her tubes tied, and my parents wound up getting divorced when I was two. I'm not very close with my father."

"I'm sorry."

I smiled. "Thank you. But there's nothing to be sorry about, even though it may sound like it when I tell the abbreviated version. My mom is super mom, so I never felt like I missed much. She retired to Florida two years ago. And I did see my dad growing up. What about you? Big family?"

"I'm the youngest of six. All boys." He shook his head. "My poor mom. We broke every piece of furniture at least once horsing around over the years."

"Ah...like your sister-in-law's chair?"

"Exactly."

"Earlier, when I asked if you lived with your mother, you said you didn't even live in the same state. So are you not from New York?"

"Nope. Originally from Washington state, but I haven't lived there in a long time—left home when I was sixteen to live with a host family to play hockey in Minnesota. Then moved to the East Coast to play for Boston University, and then on to New York to play for the Wolverines."

"What's that like? Being a professional athlete, I mean."

Max shrugged. "I get to play a game I love for a living. It's pretty much a dream. People call Disney the greatest place on earth. I'll take the locker room after a win any day of the week."

"What's the downside? Even the best jobs have one."

"Well, losing definitely sucks. My team has done a lot of it the last two years. When I was first drafted, they were a team on the rise. We made the playoffs my rookie year, but between player injuries and bad trades, the last few have been tough. It's called a *team* because you need more than a few guys to be having a good year. Other than that, the travel can be a lot. A season is eighty-two games, and that's without playoffs. Almost half are on the road. I think I see the team dentist more than I do the inside of my own apartment."

"Wow, yeah. That's a lot of travel."

Max had ordered a rum and Coke and a water. I'd figured he needed to hydrate after the game. But I noticed he hadn't touched the alcohol yet, and we'd been sitting long enough for his ice to melt. Pointing to the smaller glass, I said, "You haven't touched your drink."

"I don't drink alcohol when I have practice or a game the next day."

My brows furrowed. "So why did you order a rum and Coke?"

"I didn't want you to not order a drink because I wasn't."

I smiled. "That's thoughtful. Thank you."

"So tell me about your date tonight. Was he a total dud, or did he just pale in comparison to the first guy you met?" He winked.

"Real Adam was very nice."

"Nice?" Max's cocky grin widened. "So it sucked, huh?"

There was a napkin on the table in front of me. I crumpled it up and threw it at him. He caught it.

"I think it's time for your turn in the hot seat," I said. "Tell me about the woman you slept with recently. Is she someone you've been seeing?"

"It was just a hookup. For both of us."

"Uh-huh." I sipped my drink. "Let's talk about that. Do those happen often? I mean, you're a professional athlete and a good-looking guy—not to mention you spend a lot of time on the road."

Max contemplated me. "I told you that if you gave me a second chance, I wouldn't lie to you again. But I'd also rather not paint a picture of something you won't like. So I'm just going to say I don't have a hard time finding someone to spend time with, if I want to. But just because it's easy, and I've lived a full single life, doesn't mean that's how it has to be. I'm sure you could walk into just about any bar in this city and leave with a guy, if you wanted to. Doesn't mean you'll do it if you're in a relationship, right?"

"No, I guess not." I shrugged. "But there must be something wrong with you. Tell me your worst qualities, Max."

"Damn." He blew out a deep breath. "You're really looking for a reason not to marry me, aren't you?"

"If everything you're saying is sincere, you're too good to be true. Can you blame me for waiting for the other shoe to drop?"

He rubbed his thumb over his bottom lip, then sat up and planted his elbows on the table. "Okay. I'll give you some dirt. But afterward, I want to hear more of your dirt."

I laughed. "Okay. It's a deal."

"Shake on it." He extended his hand, and when I put mine in his, he closed his fingers and didn't let go. "Awww... you want to hold my hand."

I shook my head. "Out with it, Pretty Boy. What's wrong with you?"

Max's face grew serious. "I can be obsessive and somewhat compulsive. What normal people might call *drive* turns into overdrive for me. I can lose focus on everything else in my life, including my own health and all the people around me, when I want something bad enough."

"Okay...well, I guess that makes sense, considering your career. I've never met a professional athlete before, but I have to imagine having a fervent drive is part of what helped you get where you are."

"I also have an addictive personality. Hockey is my drug of choice. But it's why I don't drink much, and I keep away from drugs and gambling. In college, I ran up a debt of twenty grand to a bookie. My oldest brother had to bail my ass out, but not before he flew to Boston and kicked it."

"Oh goodness. How big is your brother?"

Max laughed. "I'm one of the smaller Yearwood boys."

"Wow."

"So...did I scare you away yet? So far you've had me admit I had a hookup recently, got arrested while naked hula hooping, have an addictive personality, and sometimes forget the world exists when I'm focused on hockey. What's next? Me telling you I have an irrational fear of lizards and that I once peed my pants when I was nine because my brothers brought home six chameleons and hid them in my bed?"

"Oh my God. Is that true?"

Max hung his head. "Yeah. But in my defense, you shouldn't show a four-year-old *Godzilla*. It can leave scars."

The thought of this enormous man being afraid of a tiny lizard was absolutely hilarious. But he'd won me over with the open way he'd answered my questions. He still had my hand locked in his, so I squeezed and decided honesty was a two-way street.

"You were right. I was fishing for a reason to not see you again."

"And did you find one?"

I shook my head. "Flaws don't scare me. You not knowing you have them or refusing to admit they exist would."

"So does that mean we're heading to Vegas?"

"Not quite." I laughed. "Is it my turn now? To tell you my worst qualities, I mean? Because I'm not sure I stressed how annoying my competitiveness can be when I mentioned it earlier. Like, I threw that napkin at you, and you caught it, and it's killing me that you didn't throw it back so I could catch it, too. And now I also want to tell you all my other bad qualities so mine can be worse than yours. But I'm thinking maybe I should finish my drink before I continue with my laundry list, in case you make a run for it."

Max shook his head. "Nah. You don't need to tell me anything. I already know your worst quality."

"You do, huh? I'm almost afraid to ask. What is it?"

Max's eyes met mine. The intensity in them was undeniable, and it set off a fluttering low in my belly.

"Your worst quality? Easy. I believe you said his name was Gabriel."

—Three—

Georgia

"So how was your blind date?" Maggie held out a Starbucks coffee cup and a bottle of Motrin.

There was a reason she was my best friend *and* head of marketing at Eternity Roses. "Are those both for me?"

She nodded. "I know you're trying to cut back to one coffee a day. But I'm hoping you need it this morning because your date kept you up all night."

"What are the Motrin for?"

Maggie smiled and brought her own coffee to her lips. "In case your head was banging against the headboard. I told you to get rid of that fancy wooden bedframe and get a cushioned one."

I laughed and waved off the bottle. "I'm good. No banging headboard last night. Though I will take the coffee. Thank you."

She twisted the cap off the Motrin and shook the bottle upside down. "Oh good. Because there are only two left, and my head's killing me. There's definitely no cushion on those stalls in the courthouse bathrooms."

I stopped with my coffee halfway to my mouth. "You didn't..."

She grinned. "Oh, but I did...*twice*."

I chuckled. Maggie might've lost a little of her mind. For almost a year now, she'd been embroiled in a messy divorce. A few months ago, her soon-to-be ex-husband, Aaron, didn't show up for a settlement conference at his lawyer's office. Rather than reschedule, she decided to make good use of the time by seducing his attorney. Since then, she'd made it a sport to have sex with the guy in every inappropriate place possible. I was pretty sure he could be disbarred if anyone found out.

"Was Aaron at the courthouse?" I asked.

Her eyes sparkled. "Sure was."

"What if he'd walked into the men's room?"

"Then he could have watched—same as I got to do when I walked in on him and our neighbor." She plopped down in the guest chair on the other side of my desk and sipped her coffee. "So your date was a dud, huh? I warned you that letting Frannie fix you up was not the best idea. Did he bore you to death over drinks?"

"Actually...drinks were the most exciting part of my date."

"Oh? Delicious cocktails?"

I shook my head and grinned. "Nope. Delicious man who pretended to be my date before my real date showed up."

Maggie's eyes widened.

I laughed because it was nearly impossible to shock her these days.

"Tell me everything," she said.

Over the next twenty minutes, I filled her in on meeting Max, almost walking out of the arena before finding him on the Jumbotron, and staying out until 2 AM talking. When I was done, she took out her cell.

"What's his last name?"

"Yearwood, why?"

"Because I want to Google him and see exactly what we're talking about here."

She typed into her phone, and her eyes lit up. "Holy crap. He's gorgeous."

"I know."

"When are we going out with him again?"

I chuckled at her use of *we*. "I gave him my number, but I actually don't think I'm going to go out with him."

"Are you crazy? Why not?"

I shook my head. "I don't know. It just feels...wrong."

"Because of Gabriel? Who ran away to Europe to screw other women?"

"How am I supposed to get involved with someone when Gabriel is coming back at the end of the year?"

"You're living apart, and he's dating other women. If he comes back and you two want to be together, it was meant to be. Anything that changes your mind before then just proves you weren't supposed to stay together. Take it from me, it's easier to figure it out now than after you get married. For whatever reason, Gabriel needed this time, and he's clearly taking it. So why shouldn't you?" She shook her head. "What changed? You seemed okay with it before you went out on the blind date."

I shrugged. "I guess it seemed safe and simple. The way Frannie described the guy, I sort of knew in my heart nothing would come of it."

"And now?"

"Max seems..." I shook my head and tried to figure out what bothered me so much. I couldn't put my finger on it.

"I guess he just seems the opposite of safe and simple. Max seems risky and complicated."

Maggie smiled. "Because you actually like him."

"Maybe." I shrugged. "I don't know why the thought of going out with him makes me so nervous. I think I just don't trust my own judgment anymore."

"Perhaps it seemed easier when you knew you wouldn't fall for the guy. You'd said you were going to put yourself out there, but you weren't really planning on it. You were just going through the motions and biding time until Gabriel comes home."

She leaned forward and rested her hands on my desk. "But honey, what if Gabriel doesn't come home? Or what if he does, but he doesn't want to pick up where you left off? I'm not trying to be mean. Really, I'm not. I like Gabriel, or at least I did until he pulled the crap he pulled before he left. But why should you waste more than a year of your life, when he's not?"

I sighed. "I guess. But the other thing is, it's not fair to the other person. I don't know if I can give Max the same thing a truly single person could, you know?"

"You said you told him the deal between you and Gabriel? What was his response?"

"He asked if I was looking to get even or looking to see what else was out there."

"And what did you say?"

"I was honest and said I wasn't sure."

"He was okay with that?"

I nodded. "He said he just wanted to know what he was in for."

"You want to know what I would do?"

I tilted my head. "Probably not. You're a little off your rocker these days."

"True. But I'm going to tell you anyway. I think you should fuck his brains out—have an affair, or whatever you want to call it."

I couldn't say the idea of getting hot and sweaty with Max Yearwood didn't appeal to me. In fact, the thought of it made my belly do a little dip. I was exhausted today because I hadn't been able to fall asleep when I got home last night. Lust had coursed through my veins just imagining those big, blue eyes looking down at me. I bet his thighs were muscular from all that skating, too. He was just so big and broad—nothing like Gabriel, who had a lean, runner's body. Again, I imagined what Max might look like naked. But I forced that thought from my mind with a few blinks.

When my eyes came into focus again, I found Maggie with the dirtiest grin.

"You were just imagining it, weren't you?"

"No." I answered *waaay* too fast.

She smirked. "Sure you weren't. You know what I'm going to do?"

"What?"

"I'm going to get one of those little electronic scoreboards and hang it right over there." She pointed to the wall opposite my desk. "Maybe if I tally how many times Gabriel bones someone and make it a competition, I'll get the home team off the sidelines and back into the action. You'll never be able to handle losing."

While she was right that I liked to win, I wasn't sure racking up numbers would make me feel like I was winning anything with Gabriel.

Luckily, our conversation was cut short before Maggie could delve deeper. My admin, Ellie, knocked on my office door and opened it.

"Mark Atkins has arrived for your ten o'clock meeting. He said he came early because he has a lot of prototypes to set up, so I put him in the conference room and told him I'd check on him in a bit."

"Okay, great. Thank you, Ellie."

I'd been working on a new product line with the vendor who made my vases. I thought it would be cool if people could keep their roses for a year *and* have them change colors. So we designed a vase with a removable bottom panel. Different interchangeable bottoms could be purchased that contained dye wells designed to infuse the stems of the roses with new color. After a few months with white roses, you could unscrew the bottom panel, insert a pink dye well, and twenty-four hours later, *voilà*: pink roses. It could be done a few times if you went from light colors to dark.

Maggie rubbed her hands together. "Today is turning out to be awesome already. You're going to bang a hot hockey player, and we're going to see your idea come to life."

"I didn't say I was going to see Max again."

She winked and got up. "You didn't have to. I'm going to go check if Mark needs help. You finish up your fantasy, and I'll come get you when he's ready."

• • •

I'd missed two calls during the meeting today. The first was from Gabriel, who had left a voicemail. The second was Max, who hadn't. I found myself a tad disappointed that it wasn't the other way around. Nevertheless, I waited until I got home that night to press play and listen to Gabriel's message.

"Hey, babe. Just checking in. I spoke to my publisher today, and he liked the early stuff I sent him on the book I've started working on. Of course, he liked the first one enough to buy two books and the first one flopped, so him liking it doesn't actually mean much. But it's better than him not liking it, I suppose. Anyway, we haven't talked in a while, and I miss you. I'm sure you're probably working late, busy kicking ass and taking names, but give me a call when you have time. Love you."

I frowned and unzipped the back of my skirt, tossing it on the bed. After my trip to Paris, where I'd found out Gabriel had actually started dating and had slept with other women, I'd stopped being the one to initiate contact. Seems I didn't feel like making *all* the effort anymore. So my every-other or every-third-day phone calls with Gabriel had dwindled to once a week or less. I wasn't even sure if Gabriel had noticed the change. But so much bothered me about his message today. First, "*I'm sure you're probably working late...*" It must be nice to assume that and not imagine I'm in bed with someone else. Because that's certainly what had run through my head when I thought about him lately. And second, it irked me that he was calling to tell me good news about his publisher. We'd gotten engaged when he sold his book and separated when it flopped. It made me feel like the way I was treated depended on external circumstances. Is that how it would always be? The health of our relationship relying on his career successes and failures? How had I only realized this in hindsight?

Whatever. It was eight o'clock here, which meant it was one in the morning there, so I wasn't going to call him back anyway. Plus, my phone was almost dead, so I plugged it into the charger on my bedroom nightstand and went to take a shower.

An hour and a half later, I climbed into bed and checked my phone. I'd missed another call from Max. As I nibbled on my lip and debated if I should call back, my phone buzzed with an incoming text. Normally, I had Siri read me my texts and send responses to save time because of the disconnect between my brain and letters, but when I glanced over and saw Max's name, I started to read.

Max: Are you avoiding me or busy?

I smiled and texted back.

Georgia: I had a busy day.

Max: Busy now?

Georgia: No, I just climbed into bed.

A few seconds later, my phone rang.

"I really wanted to FaceTime to see what you wear to bed," Max said. "But I figured I'd be a gentleman."

I chuckled. "I appreciate that. Because I took a shower and didn't feel like drying my hair, so I have a braid and no makeup on."

"Braid, huh? Sorta like Princess Leia..."

I laughed. "Are you actually a *Star Wars* fan, or do you just have a Princess Leia fetish?"

"I wouldn't say fetish. But what little boy wasn't hot for the princess? She was a badass."

I reached over to my nightstand and grabbed Yoda. "You know, I still have your action figure. I forgot that you put it back in my pocket when I tried to return him."

"Make sure you take care of my lucky charm."

I rolled Yoda between my fingers. "How did this little guy become your lucky charm, anyway? Is it because of your fondness for Princess Leia?"

"Nope. It all started with a girl named Amy Chase."

"A girl, huh? Why doesn't that surprise me?"

"Don't get jealous. She hates me."

I laughed. "I'll bite. What's the story with Amy and Yoda?"

"Amy was in ninth grade when I was in seventh. She was friends with my brother Ethan, who worked at the movie theater around the corner. He used to sneak people in to watch movies for free. One weekend they were running a *Star Wars* marathon. I think there were six movies back then, so it was something like twelve or fourteen hours long. I went with Amy and a few of Ethan's other friends, but everyone dropped out after two or three movies. Only Amy and I stayed for the whole thing." He paused. "Not to be disrespectful, but she had a great rack for a ninth grader. Anyway, we were sitting in the last row of the balcony during *The Phantom Menace*—which is the worst one, by the way—and we started to get a little bored, so we were talking, mostly about school and stuff. Then out of nowhere, Amy asked me if I'd ever touched a boob. I said no and asked her if she'd ever touched a dick. She said no, so of course I suggested we remedy that."

"Aren't you only like thirteen in seventh grade?"

"Yup. And Amy was fifteen. In her defense, I looked older. And I was as big as any ninth grader. Anyway, we gave each other thirty seconds to check out each other's assets. She stuck her hand down my pants, wrapped her little fingers around my junk, and gave it a good squeeze. Of course, I was fully hard and had been since she'd said the word *boobs*. After she was done, she let me play with her boobs, *under the bra*, for half a minute."

I couldn't help but crack up at the way he'd emphasized *under the bra*. "So that's why I have Yoda? Because you got to cop a feel in a movie theater in seventh grade?"

"What could be luckier than getting to watch six *Star Wars* movies for free and touching boobs for the first time?"

"You're a little nutty. Though I guess you're right—at least at that age." I laughed. "But why does Amy hate you?"

"Oh, because I told all my friends about it, and they started calling her *second-base Chase*. I was thirteen and thought I was cool. It wasn't my finest moment. My brother kicked my ass when he found out I'd told people, and Amy got even by lying and telling everyone my dick was limp when she touched it. But it did teach me an early lesson never to kiss and tell."

"I bet."

"So...were you going to call me back?"

"I..." I was about to say I would've, but why not be truthful? "I'm not sure."

"Did you not have a good time last night after the game?"

"No, I did. It was the most I've laughed in a long time."

"Not attracted to me?"

"Is your mirror broken? I'm guessing most women between eight and eighty find you handsome."

"So the problem is the dumbass then?"

"Dumbass?"

"What else would you call a guy who tells you it's okay for you to see other people while he's living out of the country for a year? *Dumbass.*"

I smiled. "Thank you."

"You didn't say you weren't going to call me back. You said you weren't sure. So that means there's a part of you that *is* interested."

"There definitely is. I'm not going to deny that I like you. That's actually the problem. I think it was easier to go out on a date when I knew the person wouldn't be someone I was into. I'm just not sure I can be invested in two things at the same time, even if there's nothing technically holding me back."

Max was quiet for a moment. I thought he might've hung up.

"Are you still there?" I asked.

"I'm here. Will you at least come to my game tomorrow night? It's at home again. You can't make me play without my good luck charm. You can give it to security if you don't want to wait around after."

I looked down at Yoda in my hand. "Sure. I suppose coming to another game is harmless."

"Bring a friend, if you want. I'll leave two tickets at the will call booth."

"Okay."

"Excellent. It's getting late, so I'll let you go."

"Goodnight, Max."

"Sweet dreams, Georgia."

— Four —

Georgia

"Hi." I stepped up when it was my turn at the ticket booth. "I'm picking up two tickets for the game tonight."

"Your name and ID, please?"

I slid my license to the other side. "Georgia Delaney."

He held up a finger. "You're Yearwood's guest. Hang on a second. He left a bag for you, too."

I looked over at Maggie and shrugged.

She grinned. "I hope it's snacks. I'm hungry. Twizzlers would be nice."

I chuckled. "We're early. We can get something inside."

A minute later the guy in the booth came back. He slid two tickets across the counter and then a logoed Wolverines bag. Since there was a line behind me, I stepped away before opening it. "Thank you."

Inside, there was an envelope on top, so I opened it and slid out a piece of thick cardstock. The handwriting was neat and very slanty.

Wear my name on your back tonight. It might be the only chance I get.

X
Max

P.S. There's a Wolverines shirt in here for your friend. Unless you brought a date. If that's the case, fuck 'em. He's not getting shit.

I laughed and handed Maggie the card.

She read it and grinned. "I like him already. He's hot, wants to put you in his seat with his name on your back, and has gifts for your friend. If you don't wind up going out with this guy, I'm warning you, I'll be giving him my number."

I shook my head with a smile. "Come on, let's go change and get you some snacks before the game starts."

We arrived at our seats carrying two hot dogs, ginormous sodas, and a large pack of Twizzlers. The same woman was sitting in the adjoining seat as last time.

"Hi, Jenna."

"Hey, Georgia. I heard you might be here tonight."

I settled into my seat with a furrowed brow. "You heard?"

"My husband asked Max if anyone was using his seats. My mother-in-law was thinking about coming. Max said his tickets were being used by his new green-eyed lucky charm. I had a feeling he meant you. By the way, thank you for being here. You saved me three hours with my horrible mother-in-law."

I laughed and pointed to Maggie. "This is my friend Maggie. Maggie, this is Jenna. She's married to one of the players."

"Great to meet you." Maggie leaned over me. "So, do you know Max pretty well?"

"Well enough that I've seen his ass more than once." Jenna smiled. "We have a summer home out east, and it has an outdoor shower. Max loves it, and I can't get him to keep his bathing suit on when he uses it."

"Nice." Maggie smiled. "Can I ask you a question about him?"

Jenna shrugged. "Sure."

"Would you let your little sister date him?"

"I don't have one. But I did try to set him up with my best friend, if that answers your question. She's a model and was very into him. They met at a party at my house, and at the end of the night she asked him if he wanted to go somewhere and hang out more. He declined, saying he had to get up early the next morning. He definitely could have had a good time and then ditched her. But instead, he kept things friendly. When I asked him the next day what he thought about her, he said she was really cool, but he wasn't into her that way and didn't want to take advantage. Not too many single guys would have done that seeing as Lana has been in the Victoria's Secret catalog."

Maggie aimed a gloating smile my way. "Good to know. Thank you."

The game started, and Maggie and I really got into it. Having someone to cheer with made all the difference. We stood when Max's team scored, booed when the visiting team did, and during intermission, Jenna brought us to some secret wives' suite where we had cocktails and everyone was super friendly. At one point during the third period, Max scored. When the camera zoomed in on his smiling face, I could've sworn he looked right at me and winked, which made the crowd go crazy. I was certain every other woman in the arena thought it was for her, too.

During the last period, the usher who had showed us to our seats came by. He handed me another envelope and two lanyards. I recognized the all-access pass from the one Jenna had let me borrow last time. The women on both sides of me grinned as I slipped the card out of the envelope.

In case you want to return my little friend in person, rather than leaving him with security.
I hope to see you.

X
Max

• • •

"Can you tell me how we got here?" I shook my head and spoke to Maggie as I stared across the bar.

"Well, we put one foot in front of the other and walked about two blocks from the Garden after the game ended." She lifted her chin toward where Max was talking to the bartender while waiting for our drinks. "I honestly don't remember much after that gorgeous beast of a man flashed those dimples and asked us to come out with him."

I sighed. "I know the feeling. One minute I was waiting outside the locker room, swearing I was returning his lucky charm and saying thank you and goodbye, and the next I was sitting here. I think the dimples are hypnotic or something."

Max returned to our booth with two glasses of wine and a bottle of water. He slid into the seat across from us and looked back and forth between Maggie and me.

"Why does it feel like the two of you sitting on one side is more dangerous than skating on an eighth-of-an-inch blade toward a three-hundred-pound defender with no teeth?"

Maggie grinned. "The man knows how to read a room."

"I wish I was better at reading your friend." His eyes shifted to meet mine a moment. "Tell me how to get your friend to go out with me."

She wagged her pointer. "Not so fast. I need to make sure you're right for her. I have a few questions first."

Max smiled. "I can see why you two are good friends already." He lifted his arms to rest along the back of the booth. "Ask away, Maggie."

"Dogs or cats?"

"Dogs. I have two."

"What kind?"

"A mutt and a Pomeranian"

I laughed. "You have a *Pomeranian*?"

Max nodded. "It wasn't by choice. My brother bought it for his kids for Christmas last year. His one daughter couldn't stop sneezing, and the other two couldn't stop crying after he told them they had to give the dog away. The younger one suckered me into taking it so they can still see it sometimes."

"How'd she sucker you?"

Max grinned. "She smiled at me."

We both laughed. "What are the dogs' names?" Maggie asked.

"Fred and Four. I adopted Fred from the pound. My nieces named the Pomeranian. I always called the girls Thing One, Thing Two, and Thing Three, so my brother started calling the dog Thing Four while they were trying to think of a name for it. It stuck, but I shortened it."

"What do the dogs do when you're on the road?"

"I have someone who comes and stays in my guest room. They take care of my apartment and my boys. It's actually two sisters who do it as a business. I give them my road schedule in advance, and they work it out between themselves for the season. They're dog lovers. It's great because the dogs get to stay in their own home, so it doesn't upset them too much when I leave for a few days. One of the sisters sells homemade organic dog treats, and she uses my kitchen when she stays, so they sample every batch. Sometimes I think they're pissed when I come back."

"Do you have any pictures of them?" Maggie leaned in. "If you do, it's bonus points. Assholes don't usually have pictures of their dogs on their phones."

Max dug his cell from his pocket. "I think there are a few videos of them snoring, too. They're bed hogs, and one snores louder than the other."

Maggie pointed to me. "Oh, so like Georgia."

"I *do not* snore."

Maggie deadpanned to Max. "She snores. *Loud.*"

I laughed. "Just shut up and let's see the dogs."

Max punched in a code on his phone and slid it across the table.

Maggie picked it up and blinked a few times. "You're just going to hand me your phone and let me look through your pictures?"

Max shrugged. "Sure. Why not?"

"I don't know. Every man I've ever met hovers nearby, ready to snatch the phone out of your hands when a woman so much as looks at one photo."

He laughed. "I don't have anything on there to hide."

Maggie started to swipe through the photos.

Max pointed. "There's a folder called dogs somewhere. My oldest niece made it. There're more pictures than you could ever want to see in it. My nieces make me text them photos. I made the mistake of deleting them once, and the little one cried. Now I keep them all."

I leaned over Maggie's shoulder as she opened the folder and started to swipe through. Most of the photos were just the dogs, but Max was in a few, too. I noticed her swipe lingered when we came to one of a shirtless Max wearing a backwards baseball hat. The man had an eight-pack carved into golden skin. She caught my eye and smirked.

"Do you have Georgia's number in here?" Maggie asked.

"I do."

She hit a few buttons, and my phone vibrated inside my purse. She winked. "I thought you might like to use that one for his contact photo. Just in case you forget what he looks like."

When we were done looking through pictures of the dogs, Maggie slid the phone to the other side of the table. "Back to my questions. I think you were trying to distract me by showing those adorable photos."

"You're the one who brought up dogs," Max said.

"Still." Maggie shrugged. "Okay, next question. What's the longest you've ever let food sit on the floor before you picked it up and ate it?"

Max raised a brow. "Are we talking sober or drunk?"

"Either."

He hung his head. "I ate an Oreo that was on the floor for about five minutes. Actually, I wound up eating it out of the sink. It was the last one, and my brother and I were fighting over it. I'd scooped it off the floor and almost had it to my mouth when he knocked it from my hand and sent it flying across the room. It landed in a pot full of greasy water my mother had been soaking from dinner. It was probably floating in there for thirty seconds or so while we wrestled over who could get to it first."

Maggie wrinkled her nose. "That's kinda gross. But I won't hold it against you since you were a kid."

Max grinned. "It was six months ago. We were at my brother's for dinner."

I couldn't help but laugh.

"You're lucky you got extra points for taking in your nieces' Pomeranian and adopting from the pound," Maggie said. "Because that just lost you one. Gross."

Max waved her on. "Hit me with another one. I can win this. I know I can."

"Alright." Maggie stared off for a few seconds while drumming her fingers against the table. She then raised her pointer in the air, and I all but pictured a giant light bulb in a cartoon bubble above her head. "I got one. Food you eat frequently."

"Easy. Cheerios."

"Really? That's weird. Not bread, or chicken, or even pasta or rice. *Cheerios*?"

"Yep. I freaking love 'em."

Maggie shrugged. "If you say so. What about your favorite book?"

"Probably *The Boys of Winter*."

"I don't know it."

"It's about the nineteen-eighty Olympic hockey team."

Maggie's nose wrinkled, and she pointed to me. "Sounds as boring as the crap she reads. A few years ago I caught her re-reading *The Great Gatsby*. Who reads F. Scott Fitzgerald unless it's assigned to you in high school? And even then, you skim and read the CliffsNotes version." She shook her head. "Okay, next question. This one's double or nothing, so you better answer it right. Do you or do you not have any plans to live in London anytime soon?"

Max flashed a dimple and looked at me. "Definitely not. I'm no dumbass."

"Good answer." Maggie grinned. "What's something you like but are embarrassed to admit?"

Max hung his head again. "I sometimes watch *Jersey Shore* reruns."

"Interesting. Would you rather hang out with Snooki or JWoww?"

"Snooki. No contest."

Maggie took a deep breath and shook her head. "I was afraid of this."

"What? Was JWoww the right answer?"

"No…not at all. You're perfect for her. That's why she won't go out with you."

"What do I need to do? Forget to hold the door and check out other women while she's talking?"

"I'm not sure that will do it."

"Umm…" I looked back and forth between Max and Maggie and pointed to myself. "You know I'm sitting right here, right?"

Maggie winked at me. She then proceeded to pick up her wine and chug the entire thing in one impressive gulp. She slapped the empty glass down on the table with a large *aahh* before abruptly standing.

"It's been lovely, boys and girls."

My face wrinkled. "Where are you going?"

"My job is done here. I think I'm going to pop over to Aaron's lawyer's for a booty call. All the testosterone in that arena got me in the mood." She leaned down and kissed my cheek. "You two have a fun evening." She wiggled her fingers at Max. "Take good care of my girl, Pretty Boy."

Without another word, she turned and strutted for the door. I blinked a few times. "Well, that was...interesting."

"Who's Aaron?"

"Her almost ex-husband."

Max's brows shot up. "She's booty calling *his* lawyer, not her own?"

"Yep." I shook my head. "There's an old saying—Never go to bed angry; stay awake and plot revenge. Maggie rewrote it as, Never go to bed angry; stay awake and have revenge sex."

Max laughed. "I like her. She seems like a no-bullshit type of person."

"She is."

"Plus..." He reached across the table and weaved his fingers with mine. "She got you to come here."

"That she did. Though I feel like I was duped. The only reason she pushed for us to come out was because she planned to duck out like she just did. I don't know how I didn't see that all along."

"Thank you for coming to the game tonight." He squeezed my fingers and looked down at my shirt. "I really like you in my jersey."

My stomach did that fluttery thing it did every time we were alone. The man was just too damn sexy for his own good. Who the hell looked that good at eleven o'clock at night after playing multiple hours of intense sports? Why couldn't he have some bruises and oozing things on his face to be at least *somewhat* hideous?

I stared down at our joined hands. "I liked wearing it. But...I don't think it's a good idea for us to see each other. You seem like a really nice guy, but things between Gabriel and me... I just don't know where they'll end up."

"But you're fine going on Tinder for a hookup or meeting a guy you knew wasn't someone you'd be into..."

"Those just seemed less complicated, for some reason."

Max looked back and forth between my eyes. "What if I told you I was moving at the end of the summer?"

An unexpected pang of disappointment squeezed my heart. "Is that true?"

He nodded. "It's not public yet. My contract here is up. My agent hasn't worked out all the details, but as of this morning, it looks like I'll be going to the Blades, out in California. I'll have better postseason playoff potential with them."

"Oh wow. So when would you go?"

"Training camp won't start until the first week in September. But I'd probably want to be settled in by the beginning of August, at the latest."

Max watched me intently as I absorbed what that meant. It was almost the end of April, so he'd only be around for a little over three months. I bit down on my bottom lip. "I don't know..."

"Enjoy the summer with me. I'm not looking for anything serious, and I can tell we'll have fun. But we'll also have an expiration date, which will keep things less—as you said—complicated."

It was a seriously tempting offer. I did want to date. At first it might've been only because Gabriel was seeing other people. But the more I've thought about it, the more I realized maybe I needed some life perspective, too. A year ago I'd had my entire life planned out. Maybe I needed to *stop* planning and analyzing and just live a little, play things by ear? Though that sounded great, it also made my palms sweat.

"Can I...think about it?"

Max smiled. "Of course. That's a hell of a lot better answer than no."

After that, we stayed at the bar talking for a few hours. Then Max hailed a cab, and we both got in. My apartment was on the way up to his, so he told the driver to drop me first. When we reached my building, he pulled out his billfold and offered cash over the seat to the driver.

"Give me a few minutes so I can walk her up."

The driver took a look at the bill and nodded. "No problem, boss."

Max and I walked side by side to the door to my building.

"I'm on the road the next four days—games in Seattle then Philadelphia. My schedule kind of blows until the season ends. But that's soon. And I'm having some people over next Saturday, if you'd be up for it. No pressure...but it is my birthday."

"Really?"

Max nodded. "You can bring Maggie or someone, if you want. That way you won't feel like it's a date, if you haven't decided on us yet."

"That's very nice of you."

He opened my apartment building door and walked me to the elevator.

"Thank you for drinks and the ride home," I told him.

After I pressed the up button, Max reached out and took my hand. He stared down at our joined hands for a long while before his eyes worked their way up. They stopped at my mouth, and he shook his head. "This is the second time I'm leaving you, and each time it gets harder not to kiss you goodbye." His eyes met mine. The intensity radiating from them took my breath away. "I want to kiss you so fucking bad."

I couldn't say anything, though it seemed like he was waiting for a response. My brain was too busy sending electric currents racing through my body.

Our eyes stayed locked as Max took a pensive step forward.

Through my peripheral vision, I saw the elevator doors slide open. It was right next to us, so we both clearly heard it, too. Yet our gazes remained steady. Max took another step toward me.

I think I might've stopped breathing at that point.

Then he took another step, and our feet were toe to toe. Slowly, Max reached out and lifted one finger to my mouth. He traced my bottom lip from one side to the other, then his finger slid down over my chin, over the length of my throat, and stopped at the hollow of my neck. He spoke directly to the spot as he traced a circle. "I'm not even going to ask to kiss you. Because I won't be able to control myself if you let me." He shook his head. "I want to leave marks."

Oh my.

Max swallowed. Watching his Adam's apple work made me feel woozy. But it was nothing compared to how the way he was looking at me made me feel. Or maybe the lightheadedness came from the fact that I still hadn't remembered to breathe.

My mouth grew dry, and my tongue peeked out to run wetness along my lips. Max's eyes followed, and he groaned. Somewhere in the distance, I heard a bell ding, but the meaning didn't register until Max held out his hand to stop the elevator doors from closing. He tilted his head toward the open car.

"You better go," he growled. "I'm not ruining my chance before I'm even given one. But I hope you'll give my summer proposal some thought."

"I will." I had to force myself to step into the empty elevator car. "Goodnight, Max."

"Sweet dreams, sweetheart." He grinned. "I know I'll be having them."

—Five—

Max

"What's up, old man? You have kids doing all the work for you again?"

Otto Wolfman turned. He smiled but tried to hide it as he waved me off. "Who you calling old? If you take a look in the mirror, you won't see the left wing who scored three goals the other night. I believe that man is enjoying a Philly cheesesteak back home in sunny Philadelphia."

Oof. That one hurt. We got our asses kicked in Philly the other day. But this ball-busting with Otto was all in good fun. It always had been. I walked over to where he sat on the penalty bench, and we slapped hands before I passed him a coffee. For the last seven years I'd been playing at the Garden, Otto Wolfman had tended to the ice, but he'd also been here thirty-one years before that. The ornery old bastard reminded me so much of my dad, though I'd never told him that. Every Saturday morning, I came an hour or so before practice and brought him the sludge he preferred from the street cart down the block. I'd made the mistake of bringing him Starbucks once. *Once.*

He pointed to the young guy driving his Zamboni. "This idiot paid ten-thousand dollars to do this. Can you believe that? Some sort of an auction where a bunch of rich, Wall Street types bid on shit. What's he, twenty-three?" Otto shook his head. "At least it's for charity."

I looked over at the ice. The guy navigating the Zamboni around the rink wore a giant smile. He was definitely enjoying himself. I shrugged. "Whatever floats your boat, I guess."

"Got the weekend off after practice this morning, don't cha?"

"Yep." I sipped my coffee.

"Any big plans?"

I shook my head and chuckled. "Apparently, I'm throwing myself a birthday party."

Otto's bushy brows pulled together. "Apparently? You sound like you're not sure."

"Well, I wasn't planning on it. But then I told a woman I was so I could get her to spend time with me."

"Would be easier to just ask her on a date, wouldn't it?"

I frowned. "I did. Multiple times. She's not sure she wants to go out with me. So I stupidly told her I was having people over tonight to make it seem casual. Figured she'd be more likely to say yes if it wasn't just the two of us."

"A woman shot you down?" Otto's head bent back in laughter. "That makes my day."

"Gee, thanks."

"What's so special about this woman that she's got you acting out of sorts?"

That was a damn good question. She had big, green eyes, smooth, pale skin, and a long, thin, delicate neck that made me feel like a damn vampire. But those felt like bonus points with Georgia. What I liked best was that she seemed to know who she was, and while she could poke fun, she was also proud and unashamed. Too many women wanted to be someone else.

I shrugged. "She's just kinda real."

Otto nodded. "Real is good. But listen, Pretty Boy. Nothing good comes easy. When I met my Dorothy, I was working security at a nudey bar downtown. I was young and handsome back then, having the time of my life with the ladies who worked there. I had to get a new *job* just so Dorothy would go out with me."

"I ain't buying the young and handsome part. But I get what you're saying."

"You players have no idea what it's like to work for a woman. I see the half-naked women who cozy up to you any chance they get. It'll do you some good to have your redwood-sized ego chopped down a bit. I like this woman already. I bet you she's a smart one."

"Might be too smart for me. Graduated from NYU business school and runs a successful company she started on her own."

"My Dorothy has been a librarian for thirty years. She's read more books than I've had beers. And you know how much I enjoy my Coors Light. So let me give you some advice."

"What's that?"

"Smart women don't believe the things you say. They believe the actions they see."

I nodded. "Good advice...for a change."

We sat side by side for a moment watching the ten-thousand-dollar Zamboni ride.

"He's doing a pretty good job." I jabbed my elbow into Otto lightly. "You better watch out. I bet he can afford to pay fifty K to replace you."

Otto scowled.

I laughed. "That's payback for the Philly comment. Now tell me how your treatment's going."

He flexed both his hands open and closed. "Not too bad. Except my hands and feet tingle all the time. Doc said it's nerve damage from the chemo. It better just be temporary."

Otto had been diagnosed with stage four colon cancer last year. He was getting treatment, but the outlook wasn't great, especially since it had spread in the months after he'd stopped his first round of treatments.

"Anything you can do for it?" I asked.

"More drugs. Doc said physical therapy might help. But I hate that shit."

I smiled. Hockey players lived in a PT office. I always dreaded going, too. *Just tell me the exercises, and I'll be on my merry way.* "What about acupuncture?"

"Pins and needles? That's what I'm trying to get rid of, jackass. But you know what might help?"

"What?"

"Warmer weather. If you happen to know anyone looking for a facilities manager out on the West Coast, put in a good word for me."

I shook my head with a grin. Otto had no intention of going anywhere, and we both knew it. But I hadn't yet told him I was in talks with the LA team, though somehow he must've gotten wind. "I would say these walls must talk, but I've never had a conversation about another team in this place."

Otto stood. He cupped his hands around his mouth and yelled, "*No fucking selfies while driving that thing*!" He grumbled as he sat back down. "Bunch of morons with those phones."

I smiled. *Yep*. There was no better way to start my Saturday than time with Otto.

• • •

"Thank you for helping me."

Jenna set a tray of veggies on my dining room table. She smacked her hands together, cleaning them off, and looked around. "*Helping* would imply you did something to contribute."

I reached to take a carrot from the tray, but she swatted my hand. "Those are for the guests."

"So I can't eat any before they come?"

"I'll let you eat one. But don't dip it in the dip. You'll mess up how nice it looks."

Jenna's husband, Tomasso, walked over. He grinned. "She won't let you dip, huh? I warned you she was bonkers about shit like this when she offered you help."

Jenna's hands flew to her hips. "You called me bonkers? Next time you want to have people over, *you* can order and make things look nice. I'm sure everyone will love Ritz crackers with Cheez Whiz." She was all of about five-two, a solid foot shorter than her tree trunk of a husband.

Yet he shoved his hands into his pockets with a sulk. "Sorry, babe."

I chuckled.

"What are you laughing at?" She wagged a finger my way. "Go do something about that little furball over there. He keeps trying to get up on the coffee table where the charcuterie board is."

I lifted my hands in surrender. "Yes, ma'am."

I took the dogs into the kitchen and fed them, even though it wouldn't stop them from trying to swipe something.

A little while later, the first guests arrived. I'd invited twelve people—or rather Jenna had. She'd said it was the perfect number to qualify as a party, but also not so many that I'd have to spend all night playing host, which would take away from my time with Georgia. I didn't argue, since she was doing all the work, but the people coming were my friends—they wouldn't give a crap if I ignored them. Which was exactly what I'd be doing once Georgia got here. The woman had gotten to me.

At about eight, almost everyone had arrived, except the person I was throwing this sham of a party for. My cell was on the charger in the kitchen, so I went to go check if maybe she'd texted.

There'd been a missed call around six thirty and then a text around seven.

Georgia: Hey. I just wanted to make sure you got my voicemail. I'm sorry for canceling last minute.

Shit.

I swiped into my voicemail and hit play next to her name.

"Hey. It's Georgia. I'm sorry to call at the last second, but I'm not going to be able to come tonight. I wasn't feeling so hot yesterday, and this morning I woke up sort of achy and wiped out. I took some Motrin a few hours ago hoping I'd feel better and laid down for a little while, and I actually just woke up. I never nap, so I didn't expect to pass out for almost three hours or I would've called sooner. Now my throat is a little sore, and I'm running a low fever. I feel awful for canceling on your birthday, but I'm not going to be able to come. I'm sorry, Max. I hope you have a great party."

I frowned. *This sucks*. When I read the text, I assumed she was blowing me off. But she didn't sound so good, and that caused an ache in my chest. So I hit *Call Back* and leaned against the counter, waiting for her to answer.

On the third ring, I thought I was about to go to voicemail, but then she answered. Her voice sounded worse than on the message.

"Hey," she croaked.

"You don't sound so good."

"Yeah, I don't feel too hot. It hurts when I swallow, and my head weighs a hundred pounds. I'm really sorry I can't come."

"It's fine. I'm sorry you're not feeling well."

"I don't think I've been sick in ten years. Not even a cold. I'm sort of a big baby when I don't feel well. You must think I'm a total wimp. Hockey players play with broken bones and injuries all the time."

"Nah. That's different."

She laughed. "Thank you for lying. How's your party going?"

"It's fine. Four is being his usual con self. He's perfected the big-eyed, pitiful stare that women fall for. He sits at their feet and looks up until they lift him and tell him how cute he is. Then he eyes whatever they're eating as if he hasn't been fed in a year. Nine times out of ten, I get yelled at for not feeding him enough. Meanwhile his bowl of dog food is full in the kitchen. If he were a human, he'd be one of those guys who run shill card games that take tourists for all their money near Penn Station."

Georgia laughed, but the laugh rolled into a coughing fit. "Sorry. Excuse me."

"No problem."

She sighed. "I was looking forward to meeting Four."

"He was looking forward to meeting you, too. You'll have to make it up to him."

I heard the smile in her voice. "Just him? Not the birthday boy?"

"Well, if you're offering..."

Jenna burst into the kitchen. "The caterer is here with the hot food for dinner."

"Hang on a second, okay?" I covered the phone. "Will you do me a favor and tell them to come in here. I'll be off in a minute."

"Sure. I also need you to open more red wine."

"Okay."

Once Jenna shut the kitchen door, I took my hand off the phone. "Sorry about that."

"It sounds like you're busy. I'll let you go."

As much as I didn't want to hang up, I knew I should. "Alright, yeah. I'll check in with you tomorrow to see how you feel."

"Have a great time at your party, and happy birthday, Max."

"Thank you. Feel better. Get some sleep."

After I hung up, I paid the caterers and opened a few more bottles of wine. I tried to keep my head in a few conversations, but my heart just wasn't in it. So when I noticed Jenna going into the kitchen with an empty tray, I followed her.

"How much of an asshole would I be if I slipped out of my own party for an hour or two?"

"Where the hell would you go?"

"To Georgia's. She's not feeling well."

"I was wondering why she wasn't here. Do you think she's lying and you want to go over and see if she's really home or something?"

I shook my head. "No, I believe her. Thought maybe I'd pick up some soup and throat lozenges."

Jenna smiled. "You really like her, huh?"

"I know I'm going to regret telling you this, but...the only reason I even had people over tonight was because she agreed to come to a party, but she wouldn't go out with me."

Her smile widened and she sing-songed her words. "*Pretty Boy got turned do-own.*"

"Why does that make people so happy to hear?"

"Because it's entertaining to watch you be treated like a mere mortal—you know, like the rest of us."

I rolled my eyes. "Will you hold down the fort for an hour or two? Just feed people and liquor them up."

Jenna waved her hand. "Go."

I leaned down and kissed her cheek. "Thanks, Jen."

As I reached the kitchen door, she yelled after me, "Wait!"

I turned back.

"Take Four with you. Women are suckers for that little guy."

• • •

I might've overdone it.

I'd bought so much crap on my way over that I had to set two of the bags on the floor to knock on Georgia's apartment door. I'd decided not to call first, which right about now I was second-guessing. The woman didn't even want to go out with me, and here I was showing up at her building and checking the mailboxes like a stalker to see what apartment she lived in. What had seemed like a good idea suddenly felt a little desperate.

But fuck it, I was here already—and with enough over-the-counter medicines to open a small pharmacy—so I knocked.

Once I did, my heart raced like I was thirteen, alone in the dark movie theater with Amy Chase. What the hell had come over me? I wasn't sure, but when no one came to the door right away, I debated whether I would knock a second time. What if she was sleeping? I didn't want to wake her if she was resting. Just as I'd decided to head back home if she didn't come to the door in the next minute, someone opened the door to the apartment next to hers, and Four started to bark like a lunatic. His high-pitched chirp echoed through the hallway, and the old man who'd stepped out jumped. He was so startled, he nearly fell over. I tried to calm my six-pound guard dog while apologizing.

Then before I could shut Four up, Georgia's door whipped open.

"Max?" Her brows pulled together. "What are you doing here?"

I bent and scooped up the bags of supplies, holding them like a peace offering. "I brought you some soup. And throat lozenges. And...other stuff."

She patted a big knot of hair on top of her head. "I look like crap."

Georgia had on a fluffy pink robe, not a stitch of makeup, and oversized, dark-rimmed glasses that were crooked on her face. Her eyes were puffy and her nose red, yet she still looked beautiful.

I reached out and straightened her glasses. "You look adorable."

"You'll get sick."

"I'll risk it." She looked clammy, so I felt her forehead. "You have a fever."

"I ran out of Motrin."

"Well, then it's a good thing I came. Can I come in?"

Her eyes dropped down to Four. "Oh my God, he's the cutest thing I've ever seen."

I inwardly fist pumped. *Nice call, Jenna.* I'd have to remember to send her flowers.

Georgia opened the door all the way and stepped aside with her hands out. "Can I hold him? Or maybe keep him forever?"

Or a car. I might owe Jenna a car.

Inside, her apartment was really nice—exposed brick in the living room, a decent-size kitchen with stainless-steel appliances, high ceilings, and not surprisingly, there were flower arrangements all over. It also smelled pretty incredible. I walked to the kitchen counter and started to unpack the stuff I'd picked up at the drug store. Finding the Motrin, I peeled open the bottle and shook out two pills. Then I helped myself to the refrigerator and grabbed a water, twisting open the cap as I walked to the living room where Georgia already had Four on her lap on the couch.

"Take these," I said.

"Thank you." She swallowed the pills and chugged some water.

"Are you hungry? I brought some chicken soup."

Georgia shook her head. "I haven't had much of an appetite at all today. But maybe I'll force myself to eat some in a bit, when I'm done loving on this little guy."

She dug her nails into Four's head, and he nuzzled against her chest. With his head in her cleavage, the little furball glanced back in my direction. I could've sworn he was gloating.

Yeah, I am jealous, you little shit.

I grabbed the other bag I'd brought and sat beside Georgia on the couch.

"There's an old record store next to the pharmacy I stopped at. The sign in the window said they also sold movies, but the pickings were pretty slim." I reached into the bag and pulled out two of the three movies I'd bought. "This one is silent, and this one isn't. I didn't know if you preferred one over the other."

Georgia's mouth hung open. "Black and white? How did you know I loved old movies?"

"You mentioned it the night we met."

"I did?"

I nodded. "I think it was when you were telling me how little you had in common with your blind date."

"I don't even remember that."

I shrugged. "I also got this one."

Georgia took the movie from my hand, laughing. "*The Phantom Menace?* Didn't you tell me this one is the worst of all the *Star Wars* movies?"

"It is. But I was hoping maybe it would bring me luck again." I wiggled my eyebrows.

Georgia smiled. "You're going to try to feel me up when I'm sick?"

I held up my hands. "I wasn't going to, but if that's what the powers that be wanted..."

She laughed and then grabbed her throat. "Oww... Don't make me laugh. It hurts."

Damn, her smile made my chest feel funny. I wondered if I might be coming down with something, too.

Georgia held Four up in the air, smiling at his tiny face. "I can't believe this little guy is your dog. He's so freaking cute. What you must look like walking the streets with him. Do you even notice the women fainting as you pass?"

When I smiled, she pointed to my cheeks. "Put those things away, Yearwood. I'm weak. Flashing those dimples isn't playing fair."

"Yes, ma'am." I smiled more, making sure to showcase what she apparently liked.

Georgia stroked Four's head. "I'm surprised your party ended so early. It's barely nine o'clock."

I shook my head. "It's not over. I just ducked out for a little while."

"You left your own birthday party?"

I shrugged. "There's plenty of food and booze. Most of them won't even notice I'm gone."

"I cannot believe you left your own birthday party to come nurse me."

I leaned to her. "Can I tell you a secret?"

"What?"

"I only threw the party so you'd come anyway."

Georgia stopped petting Four. "Are you serious?"

I nodded. "It didn't work out too well, did it?"

"I don't quite get you, Max Yearwood."

"What do you mean?"

"You have to be able to walk into a room full of beautiful, single women and cozy up to almost anyone you want. So why are you over here risking getting sick for someone who comes with a truckload of baggage?"

I shrugged. "I don't know. We can't control chemistry, I guess. Can you honestly say you don't feel anything when we're near each other?"

"I'm attracted to you, yes. I've admitted that."

"Chemistry is more than an attraction. I want to spend time with you, even if it's just sitting here right now."

She studied me. She still seemed to be trying to figure out if I was feeding her a line of shit. I'm not sure if she made it to a final conclusion on the subject, because she suddenly started sneezing. Not once, not twice, but at least a dozen times. Each time, the pile of chestnut hair on top of her head bounced around and jerked back and forth. She reached forward to the coffee table, grabbed a box of tissues, and buried her face in them until she finally stopped.

"God bless you," I said.

"Thank you." Her nose and mouth were still covered when she looked over the tissues with watery eyes. "Still feeling that chemistry?"

I grinned. "I do find the way your bun flops back and forth kinda cute."

She laughed and blew her nose. "You've taken one too many sticks to the head, Pretty Boy."

"Maybe." I felt Mother Nature calling, so I looked around the room. "Is it alright if I use your bathroom?"

Georgia pointed to a hallway. "Of course. First door on your right."

After I relieved myself and washed my hands, I turned to find a hand towel. But the bar that usually had one was filled with something else. *Thongs. Lace ones.* Two black, two cream, and a red. I stared down at them longer than was likely appropriate. For a few seconds, I might've even wondered if she would notice one missing. But then I dried my hands on my pants and forced myself to exit the bathroom like a respectable human being.

Georgia was slouched on the couch in the middle of a yawn when I walked back in.

"Why don't you have a little soup, and I'll put on one of the movies I bought so you can rest, and I'll get going."

"Will you have some soup with me?"

I hadn't eaten anything before I left the party, so I nodded. "Sure."

Georgia went to stand. I put my hand up. "Stay there. I'll bring it to you."

"Thank you."

In the kitchen, I rummaged through her cabinets until I found the bowls. Then I searched some more to see if she had any saltines. She didn't, and I noticed her food stock was pretty sparse overall.

"I take it you don't cook much?" I passed her a bowl of soup and a spoon and sat down with my own on the couch next to her. "Your cabinets are pretty bleak."

"Yeah, not really. I work late a lot, and it sort of sucks to cook for one person."

"Are you hinting that you'd like to make dinner for me? Because if you are, I accept."

She laughed. "What about you? Do you cook?"

"Now you want me to cook for you? Make up your mind, woman."

Her smile widened. I could sit here all night breathing in her germs if she kept that smile on her face. Even her pale skin and puffy eyes didn't stop me from wanting to kiss her. I had to force my eyes back to my soup.

When we were done, I took the bowls to the sink and washed them. Then I pulled out one of the movies and looked around.

"Do you have a DVD player?"

She pointed to the cabinet under the TV and nodded. "In there."

"I'm glad you have one. I'm not sure why I assumed you did when I bought these. I don't have one. I just rent stuff on TV if I want to watch something."

"They don't put too many of the really old movies on the streaming services. I have to order them on DVD."

The cabinet under the television was jam-packed with videos and books. On top were a few framed pictures I hadn't noticed before. I crouched down and picked up one of her and Maggie—from Maggie's wedding, I assumed, since she was dressed in a wedding gown.

"You look beautiful here."

Georgia smirked. "As opposed to what I look like now?"

"Nah. You still look good. You can pull off snot on your face like a champ."

Her eyes bulged, and she wiped at her cheek.

I grinned. "I'm kidding."

She squinted and shook her head.

I checked out the other framed photos. There was one of her dressed in a cap and gown with her mom at her college graduation, one that she said was her grandmother, and another of Georgia cutting a ribbon with big scissors, which she said was at the opening of her first distribution center. But the one at the very end was face down. I eyed it and looked over at Georgia.

"Did this one fall?"

She shook her head. "It's of Gabriel and me. I laid it face down before he left after an argument we had, and I guess I forgot it was even there."

Considering she'd said he left eight months ago and there wasn't dust on the frame, I wasn't sure she'd actually forgotten at all. But I was curious about the guy, so I put my hand on the photo and caught Georgia's eye.

"Mind if I take a look?"

She shook her head, so I turned it over. I don't think I had a picture of her ex in my mind, yet he looked exactly like I would've expected. Tall, thin, good-looking enough... He wore horn-rimmed glasses that made him look like the English professor he was, and he was dressed in a button-down shirt with a cardigan sweater over it and slacks. Georgia was turned to the side and looking up at him with a revered smile on her face. Jealousy coursed through me.

When I looked over at Georgia, I found her watching me. Rather than set the frame back down where it had been, I tucked it inside the cabinet between some books. Turning back, I winked. "I put it away for you."

She smiled. "You're so helpful."

After I finished setting up the DVD player, I grabbed the remote and went back over to the couch. Georgia looked better, so I felt her head.

"I think your fever broke."

"I actually feel a little better. The soup and Motrin must've done it. Thank you."

Four was stretched out on her lap snoring while she ran her fingers through his fur. I shook my head. "He's such a ham."

During the movie, we sat side by side. Georgia rested her head on my shoulder, and at one point, I realized it was no longer only Four snoring. She had conked out, too. So I turned off the TV and attempted to extricate myself without waking her. But when I stood, Four started to dance around on her lap and woke her up.

I lifted him into my arms. "Go back to sleep. Me and furball are going to get going."

She rubbed her eyes. "Oh, okay."

"Do you want me to carry you to your room?"

"I think I'm just going to sleep here."

I picked up a throw pillow that had fallen to the floor and laid it at one end of the couch. Then I lifted her legs and guided her to turn and lie down.

She tucked her hands between her cheek and the pillow and brought her legs up into the fetal position.

I leaned down and kissed her cheek. "Goodnight, sweetheart. Feel better."

"Thank you." She closed her eyes. "And Max?"

"Yeah?"

"Happy birthday. I owe you a night out to make up for spoiling your party."

I smiled. "I'm going to hold you to that."

— Six —

Max

"So I have two things to talk about today." My agent, Don Goldmann, leaned back in his chair and clasped his hands behind his head with a cocky smile. "Do you want the good news first, or the really, really good news?"

"Surprise me."

"Let's start with endorsements and work our way up. ProVita wants to extend their Powerade drink deal. I also have offers from Nike, a sports watch company, and Remington, who wants to put your ugly mug in their electric razor commercials for some unknown reason. All told, it's just shy of three-point-five million."

"Jesus Christ."

"And you're on a team that isn't even making the playoffs. Think about what you could get if you were on a winning team."

"Yeah, that's crazy."

"I know you like to check out the products before you decide. So I had Samantha make you a nice little care package you can take with you today, or I can have her ship it to your place, if you want."

"Sounds good."

Don sat up and folded his hands on his desk. "Now for the real money. We discussed three numbers—the minimum you'd take, what you'd like to get, and your pie in the sky." He grabbed a pen, jotted some numbers on a Post-it, and slid it across the desk to me.

I lifted it to make sure I was seeing the number correctly. "You're serious?"

"Eight-year contract. Congratulations, you're about to become one of the top ten highest-paid players in the National Hockey League."

I'd been expecting a solid number, but nowhere near this. I wasn't a twenty-three-year-old spring chicken anymore. Contracts at twenty-nine that span that long aren't easy to come by. "Wow. That's fucking amazing."

Don smiled. "You mean, your *agent* is fucking amazing."

"Whatever. Take all the credit, if you want. For that money, I'll wear a T-shirt that says my agent is fucking amazing."

Don laughed. "You know I'm getting that shit printed."

"What about the physical exam? Anything special I have to submit to with that chunk of change?"

"The usual. Labs, EKG and stress test, and a physical exam from an ortho." Don squinted. "But this isn't the first time you've asked me about the health checkup. Anything you want to tell me?"

I shook my head and swallowed. "Nope."

He looked me in the eyes. "You sure?"

"Yep."

"Alright, good. It'll take a while to hammer out the details, and they have to make some moves to stay under the salary cap. But they want you, and the number is a done deal."

I stuck around after that to talk about all the deals rumored to be in the works with other agents. Don loved to talk shop, mostly because his roster of clients was filled with heavy hitters, and most other deals paled in comparison. But he deserved to pat himself on the back. He worked his ass off and was damn good at his job.

After, I was on my way to practice when my brother called.

"What's up, Altar Boy?" he asked.

Tate had nicknamed me that after an unfortunate incident when I was six and he was eleven. My parents were out one night, and he'd convinced me that we had another brother I had never met, who was a year older than him. He'd told me this brother had gone mad and lived in the shed in our yard. Unbeknownst to me, there *was* someone, or rather some*thing* living in there—a family of raccoons that my dad had just discovered that day and had yet to get rid of. He'd left the door open that night, hoping maybe they'd find their own way out.

Anyway...when it got dark, Tate made me go out into the yard and then locked me out. I started to cry and bang on the door because I was scared the brother who had gone crazy was going to get me. At one point, I heard a loud bang from behind me, and when I turned around, all I could see were two glowing eyes standing at the shed. I freaked out, crying and screaming, but Tate wouldn't let me back in until I got on my knees and said three Hail Marys. Of course, he videoed it from the window. When he showed it to my other brothers, my nickname became Altar Boy.

"What's up, asswipe?"

"I called you for your birthday, but you didn't pick up."

"Sorry. I was watching a movie and turned my ringer off. Four fell asleep, and when he gets woken up scared, he pisses. I didn't want to be pissed on."

"Ah...so your dog is a lot like you when you were little."

"Fuck off."

Someone listening to our conversation might think we didn't get along. But Tate and I were tight.

"You watched a movie on your birthday? Damn, you're getting old. I figured you didn't answer because you were out with some puck bunny. Anyway, I just called to make sure we're still on for dinner tomorrow night? Not that I want to see your butt-ugly face, but my girls are bugging the crap out of me, asking if Four is coming."

"We'll be there."

"Alright, good. I'll see you tomorrow."

I swiped to end the call as my phone buzzed with an incoming text.

Georgia: Hey. I wanted to say thank you again for last night. It was really thoughtful of you to bring me everything you did.

I typed back.

Max: My pleasure. How are you feeling today?

Georgia: A lot better. My fever is gone, and my throat is almost back to normal. My energy is coming back, so I might even run out to Home Depot to get a cock gun to fix my tub.

My brows shot up. *A cock gun?*

Before I could ask, another text came in.

Georgia: Oh my God. Autocorrect. A caulk gun. I meant a caulk gun. LOL.

I chuckled and typed back.

Max: That's too bad. I was going to offer to come over and bring my cock gun to help with whatever you need.

Georgia: LOL. Anyway, I'm feeling a lot better. Thank you.

Max: Glad to hear it.

Georgia: I feel bad about ruining your birthday.

That gave me an idea.

Max: How bad? Want to make it up to me?

The circles started to jump around as she typed. Then they stopped for a full minute before they finally started again.

Georgia: I don't think it's smart for me to answer yes to that question, without knowing what you have in mind.

I smiled. *Smart woman.*

Max: Nothing too devious. But I could use some company tomorrow night. I have a birthday dinner at my brother's. You coming will ward off my sister-in-law spending half the night telling me about her friends and trying to set me up.

Georgia: LOL. Birthday dinner at your brother's. That sounds harmless enough. Sure, I'll come. It's the least I can do for ruining your birthday.

Max: Can you cut out of work at four? It will take us an hour or so to get there.

Georgia: I think I can arrange that. My boss is pretty cool.

Max: She also has a great ass. ;) I'll see you tomorrow.

And here I thought my day couldn't get any better.

Seven

Georgia

"So how did things go with your cock gun?" Max flashed a grin before returning his eyes to the road.

I chuckled. "It went well. But I guess I have a confession to make. My texts sometimes get mangled because I use Siri to read them to me and voice text to respond. It's quicker because of my dyslexia. I guess I should be more careful."

Max shrugged. "Nah, not with me. Do whatever is easiest for you. I figured it was autocorrect. Though if you ever do need a cock gun, I'm your man."

I smiled. "I'll keep that in mind."

"What's it like, anyway? Having dyslexia."

"It's frustrating at times. Have you ever gotten really drunk and tried to read something? You can't quite make out the words, so you're squinting at the paper, but you're also rocking back and forth so you just can't grasp the letters with your focus? It kind of looks like a bunch of symbols that don't make too much sense."

"Is this a trick question to assess my character?"

My brows drew together. "No."

"Then the answer is yes."

I laughed. "Well, that's sort of what reading can be like for me."

"Doesn't seem like it's stopped you from doing much."

I shook my head. "In some ways, I think it actually helped me. It taught me a work ethic at a young age."

Max put on his blinker and got off at the next exit—the Van Wyck Expressway.

"Umm… Where are we going?"

He grinned. "I told you. My brother's for dinner."

I looked around. "Does your brother live at *the airport*?"

Max had arrived at my apartment in a sleek, black convertible Porsche with Four in a small travel caddy in the backseat. He'd said it took about an hour to get to his brother's, so I'd assumed he lived in Westchester or Long Island.

"I have practice at eight AM tomorrow. I promise I won't have you out too late."

"But where are we going?"

"You'll see."

We passed a dozen color-coded signs for all the different terminals at JFK, yet Max never turned. Instead, he exited onto an area that looked industrial, a combination of airplane hangars and office buildings. A few blocks down, he pulled into a parking lot.

"Are we here?" I looked at the sign hanging from the building. "What's Empire?"

He smirked. "It's driving you crazy, isn't it?"

A guy in Dockers and a polo walked out from the building. He strolled directly to Max's car and opened the driver's side door.

"Good afternoon, Mr. Yearwood. We're all ready for you."

Max shut off the ignition and tossed the keys to the guy. "Thanks, Joe." He got out of the car, jogged around to my side, and opened my door, extending a hand to help me out. Then he grabbed the dog from the backseat.

"Did I forget to mention that my brother lives in Boston? Empire is a private jet company."

"You have a private jet?"

He shook his head. "The owner of my team does. He lets us use it whenever we need to."

Max kept my hand after helping me out of the car. He entwined our fingers, and we walked hand in hand to the door.

"I've never been on a private plane. So I'm impressed," I said. "But I'm still not sleeping with you."

"So I should have them take the rose petals off the bed in the back then?"

I stopped. "You're kidding, right?"

Max winked. "Of course. The flight up to Boston is only forty minutes. I need way more time than that when I get you under me."

• • •

A black Town Car waited on the tarmac when we landed. It scooped us up and began the drive into downtown Boston. A half hour later, we pulled to the curb in a residential neighborhood—a really nice one on the outskirts of the Charles River in an area called Back Bay.

"Are we here?"

Max nodded and pointed to a beautiful, old building. "Remember how I told you my oldest brother had to come bail my ass out when I got into a little trouble gambling during college?"

"Yes?"

"Well, I don't think I mentioned that Tate stuck around for a few days after that. On the last night he was supposed to be here, we went out to a local bar, and he met a girl named Cassidy. They hit it off, so he wound up canceling his flight and staying three weeks longer. He's a programmer, so he can work from anywhere. When he finally went back to Washington, he lasted two weeks before he packed his shit and moved to Boston. They've been married seven years and have three daughters."

"And they're the ones who had Four?"

"Yep. Katie is allergic, but her mom doses her up with antihistamines when I come so the girls can at least have him visit."

I shook my head. "I still can't believe you took me on a private plane to Boston for dinner."

Max smiled. "Are you mad?"

"No. You make things into an adventure. But it is a little odd to be traveling to meet a guy's family when we've only just met ourselves."

"It won't seem so strange if you stop thinking of it as meeting the family of the guy you just met and start thinking of it as meeting the family of the guy you're gonna date all summer."

I laughed. "Pretty confident of yourself."

"You gotta put things out there to the universe if there's any shot you're gonna get them to happen."

Through my peripheral vision, I caught motion at Max's brother's front door. A woman walked out and smiled and waved. I knew Max had said his brother was older, but this woman looked old enough to be his mom. Still, who was I to judge?

"Is that your sister-in-law?"

"Nope. There's one more thing I forgot to mention about dinner tonight."

Max looked a little nervous, which made me nervous. "Oh, God. What else is there?"

His eyes lifted over my shoulder to his brother's house, and then he brought out the big guns—flashing his dimples the way a little boy who got caught with his hand in the cookie jar might.

"My mom's in town visiting, too. And all of my brothers and their wives."

• • •

A little while later, Tate's wife, Cassidy, and I were alone in the kitchen. "Do you want something to drink?" she asked. "I'm sure you could use something after meeting the entire family."

"Oh, thank God," I said, only half kidding. "I'm about thirty seconds from searching your bathroom for perfume or mouthwash and chugging the bottle."

She chuckled and took out two wine glasses. "The Yearwood family is...a lot."

I sighed. "I had no idea I was meeting the entire family until five minutes ago when we were in the car out front."

Cassidy smiled. "That sounds about right, though we knew about you. You know why?" She filled two glasses and passed me one.

"Thank you. I'm a little afraid to ask how you knew."

"Because Max called us at *six AM* one morning to tell us all about you."

I'd been sipping my wine and coughed it down the wrong pipe. "What?"

"Yep." She nodded. "Six fifteen, actually. Don't get me wrong, he knows we're up, but he doesn't usually call at that hour. In fact, he doesn't usually call. It's Tate who has to track his brother down to check in." Cassidy tilted her wine glass at me. "You're also the only woman he's ever brought over."

I wasn't sure what to say to that. So I drank some of my wine instead.

"The Yearwood men are sort of like large trees," she continued. "You can't chop them down very easily, but when they fall, they're sort of immovable." Her voice softened. "They're good men. I can vouch for that. As loyal as they come and honest to a fault. They say if you want to know how a man will treat his wife, you should watch the way he treats his mother. Those boys won't even curse around Rose because she doesn't like foul language."

Suddenly the kitchen door burst open, and two enormous men rolled in. Literally rolled. Max and his brother Tate were on the floor, wrestling around like two teenage boys.

Cassidy pointed to them, completely unfazed by the scene. "Whichever brother gets all the other brothers in a headlock first doesn't have to help with the dishes. A few years back they upended my tree on Christmas Eve. Somehow they snapped the thing in half, in addition to smashing three quarters of the ornaments. I have three little girls who get up at the crack of dawn to run and see what Santa left under that tree. So I made them march over to the tree lot, pick up a new one, and see if they could find replacement decorations so the kids wouldn't be devastated in the morning. Most stores were closed by then, except for Lalique. Do you know the brand?"

"They sell expensive crystal vases and fancy bowls, right?"

Cassidy nodded. "That's the one. But apparently they also sell collector's ornaments for the holidays. Max bought all their remaining stock. I almost died when I saw the receipt. He spent twenty-seven-thousand dollars on decorations for the tree so it would have ornaments. And he wasn't even the one who'd knocked it over."

My eyes widened.

Cassidy nodded. "I told you—they are *a lot*."

A few minutes later, Max flipped his brother on his back and wrapped him in a headlock. Tate had started to turn red when Mrs. Yearwood walked in and yelled at them. They stopped, both panting, and Max pointed at his brother.

"That counts. You would've tapped if *your mommy* didn't have to come in and save you."

"No way, Altar Boy."

Mrs. Yearwood rolled her eyes. "You'll *both* do the dishes for being idiots."

As I stood in the kitchen watching the antics, I realized something strange. I should've been freaked out that a man I wasn't dating had flown me to Boston to meet his entire family. Yet here I was, inside their home for only fifteen minutes, and instead of being nervous or anxious, I felt warmth in my chest.

Max walked over and hooked his big arm around my neck. Leaning in, he whispered, "You good?"

I smiled back. "Yeah, I think I am."

Dinner with the Yearwoods was one of the most entertaining meals I'd had in a long time. The brothers argued, their mom told embarrassing stories, and we laughed more times than I could count. After, I got up to help clear the table. One of the chairs had a place setting no one had used. I'd assumed someone was late for dinner.

"Do you want me to leave this setting?" I asked Mrs. Yearwood. "Is someone still coming?"

Her eyes caught with Max's briefly, before she smiled at me. "You can take it, honey. That's Austin's seat, my second youngest. He passed years ago, but I like to include him in family dinner when we're all together. On the holidays when dinner is at my house, I usually invite someone in need of a warm meal from my church to share Austin's seat. Otherwise we leave it empty for him."

I swallowed. "Wow. That's...beautiful."

She smiled. "I'm glad you think so. A few of my boys thought it was creepy for a long time. But they've come around after all these years. Now they just like to tease me that I only set a plate for my son and not their dad, so clearly I liked him better."

After dinner was cleaned up and the dishwasher loaded, Cassidy suggested we go sit out back on the deck and make a fire in their chiminea. It was a beautiful night, one that reminded you warm weather was coming soon.

Tate built the fire, and the ladies made a semicircle around it while the other brothers went out on the lawn to toss a football around. But the nice game of catch quickly escalated to tackling each other and rolling around on the lawn.

Mrs. Yearwood shook her head. "Still acting like they're twelve."

"Except now they get bruised and ache for a week after," Cassidy said. "Tate will never admit it, but he had to go to the chiropractor after their shenanigans on Easter."

Another of the wives chimed in. "Lucas wore a knee brace for a month."

Yet another wife laughed. "Will dislocated his elbow at Christmas. The only one who isn't out of commission after a family holiday is Max. He's the youngest and gets slammed into walls for a living."

"Speaking of making a living," Cassidy said. "Did you ladies know Georgia owns the company that made the beautiful flowers that are always in the center of my dining room table? The ones Max sent a few months back that last a year?"

"Really? Is that how you two met?"

I shook my head. "He actually sent those before we met."

"How did the two of you meet?" Mrs. Yearwood asked.

"Well...I guess sort of on a blind date."

One of the wives scoffed. "Really? Max went on a blind date? We're always trying to fix him up, and he refuses to let anyone play matchmaker."

"Well, Max wasn't actually who I was supposed to meet. He just pretended to be until my real date showed up and blew his cover."

Everyone laughed.

"Now that sounds more like our Max," Cassidy said.

The sound of bodies colliding and men grunting turned everyone's attention to the grass once again. Two of the brothers were lying on the grass while Max and Tate high fived. They'd been playing all of about ten or fifteen minutes, yet they were all sweaty and their clothes had grass stains. Max lifted the hem of his shirt and wiped sweat from his forehead, and it suddenly felt warm where I sat, too.

Damn. What a body. I wasn't sure I'd ever seen abs like that on a real, live person. For the most part, the men I'd been with had been physically fit. But there was a hell of a big difference between physically fit and *that*. Each rippled muscle on Max's torso was so defined, it was like he'd been hand carved. I found myself thinking about what it would be like to scrape my nails over each one and watch his face for a reaction. That made my mouth go dry. Without thinking, I ran my tongue over my bottom lip, and as luck would have it, Max picked that moment to look over at me. A devilish smirk spread across his handsome face, one that made me question whether he might know exactly what I'd been thinking. I tried to pull off casual by smiling and looking away. But something told me I'd failed miserably.

An hour later, we were already getting ready to leave. I went to use the bathroom before our trek home, and when I came out, Max and his mom were alone in the kitchen. They didn't hear me come in.

"I really like her. Please tell me she knows."

"Can we talk about this another time, Mom?"

She frowned. "Max..."

He looked up and saw me. "There she is. It was good seeing you, Mom. I'll call you next week."

"Okay." She smiled and turned to me. "You're a breath of fresh air. I hope I see you again real soon."

"You, too."

She hugged me, and then it took another fifteen minutes to say goodbye to everyone else. Poor Max had to practically pry Four from his nieces' hands. He soothed away the oldest girl's impending tears by promising her he'd bring the dog when he came to town for his next game.

Once we got back in the Town Car, I took a deep inhale and exhaled audibly.

Max smiled. "That bad."

"No, no...I had fun. It was just...a little overwhelming with so many people. Since I'm an only child, my family gatherings are usually just my mom and me. She has one sister, who lives out in Arizona, and we see her maybe once every two years. But I had a good time. Though for a minute there, I thought we were going to go out in a ball of flames with your three nieces crying about Four. It works out great that you're able to bring him to the game with you."

"I'll wind up getting fined for sneaking him on the team plane again. But I'd rather that than tears. Thank God I only had brothers, because I can't take seeing girls cry. Keri, the woman I dated for eighteen months a couple of years back, cried when I told her I wanted to end things. I gave her my car."

I laughed, but Max didn't. "Oh my God. You're joking, right?"

He shook his head and shrugged. "It made her stop crying."

"Wow. Okay...well, I'll keep that in mind if I'm having a hard time getting my way with you."

Max looked at me tenderly. He brushed his knuckles along my cheek. "Trust me, you won't have a hard time getting anything from me."

Warmth flooded my belly. I had the strongest urge to rest my head on his shoulder, so I gave in and did. We were mostly quiet the remainder of the way to the airport, but it didn't feel awkward, which was nice. Once we boarded the waiting jet, Max and I sat across from each other.

His eyes pointed down to my ankle, where I had a big bruise on the inside of my leg.

"How did you get that?"

"I, uh, jumped out of the shower to write something down that I'd thought of while I was washing my hair, and I slipped on my way back in. My leg hit the side of the tub. I have a matching one on my hip."

Max looked amused. "Do you run out of the shower often?"

I sighed. "I do, actually. I don't know why, but I think of things I forgot to do at work when I go in the shower. I could sit at my desk for an hour, and nothing. But the minute I'm lathered up, things start popping into my brain. Does that ever happen to you?"

"Nope. I put on music and enjoy the down time."

"Yeah. I'm not so good at that."

Max smiled. "So did my mother and my sisters-in-law tell you stories about how rotten I am while you were sitting on the deck?"

"You mean like when you and your brothers snapped Cassidy's Christmas tree in half while wrestling?"

Max hung his head. "It was an accident. We bought her a new one, even if it was pretty sad looking because that was all they had left on Christmas Eve. That year was a shitshow. Did she also tell you about the stolen presents?"

My forehead wrinkled. "Someone stole gifts?"

He nodded. "Ever since my mom started getting really into the church, she brings around strangers for the holidays. Usually it's when she has us at her house in Washington, and they're people her church knows. But a few years ago, we started having Christmas at Tate and Cassidy's, because they're the only ones with kids. Mom went to some local church near them on Christmas Eve morning and came home with a woman she met. Not to be a jerk, but the woman looked like an addict. She was scratching her arms constantly, and she didn't meet your eyes when she spoke to you. But Mom had invited her for dinner, so everyone was polite. After we finished eating, my brothers and I went to the garage to put together some toys the girls were getting for Christmas, and the ladies were all clearing the table and doing whatever. When we were done, we came back in, and I asked where the woman was. She was gone, but she hadn't said goodbye to anyone. Then Cassidy noticed half of the presents under the tree were gone, too."

"Noooo."

Max nodded. "Mom's a little too trusting at times. It's great that she wants to help people who are less fortunate, but she needs to sprinkle a bit of safety into her decisions."

"Yeah, definitely. Is her growing more involved with the church something new?"

"She's always been religious. We were raised Catholic and went to religion classes growing up, and Mom always went to church on Sundays. But ten years ago, she started to go daily and get involved in outreach programs and stuff."

"Did something happen to make her turn to the church?" After I asked the question, I realized maybe it wasn't polite.

Max looked out the window and nodded. "It started when my brother Austin died. He was only twenty one."

"Oh gosh, I'm so sorry."

Max continued to stare out the window. "He had an abdominal aortic aneurysm. We both went to BU. He was a year ahead of me. We were only thirteen months apart."

I had no idea what to say, so I took his hand and squeezed. I'd wondered about the conversation I'd walked in on between Max and his mom. I guess I understood what he didn't want to talk about now. We were both quiet for the rest of the plane ride, only this time, the silence wasn't quite as comfortable.

In the car on the way back to my apartment, we made small talk. But something had changed. So when we pulled up near my building and Max parked, I felt compelled to say something.

"Max?"

I waited until he looked over to continue.

"I'm sorry if I overstepped and took our conversation in a direction that ruined your evening."

He shook his head. "You didn't. I apologize if I made you feel that way. Sometimes I just get stuck in my head."

The sound of my phone vibrating in my purse interrupted our conversation. I didn't intend to answer, but I dug it out to see who it was and send the call to voicemail. *Gabriel* flashed on the screen. After I hit decline, I looked up, and Max's face told me he'd read the name, too.

He smiled sadly. "It's late. I'll walk you up with Four."

Unlike last time, Max didn't hold my hand as we walked to my building. He had Four in his arms, but that didn't feel like the only reason there was distance between us. When we reached the elevator, I didn't press the button. Instead, I turned to face him.

"I had a good time. Thank you for bringing me tonight."

Max bent and set Four down to the floor. When he stood back up, he took my hand. "Listen, Georgia. I'm just going to put it out there once more. I'd love to spend the summer with you. After next week, there won't be any more games or traveling I have to do. Other than keeping in shape, I pretty much have no plans except to find somewhere to live by August. We could have some fun. No strings attached. I get that you have some unsettled stuff going on, but you know I'm going to be out of here in a few months. To me, it keeps things pretty simple." He held up his hands. "But I won't push it anymore. If you change your mind, you have my number. All you have to do is say the word."

My face fell. "We can't just be friends?"

Max's eyes dropped down to my body. They took their time caressing their way up and over each curve. "Friendship between two people who are the opposite sex doesn't work when one of you wants to see the other naked. That might be an asshole thing to say, but it's the truth." He pushed the button to call the elevator. It must've been waiting, because the doors slid right open. Max lifted my hand to his mouth and kissed the top. "I hope you call."

I swallowed and nodded. But as I stepped into the elevator, a heavy feeling came over me. The thought of never seeing Max again made me panicky, so when the doors began to slide closed, I stuck my hand out to stop them at the very last second.

"Max, wait!"

He looked up at me, and I stepped forward, holding the doors open.

"I never do anything without spending forever debating all the pros and cons." I shook my head. "And I'm not sure what the right thing is for us, but I am sure it's not never seeing you again. Could we...take it slow?"

The biggest grin spread across Max's face. "I like it slow."

I chuckled. "You know what I mean."

He nodded and took my hand. "We can go at whatever speed makes you comfortable."

I took a deep breath and blew out a rush of air. "Okay."

He lifted a brow. "Okay?"

I nodded. "Let's do it—spend the summer together, I mean."

Max yanked the hand he was holding, and I stumbled against his body, crashing into what felt like a brick wall.

"Oww..." I said, laughing. My palms landed flat against his chest, and I patted it twice. "This thing hurts. It's really hard."

"Oh, I can't wait to show you hard. Now give me that mouth. I said I'm good with going slow, but I'm going to lose my mind if I can't at least have a little taste."

I didn't get a chance to respond before his lips crashed down on mine. He squeezed me tightly against his hard body, making my knees feel weak. There had been an intensity about the way Max looked at me from the moment we'd met, but this kiss... It was a whole other level. He licked my lips and nudged my mouth open while one of his large hands slid up to my neck and wrapped around my throat. I'd never had a man hold me like that. It felt desperate and needy and just on the right side of dominant. My hands threaded through his hair, and he lifted me into the air and walked us until my back hit a wall. I lost all sense of where we were when I felt his hard-on push up against my stomach.

Oh God.

We stayed wrapped around each other for the longest time, groping and grabbing like two horny teenagers. Max used my hair to pull my head back and sucked along my pulse line, which had to be beating frantically. When we came up for air, he leaned his forehead to mine and used his thumb to wipe at my bottom lip.

"I knew it."

I could barely form words, and I was glad he hadn't set me down yet, because my legs felt like jelly. "What?"

"Magic, sweetheart," he said. "We're going to make magic."

The smile on my face was so big, I thought my skin might crack. "Would you...like to come up for a little while?"

Max gripped both of my hands in one of his behind my back. “I’d love to come up. But you’d probably never get me to leave, and I also have practice in the morning. Besides…” He pressed closer to me, and I felt his erection dig into my hip. “My brain understands going slow, but my body isn’t quite getting the message. Have dinner with me Friday night. Let me take you out on a real date.”

I nodded. “I’d love that.”

Max pushed the elevator button again, and the car doors immediately slid open. He leaned down and brushed his lips against mine once more. “I didn’t even leave yet, and I can’t wait to see you again.”

I stepped into the car with a fluttering heart and smiled as I shook my head. “No strings attached, right?”

He winked. “The only string might be one I use to tie you up.”

It all sounded perfect. *Too perfect.* As the doors slid shut, I felt sweat tingling my palms. I rubbed them together and squeezed my eyes closed a moment. I mean, what reason would there be for something to go wrong?

— Eight —

Max

Ten years ago

"Ummm...what are you doing?"

I shrugged without turning around. "What does it look like I'm doing?"

"It looks like you're filling an empty, half-gallon container with milk from that milk dispenser that's supposed to be for coffee."

"There's no sign that says there's a limit." I held up the empty coffee cup in my hand. "I paid for a coffee."

When the milk reached the neck of the plastic bottle, I pulled the jug away and twisted on the cap. I turned, expecting to see one of the ladies who worked here wearing her cafeteria uniform, but instead my eyes landed on a gorgeous blonde I'd never seen before. She looked a few years older than me. I glanced around the room to see if whoever had started with me about the milk might've walked away, but nope... No one was around except her.

She had her feet propped up on the chair in front of her, and I did a double take catching a look at her ankle.

"What's going on there?" I motioned to her leg. A dozen or so colorful ice pops were taped around her ankle with black electrical tape.

"I twisted my ankle playing volleyball. It's starting to swell, and no one has an ice pack. So it was these or beers. I figured ice pops are colder and plus, Andrea will let me return them if I bring them back unopened."

"Andrea?"

She lifted her chin toward the cashier. "The woman you handed a dollar for your empty coffee cup to justify stealing a half gallon of milk."

I chuckled. "You're a stickler for rules when it comes to me, yet you're stealing ice."

"I'm not stealing. I paid for them. I'm just going to return them when I'm done, unharmed."

"But they will no longer be frozen, correct?"

"Probably not."

"Right. So you're stealing the ice. The school is going to have to pay the electric bill for that freezing a second time."

She rolled her eyes. "Whatever."

"I'll tell you what, why don't you return them while they're still frozen to avoid becoming a thief? I have plenty of ice packs in my room. I'll give you a few to ice your ankle properly."

"Why do you have so many ice packs?"

"I'm on the hockey team. I'm always icing something."

"You're not just trying to lure me to your room, are you?"

I chuckled. "I'll go get them for you. You can wait here."

She tilted her head. "Why would you do that?"

"Because swelling should be iced and..." I shrugged. "You're hot."

She smiled, suddenly more shy. "Okay. Thank you."

I lifted my chin. "What's your name?"

"Teagan Kelly. What's yours?"

"Max Yearwood. I'll be back in a few minutes, Teagan Kelly."

I jogged up to my room, grabbed a few instant cold compresses and a box of Cheerios, and went back to the cafeteria. Teagan was still sitting in the same place, but she'd removed the frozen ice pops from around her ankle and was now in the process of trying to unstick the pops from the tape.

She looked at the crap in my hands. "What are the Cheerios for?"

"Breakfast."

"But where's your milk?"

I grinned and lifted the empty coffee cup I'd bought earlier, pointing to the machine. I'd left my nice, full half gallon in my fridge back in my room.

Teagan laughed. "What's your major, Max?"

"Math."

Her eyebrows shot up. "Really?"

"Why do you look so surprised?"

"I don't know. Just doesn't seem to go with hockey."

"Ah." I nodded. "Dumb jock stigma."

"That's not what I meant."

"So you expected me to be stupid because I'm so pretty?"

She laughed. "Sorry. I guess I was kind of labeling you."

I shrugged. "It's okay. I'll give you a pass. What's your major? Baton twirling? I mean, you are hot."

Setting everything except one of the ice packs down, I whacked the plastic bag against the table to activate the cold. The inner bag made a popping sound and began to swell. After I finished getting the second one ready, I pointed to her foot. "Can I take a look?"

"I'm a third-year med student. I can get it checked at the hospital later. I just started ER rotations, and I stand for hours at a time. I just wanted to keep the swelling down before I had to go over there in a little while."

My brows shot up. "You're a third-year med student, and your treatment plan of choice was ice pops and electrical tape?"

"Shut up. It's what was available."

"Can I take a look anyway?"

She sighed. "Sure. Why not?"

Fifteen years of playing hockey, with doctors feeling all of my battered bones, had made me pretty damn good at guessing the extent of an injury. I put my hand on her anklebone and pressed. "Does this hurt?"

"Not really."

Sliding my hand to the soft part of her ankle, I pressed again. "What about this?"

"Oww—yeah, that's right where it hurts."

"Any numbness or tingling?"

She shook her head. "No. It's just sore right where you touched."

I nodded. "Good. It's probably not broken. You'd feel it in the bone if it were. My money is on a bruise."

"Your money? You just bought an empty cup to steal milk. I hope you're not insulted if I don't think that statement holds a lot of weight."

"Good point." I held out the ice packs to her. "Where's your sock? You should put it on and tuck these inside. It works a lot better than electrical tape."

Teagan leaned to the floor and scooped up her backpack. She found her sock, pulled it on, and planted the ice packs inside. While I watched, my stomach growled, so I tore open the box of Cheerios, filled my trusty coffee cup, and poured in some milk from the dispenser before pulling a big spoon from my back pocket and taking a seat across from her.

She laughed. "You brought your own utensil, but not milk?"

I shoveled a heaping spoonful of cereal into my mouth and spoke with it full. "The spoons down here are too small."

"Oh, I see." She nodded. "You prefer a shovel."

"I just burned twenty-five-hundred calories at practice. I'm starving." I pointed to her colorful collection of ice pops on the table. "You better move those, or I might eat them next."

When I finished the first cup of Cheerios, I immediately poured a second.

"Are you going to eat that entire box?"

"Do you want some?"

"No."

I shrugged. "Then yeah, probably."

Teagan laughed. She thought I was joking, but I did eat the entire box most of the time. I freaking loved Cheerios.

"So are you any good?" she asked.

"I'm good at pretty much everything, so you're going to have to be more specific."

She rolled her eyes. "At hockey. I mean, if you get injured so much that you can tell if bones are broken, that probably means you aren't, right?"

I grinned. "You don't know shit about hockey, do you?"

"Not really."

"Injuries are part of playing. If you aren't icing something, you're not getting much playing time. I'm the team captain."

"Are you a senior?"

"Freshman."

"I didn't think they named freshmen as captains."

"They don't. Usually."

Teagan tilted her head. "Should I be impressed?"

"Nah. Got plenty of better things for you to be impressed about."

"Like what?"

"Go out with me and I'll show you?"

She laughed. "Smooth, Captain Yearwood."

"So is that a yes?"

"How old are you?"

"Nineteen. Why?"

"I'm twenty-four."

I shrugged. "So? Doesn't bother me. Does it bother you?"

She tapped her finger to her lip. "I'm not sure. If we did go out, where would we go? Is *go out with you* code for hookup in your dorm room? Or do you really want to take me out?"

"I'll take you wherever you want." I held up my cup of Cheerios. "Though I'm not a fan of eating O Toasties, so make it within reason."

"O Toasties?"

"Yeah, you know, the knock-off brand. I eat a lot of Cheerios, and if I'm broke, I'm going to have to eat those things, and they taste like cardboard."

Teagan grinned. "Too bad people don't put Cheerios in their coffee and there's no cereal machine you could rob, huh?"

I finished my second cup of Cheerios and downed the milk from the cup before shaking a third helping from the box. I looked around the empty cafeteria. "No Cheerios machine, but there must be a sarcasm dispenser somewhere, since you're so full of it."

Teagan tried to hide her smile. "How about a party with your friends?"

"As a date?"

She nodded. "I don't go to a lot of parties anymore. But I think you can tell a lot about a person by the company they keep. It's also cheap—and will keep you in those oh-so-important brand-name Cheerios. So why not a party? It'll help me figure out if our age difference is just a number or a maturity gap."

Shit. Most of my friends were immature idiots. A party wasn't a good idea.

Teagan noticed my less-than-excited face. She arched a brow. "Unless you don't want me to meet your friends for some reason?"

It seemed like she was daring me to say yes. I was nineteen and played hockey, which meant I never met a challenge I didn't like. So I smiled. "How about Saturday night?"

Nine

Georgia

I spent the next morning making lists, deliberating over the decision I'd already told Max I made last night. Obsessive overanalyzing didn't stop after I came to a conclusion; it only meant I shifted from deciding how to handle a situation to wondering if I'd made the wrong choice. It wasn't something I could stop. The problem was... I was having a hard time seeing any outcome other than me getting hurt at the end of this summer.

However, one of the many benefits of hiring my best friend to work in my office was that I had a built-in therapist whenever the need occurred. Maggie strolled into my office at 11 AM, assuming we were going to go over the latest graphics she'd been working on for an upcoming ad campaign, but right now she wasn't going to get to show me even page one of what she'd brought with her.

Ready for business, she pushed a four-inch-thick deck of papers across my desk and looked up at the frown lines cutting into my forehead. "Don't worry. It won't take that long. It's only a couple of concepts, but I did a few different colorations of each, so that's why it's so many pages."

"I told Max I would have sex with him."

Maggie blinked a few times. "Can you repeat that?"

I rubbed my temples. "He has an adorable little furry dog, kneels down to play with his three young nieces, and he wipes his stupid, sweaty head with the hem of his shirt, and underneath are rock hard abs. It's awful."

Maggie's brows furrowed. "Yeah, sounds it. I like my men to kick puppies, be mean to children, and have soft, mushy beer bellies."

I dropped my face into my hands. "He also makes me laugh—like, all the time—and he brings me chicken soup when I'm sick. Chicken soup! *And drugs!*"

"You lost me with that one, honey. Did he bring you crack? Is that why you're so upset?"

I shook my head. "What am I going to do when Gabriel comes home, Mags?"

"Oh..." She nodded as if everything made sense for the first time. "You're afraid you might grow feelings for Max, and that will complicate things when Mr. I-Want-an-Open-Relationship floats back into your life."

"I love Gabriel, Maggie. I know you've had your doubts about him since he pulled what he pulled, but I said yes when he asked me to spend the rest of my life with him. You know I don't rush into things until I'm sure where I want to go. Last year I was absolutely certain I wanted to wake up next to him every day and have a family together. I'd agonized over whether it was the right time for me, whether Gabriel was ready, and if he was truly the one. I didn't have any doubt."

Maggie studied me for a moment before leaning forward in her seat. "What is really freaking you out here?

The fact that it will be tough to say goodbye to Max when the time comes, or that you might not *want* to end things with him, which would mean the decision you made to say yes to Gabriel a year ago might not have been the right one?"

I rubbed my temples. "I have a headache."

"That's because you're wound up so tight." She grinned. "I bet sex with Max would fix that. Something tells me you'll be a bowl full of jelly when that man is done with you."

I sighed. "I've never had sex with anyone I wasn't in a relationship with."

"I know, honey." Maggie reached across the desk and patted my hand. "But don't worry, I've done that enough for both of us. So this is a subject I can help with."

I smiled sadly. "When I'm with Max, I'm so caught up in things that I don't think about anything else. But the minute he leaves, all the guilt and questions set in. I feel like I'm cheating on Gabriel."

"Okay, let's start with the simple stuff here. You are *not* cheating on Gabriel. That fucker is in England boning Brits. He's the one who forced this situation. You can't cheat on someone when you aren't in a relationship."

"I know I wouldn't be technically cheating, but my heart still feels like it is."

Maggie shook her head. "God, I can feel the tension radiating from you. You're making me feel stressed just sitting in the same room. I think you need to put the meditation you learned a while back to some use so you can relax, and maybe things will become clearer."

"I did meditate! For an hour this morning. That's why I was late getting in."

Maggie arched a brow. "So this is calm you?"

I took a deep breath and heaved a loud sigh. "I don't know what to do."

"Do you remember when you came home from that meditation retreat? You told me about these sessions you went to for over-thinkers and said they suggested implementing some rules to make decisions less stressful."

I nodded. "The serenity six, they called them."

"What were they?"

"Umm... There was an acronym. What was it again?" I tapped my finger to my lip. "Oh, I know. STEP UP. S was for spontaneity, to work on being more spontaneous. T was for timeline. They suggested setting a timeline to make decisions and move on. Thirty seconds for little things like what you should have for lunch. Thirty minutes for bigger decisions, and to the end of the day for the biggest stuff. E was for exercise, which is self-explanatory. P was for present, to work on being in the present and not looking back at things. U was for ubhaya padangusthasana, which is a yoga balancing pose that they suggest you do when you're under a lot of stress because it's supposed to center your core, and the last P was for people. They suggest only associating with people who aren't over-thinkers when you're struggling."

"Okay, well...I didn't remember any of that, and honestly I just zoned out while you were explaining half of it, but the parts I heard sounded useful. Like setting a timeline—I'm sure you see this as a big decision, so maybe give yourself until the end of the day today, and then don't look back. You're either in or you're out. If you're in—stay in the present. Don't think about Gabriel. He's not here, and he's not part of today. And I definitely think you could use some spontaneity. If you decide yes on Max, make a commitment to have fun with him and try new things. If not, you and I will make some plans. I've always wanted to jump out of a plane."

I smiled. "I don't know about the plane part, but I guess the other stuff is good advice."

"You are great at making decisions, but sometimes circumstances change. You need to loosen up and be able to roll with the unexpected punches. It's okay to just go out there and have fun without knowing what tomorrow will bring."

Reluctantly, I nodded.

Maggie leaned back in her chair and stretched her arms out on the armrests. "Look at me. I'm the normal one now."

I snorted. "Let's not go that far. Are you still sleeping with Aaron's lawyer?"

"We did it in a conference room in his office, right before Aaron was coming for another settlement meeting. He sat down in the exact spot where my bare ass had been not ten minutes earlier. I'm pretty sure if he had paid attention, he could have recognized my ass-cheek print on the glass tabletop."

"I rest my case."

Maggie took a deep breath. "Alright. Well, are you ready to get started? We're on a tight deadline with the printer."

"Yeah, sure."

Two hours later, we'd finalized the new ad campaign, and Maggie stood to head back to her office.

When she reached the door, I called after her, "Mags?"

She turned back. "Yeah?"

"Thank you for talking me down."

"My pleasure." She winked. "Now I only owe you a million more for all the times you've helped me. I'll be back this afternoon to hear your decision."

• • •

My supplier meeting ran late, so by the time I got back to the office, people were already leaving for the day. Ellie, my assistant, was putting her jacket on as I walked by her desk.

"Hey, Georgia. I left a delivery that came for you in your office."

"Oh, okay. Thank you."

"And I summarized all of your messages in an email. Nothing sounded urgent, but I'm sure you'll check."

"Thanks, Ellie. Have a good night."

I expected to see a brown cardboard box on my desk, the usual delivery of samples or something from Amazon. I was surprised to find a white gift bag, decorated with ribbons. Curious, I didn't even take off my jacket or sit down before I tore into it.

Inside was a plastic gift box with a pad and pencil set. Upon closer inspection, I noticed both had suction cups attached to them. I wasn't quite sure what I was looking at. A sample of some sort sent in a pretty bag by a supplier? There was an envelope, so I sliced open the back and slipped out the card.

Georgia,
It's waterproof. No more slips and falls.
Looking forward to Friday night.

X
Max

Damn it, that Max. Did he have to go and be so great? While a gift like this seemed like it should go in the pros column, there was also a reason to put it in with the cons. Any man who took time out of his day to find me a water-resistant pad and pencil was someone I could grow attached to. Now, if the bag had contained a black-lace teddy, that would actually have seemed safer—that type of gift screamed *summer fling only*.

So I sat at my desk, staring into space for the next half hour, doing what I did best—analyzing and overanalyzing. Eventually a knock at my door interrupted my thoughts.

Maggie held up two of those tiny bottles of wine you get on an airplane.

"Decision time. I'm going to assume you haven't come to one—or rather, you haven't settled into the one you told Max you already made. So I'm here to rip the Band-Aid off. The wine will help take away the sting."

She plopped down in one of my guest chairs, twisted the cap off one bottle, and passed it to me. Maggie held her bottle out to me to clink. "To being lucky enough to sit in a beautiful office with my best friend whose biggest stress right now is whether to fuck a hot hockey player."

I laughed. "Thanks. When you put it like that, it seems a tad bit ridiculous how much anxiety this is causing me. Especially after this..." I pushed the gift bag to the other side of the desk and explained the gift as she looked it over.

Maggie put her hand on her lower belly. "I'm pretty sure my ovaries just fluttered. Do you still have that picture of him with no shirt on that I sent you from his phone? That might help lower the sensation to *right where I need it*."

I snorted. Even if I was stressing, sharing it all with Maggie at least made it fun.

"So what's it going to be, girl?" She looked at her watch. "It's six thirty. I'd say we're past the end of the business day. Are you going to have a summer to remember or up your battery subscription on Amazon?"

I closed my eyes. My brain still told me to keep my distance from Max Yearwood. Though my body said my head needed to be examined. But for the most part, I'd done really well for myself by using my brain and making logical decisions, hadn't I? Though not with Gabriel. So maybe it was time to do like Maggie said and have some fun without knowing what tomorrow would bring...

My phone buzzed on my desk, interrupting my thoughts. I swiped to see who had sent me a message.

Max.

Perfect timing.

He'd sent a selfie from the plane. He had a small duffle bag on his lap, with Four's tiny head peeking out the top while he leaned in and held his finger to his lips, giving the universal *shhh* sign. His dimples were on full display. It was impossible not to smile.

I turned the screen to show Maggie. "He's sneaking Four on the team plane to Boston where his nieces live, so they can see him."

She grabbed the phone out of my hand and looked down at the screen, shaking her head. "I wanted to have you come to a decision on your own. But I'm afraid you're going to chicken out. So now I'm going to give you my opinion. Have I ever steered you wrong?"

I shook my head.

"Do it, Georgia. He knows the deal. You're both going into this with your eyes open. I have no doubt you'll enjoy the shit out of this man, but you also might learn some things about yourself."

I took a deep breath, picked up my little wine bottle, and drank the entire thing in one gulp. "Okay. I'll do it. This is going to be one interesting summer."

Ten

Georgia

I was nervous. *And late.*

This afternoon, Max had texted that he'd gotten stuck at some photo shoot for a sponsor, and he'd have to meet me at the restaurant for our date. He'd tried to insist on sending a Town Car to pick me up, but I'd convinced him it was faster to take the subway with Friday evening crosstown traffic. However, the block-and-a-half walk from the station in the heels I had on had me wishing I'd relented. But the look on Max's face as I walked up to the restaurant made the pain from the strap cutting into my pinkie toe worthwhile.

God, he looks so handsome. Max was dressed in dark slacks and a white dress shirt. But the way they fit, I suspected they were probably custom made. Yet it was more than the perfectly tailored clothes and his large stature that caused him to stand out. His stance was just so dominant and confident, with legs spread apart, shoulders squared, and one hand casually tucked into his pocket. Unlike every other person waiting for anything these days, he didn't have his phone out or earbuds in his ears. He just stood there, waiting and looking around, and when he saw me, his lips curved to a smile. He watched my every step intently.

"Hi," I said. "Sorry I'm a few minutes late."

He looked me up and down. "You look incredible. While I was watching you come up the street, I was trying to decide if I want to show you off or wrap my jacket around you so no one else gets to look at you."

I smiled. "And?"

"I want to show you off. But I might growl at anyone who takes more than a polite look."

I laughed. "You look very handsome yourself. Though I'm positive my growl isn't half as scary as yours." I pointed to the door. "Should we go in?"

Max stepped forward and wrapped one hand firmly around my waist, while the other encircled my neck from the front. "Nope. Want that mouth first. C'mere."

Before I could respond, his lips were on mine. His tongue dipped inside, and I felt the raging beat of my heart against his hard chest. He kissed me like we were the only two people in the world, even standing on a busy Manhattan street, like he *had* to kiss me, rather than wanted to. I couldn't remember the last time I'd been kissed hello with so much passion. Sadly for me, I wasn't sure I'd ever been. As corny as it might sound, the man made my knees weak.

Before releasing me, Max caught my lower lip between his teeth and gave it a tug that I felt between my legs. He used his thumb to wipe beneath my lip as he cleared his throat. "We better go in before I get us arrested out here."

Inside, the restaurant was dark. We followed the hostess down a long corridor and through another door.

Max held out a hand for me to walk through first, and I was surprised to find we'd stepped outside into a small courtyard. A large tree stood in the center, decorated with strings of twinkling white lights that draped overhead and illuminated the area. Tall bamboo in long planters created individual, secluded dining areas.

The hostess led us into one and held out her hand. "Our wine menu and specialty drinks are on the table." She pointed to a tall lantern a few feet from the table. "If you get chilly, just let your server know, and we can turn on the heater. I'll give you a few minutes and then send someone over to take your drink order."

"Thank you."

Max pulled out a chair for me.

"This is so unexpected," I said. "I had no idea there was an outdoor area when we walked in. It's so pretty. I'm glad I came."

"Were you considering not coming?"

I hadn't meant to let on that I'd had doubts, so I tried to sweep my comment under the table. I shook my head. "I wouldn't have stood you up."

He cocked his head. "But you *were* considering not coming?"

Great. Two minutes into the date, and I'd already stuck my foot in my mouth. "I second-guess everything, weighing the pros and cons. It's my nature. It's not you."

"That sounds pretty exhausting."

I smiled. "It is. I'm trying to work on it."

"I'm just the opposite. I tend to go with my gut and don't always think things through enough." He winked. "I'm trying to work on it. But now I want to hear your pros and cons. I'm curious to find out what tilted things in my favor."

The waiter walked over, and we hadn't even picked up the wine menu yet. I looked at Max. "Are you having something?"

He lifted the menu and held it out to me. "No practice tomorrow. You pick a bottle."

I perused the menu and settled on a full-bodied red. When the waiter disappeared, Max looked at me expectantly.

"What?"

"You were about to tell me about your pros and cons analysis."

"You just want to hear all the pros to stroke your ego."

Max grinned. "That would normally be true. But I'm more curious about the cons when it comes to you. If I don't know what's broken, I can't fix it."

The waiter came back to deliver our wine. After a taste test, he filled both glasses and left us with dinner menus.

"None of the cons were about you, really. The cons were more about me. I've never had a no-strings-attached relationship, and I'm not sure I know how." I sipped my wine. "You said you've had hookups before. How do you keep things simple?"

Max shrugged. "I guess we're both just upfront about what it is we want."

"Okay." I looked into his eyes. "Tell me what you want from me."

Max lifted his wine and drank. His eyes flickered to my lips. "That might get me smacked."

I laughed. "It won't. I promise."

He leaned in, lowering his voice. "I want to spread you out on my bed wearing nothing but those shoes you have on right now and lick you until you beg."

I swallowed. "I don't beg."

A wicked grin spread across Max's face. "Then you haven't been eaten properly."

I felt my face flush, so I grabbed my wine again. But the sparkle in Max's eyes told me he knew exactly what he was doing.

I cleared my throat. "So is that it? What you want from me, I mean? Just sex?"

"I like you, Georgia. I enjoy your company." His eyes roamed my face. "You're the one who seems to need things defined. So why don't you tell me what *you* want?"

I blushed again. "What you said sounded pretty good."

Max laughed. "What else do you want, Georgia? Because I get the feeling I could scare you away pretty easily and not even know why."

"I just want to have fun. I guess, feel free? Do things I've been putting off and enjoy this summer."

He nodded. "I'm game for fun. But tell me what kind of things you've been putting off."

"Do you remember the night we met I mentioned I had a list of things I'd been putting off, and dating was at the top of it? That's why I forced myself to go on my blind date even though I hadn't really wanted to?"

"Yeah."

"Well, I actually do have a list. It's not a bucket list with crazy things like jump out of an airplane or anything that exciting. It's more about making things I've been meaning to do a priority over work and cutting back on overanalyzing. For the last four years, I've worked seventy to eighty hours a week, and the highlight of my week has been going to a late dinner on Friday night. A few months ago I hired a director of operations, so now I can delegate more and work less. I want to unplug more, be more spontaneous, stay out all night, watch the sunrise, go to an after-hours club, volunteer somewhere, take a staycation here in the city. I've lived here my entire life, and I've never even been to the Statue of Liberty or walked the Brooklyn Bridge. I also have dye my hair red on that list." I shrugged. "I love red hair, and I've always wanted to try it."

"A redhead, huh?" Max smiled. "I think you'd look hot."

I smiled back. "Thanks."

He ran his finger along the top of his wine glass. "How about we hit your list together?"

"Really? You want to go to the Statue of Liberty with me?"

Max shrugged. "Sure. Why not?"

"Are you truly this easygoing?"

He laughed. "I don't know about easygoing, but I'm up for an adventure with you."

"An adventure, huh?" *God, why can't I see things this simply?* I bit down on my bottom lip.

Max leaned forward and used his thumb to gently rub it loose. "Don't overthink it. Just say yes."

I took a deep breath. "I know you proposed spending the summer together. But could we just see how it goes? It's less intimidating if it's...I don't know...*less,* I guess."

"Whatever you want."

I nodded nervously. "Okay. Screw it. Let's hit my list."

"*Nice.*" He hooked a hand around my neck and pulled me to meet his lips for a kiss. "This might be the first time since I was a kid that I've been glad hockey season ended."

The waiter interrupted to take our order, but yet again we hadn't even looked at the menu. So we asked for a minute and quickly decided to order two dishes and share them. After we'd ordered, I shifted the conversation to something that wouldn't freak me out as much as what I'd just agreed to...*again.*

"So tell me about your photo shoot today? Was it for a sports magazine or something?"

"Underwear ad." Max shook his head. "I called my agent on the way back and told him that was my last one of those."

"Why?"

"They wanted me to wear a Velcro strap around my junk. Not just the frank, the beans too."

I chuckled. "What?"

"Apparently it's a thing underwear models do to make the package more pronounced." He shook his head. "I wasn't doing it."

I covered my smile with my hand. "Oh my God. What did they say when you refused?"

He shrugged. "They took the pictures. My junk's just fine on its own."

"When will the ads run? I'm curious to see them now."

"They said they would send proofs to my agent in a few days. He negotiated approval rights. But if you'd like to take a look at my junk sooner..."

I laughed. "I was asking for business purposes. If you look good, maybe we can have you hold up some flowers in tightie-whities. I'd need to check out the merchandise before deciding, of course."

Max winked. "Anytime, sweetheart."

I drank the rest of my wine. "So how long does a hockey player usually play professionally? I know football players must retire pretty early because of how big a deal everyone makes out of Tom Brady still playing in his forties."

"The average retirement age in the NHL is something like twenty-nine."

"Twenty-nine? But that's your age."

"Don't remind me."

"That's so young."

"It's not by choice. Hockey is rough on the body. Between injuries and joints and ligaments not holding up, a lot of guys are forced out earlier than they'd like. But there've been a few dozen guys who have played into their forties. Gordie Howe played until he was fifty-two, but that's definitely not the norm."

"Then what? If the average player is done by thirty, what does he do after?"

"Some guys stay in the business—coaching, broadcasting, fitness, that type of thing. Some go into sales. If they have a well-known name, it opens a lot of doors for the company they represent. A lot actually buy businesses. They know the odds of an early retirement are pretty high, so they stash away money and buy into a business once they hang up their skates. I know guys who own gyms, car dealerships, restaurants, a little bit of everything."

"What do you think you'll do?"

"I'd like to stay in the sport in some way. But I'd also like to open a small business. My brother Austin was a really talented woodworker, like my dad, who was a carpenter. Do you remember Lincoln Logs?"

"I think so. They came in a bucket and you could build little log cabins, right?"

"Yeah, that's them. My brother loved them as a kid. He was obsessed with building. When he was maybe ten, he and my dad made big Lincoln Logs together. Life-sized ones my brothers and I used to build forts and stuff in the yard. Austin wanted to make a business out of it. The two years before he went to college, he perfected a set of large-scale pieces and illustrated a book of fifty different structures you could build with just one set of interconnecting wood logs—everything from a swing set to a fort to a tiny two-story house. Most kids love to build, so these were a way to teach them how to build their own stuff. When they're done, they also have something to play with. And once they grow bored with whatever they build, they can reconfigure it into something else."

"That's a really cool idea."

Max nodded. "Austin was smart. He was a dual major in architecture and architectural engineering. I have his prototypes and illustrations. He never got to see his ideas become more, so I'm hoping maybe I can finish things for him."

"Wow. I think it's pretty amazing that you want to honor his memory by bringing his ideas to life."

The waiter came with our meals. We'd ordered the pan-seared sea bass and the risotto Milanese with asparagus and shrimp. I salivated as the plates were arranged on the table. Max split up the dishes and passed one over to me.

"This looks delicious," I said. "Though it also reminds me of another thing on my list. I need to find some sort of hobby that incorporates exercise I enjoy, because I hate going to the gym. I run so I can keep in shape and eat what I want, but I'd love to find something I actually like to do. Maggie's gotten into rock climbing, mostly indoors, but she loves it. I'm not sure that's for me, but there has to be something I can find that will burn calories and be more fun than running."

"I can think of a few enjoyable ways to burn calories." Max wiggled his brows.

I laughed. "I walked right into that one, didn't I?"

"You did. But in all seriousness, that's right up my alley. I'm always game to try new workouts. I'll tell you something, but you can't laugh."

"What?"

"There's one of those aerial yoga places on my block—the kind where people hang from what looks like sheets suspended from the ceiling. I secretly think about trying it whenever I see them doing it in the window."

"So why don't you?"

Max shrugged. "Because I'll probably make a fool of myself. I'm strong, but I'm not the most limber guy. Plus, all I'd need is for the guys on my team to get wind of it. I'd never live it down. One of the players has a daughter who takes mommy-and-me ballet classes. His wife got the flu right before a dress rehearsal for their recital. Yuri filled in for his wife so his daughter could practice being on stage. Some pictures got leaked, and the entire team came in dressed in tutus the following Monday, including me. We're a bunch of ball-busting assholes. To this day, Yuri Volkov is nicknamed Twinkle Toes."

I laughed. "I guess Pretty Boy is better than Twinkle Toes."

Over the next few hours, we polished off the bottle of wine and shared a dessert. Max was signing the credit card slip when my phone vibrated in my purse. I'd missed a call from Maggie, but I also noticed a few texts from her, so I swiped to make sure everything was okay.

The first one must have been sent a few minutes before I arrived at seven.

Maggie: Just making sure you didn't back out.

An hour later, another one came in.

Maggie: You better be enjoying yourself on your date and not just ignoring me while watching some dumb, old black-and-white movie and eating a pint of Ben & Jerry's Chunky Monkey.

Maggie: Mmmm…now I really want Chunky Monkey. Thanks a lot.

The next text read:

Maggie: Okay, now I'm starting to get worried. It's been almost three hours and no response. The only time you don't check your phone for that long is when you're sleeping. You better not be sleeping. I had such high hopes for tonight! Should I be worried? What if Mr. Hot Skates turned out to be an axe murderer and you're lying with your head chopped off somewhere? That would suck. For me. I don't want to make a new friend. So text me and let me know you still have a pulse when you read this.

The last text had come in ten minutes ago.

Maggie: Earth to Georgia…come in, girl.

"Shoot," I mumbled.

"Everything okay?" Max asked.

"Yeah. I just need to text Maggie back. She was checking on me, and I didn't respond right away, so she started to get worried." I shook my head. "I had no idea we'd been sitting here for almost three-and-a-half hours. It's rare that I don't check my phone for that long."

Max smiled. "That's good. You said you wanted to disconnect more."

"Yeah. I guess that will take a while for some people to get used to."

I shot off a text to Maggie, letting her know I was fine and still on my date with Max.

She responded ten seconds after I pressed send.

Maggie: Oh good! Climb that man like a tree.

I smiled and tossed my phone into my purse.

"Whatever she said, you should listen to her."

I hadn't thought he could see my screen. "What makes you say that?"

He pointed to my mouth. "Your smile had a dirty edge to it when you read that last text."

I laughed. "You're very perceptive, and my best friend has a dirty mind."

"I knew I liked her. You ready to get out of here?"

"Sure."

Max stood and offered his hand to help me up. He didn't let go once I was standing. Instead, he maneuvered my hand behind my back, and used it to draw me close. "I'm not ready for the night to be over. But I have to stop back at my apartment to let the boys out. I was running late and came here straight from the shoot. We could hang out there, or I could just walk them quick, and we could go somewhere for a drink. Whatever you want. Just don't leave me yet."

I was definitely not ready for the night to be over, either, and I'd spent enough time with Max to be comfortable going to his apartment. So I nodded. "I'm good with your apartment. I just...would still like to take it slow."

He kissed my forehead. "Understood. I'll be a perfect gentleman until you're ready. Then all bets are off."

• • •

If I'd had any doubts that Max was lying about the dogs needing to go out in order to lure me up to his place, that thought was put to rest the minute the elevator doors opened—directly into his apartment. The moment we stepped off, Four bolted into the waiting car. And the bigger dog, who I assumed had to be Fred, kept running in circles right outside of it.

"You want to wait here?" Max looked at my shoes. "Those don't seem like they're made for dog walking. And I have to do once around the block or they'll be maniacs all night. I won't be more than fifteen minutes." He walked to a round table in the entryway and opened a drawer, pulling out two leashes.

"Aren't you afraid I'll snoop if you leave me here all alone?"

Max smiled. "Have at it. I keep the whips and chains in the drawer next to my bed, if you want to check them out."

He was kidding. Wasn't he?

Max chuckled. He leaned down and brushed his lips with mine, then spoke against them. "I'm kidding. But you're welcome to look around. I don't mind. Make yourself at home."

"Thank you."

After the doors slid closed behind Max and the dogs, I turned around to check out the apartment. A few steps down from the marble entryway was a ginormous living room.

"Holy crap," I mumbled as I walked in. I didn't live in a typical, small New York apartment, yet my entire place could fit in this living room. Floor-to-ceiling windows acted as artwork, showcasing the city illuminated outside. I headed to check out the view first. Max lived on West 57th, so in front of me was the twinkling city, but to the left was the river. It was a clear night, and a full moon glittered a straight path across the water. Absolutely stunning. I could've stayed here all evening staring, but I tore myself

away so I could sneak a peek at the rest of the place before Max got back. Of course I wanted to snoop a bit.

The living room was open to the kitchen, which was equipped with state-of-the-art appliances, a built-in coffeemaker, and a glass-front wine refrigerator. On the opposite side of the room, a long hall opened to a few doors, including a large bathroom and an office. At the very end was the master bedroom. I flicked on the light and found a beautiful, masculine, carved-wood bed elevated on a platform to take full advantage of yet another wall of windows—this time with a view of Central Park. I stood at the edge of the doorway, not wanting to invade his privacy, even though he'd invited me to look. But I did note a stack of books on his nightstand. All in all, his apartment was nothing like I'd expected. It had a mature vibe, not the bachelor pad I'd envisioned.

When Max returned, I was back in the living room enjoying the view. The dogs ran right to their water bowls while he came up behind me and wrapped his arms around my waist, dropping a kiss on my shoulder. "Did you check out my nightstand to make sure there weren't any whips?"

I turned around in his arms and ran my fingers through his hair. "Who says I'm not into that? Maybe I'm disappointed I didn't find any."

Max's eyes sparkled. "Then I guess you didn't look in my closet."

My eyes widened, and he chuckled. "I'm kidding."

Four and Fred finished their drinks and came to sit at our feet. Four nuzzled his wet face against my bare leg, like a cat.

"They weren't interested in me when we walked in, so I didn't get to say hello." I bent down and lifted Four, scratching the top of his head with my nails while using my other hand to pet Fred. "Hi, Fred. I'm Georgia. It's nice to meet you."

Fred leaned in and licked my cheek. I laughed. "Ah, I see you take after your father with the ladies."

Max smiled. "What can I get you to drink?"

"I'll take a glass of wine, if you're having one."

While Max opened a bottle, I spent a little time with the dogs. After he poured two glasses, he tossed a ball down the hall, and Fred took off running.

I stood with Four in my arms. "Boy, and here I thought I was winning him over. All it takes is a ball and he loses interest."

I walked into the kitchen, and Max held out his arms. "Come on, puffball, you too. It's my turn." He set Four on the floor and bribed him with a biscuit before passing me wine.

"I'm glad I didn't walk them with you." I lifted my foot into a flamingo stance and rubbed at my toes. "The strap on this shoe has a sharp edge and feels like it's trying to cut into my toe."

Max set down his wine and took mine from my hand, placing it on the counter. "Let me take them off for you." He gripped my waist and lifted me up onto the kitchen counter, then raised my foot and unbuckled the strap to my sandal. "These are sexy as shit. But I'd rather you be comfortable here."

I really loved watching him take my shoes off for some reason. It was a sweet gesture, but perhaps also a prelude to him removing other articles of clothing sometime in the near future.

I took a deep breath to focus. "Your apartment is nothing like I thought it would be."

"No? What did you expect?"

I shook my head. "I'm not sure. You're an athlete, so I guess a big-screen TV and maybe a room with a workbench and exercise equipment. I think I was expecting more of a bachelor pad."

Max lifted the foot he'd freed from the angry buckle and kissed the red welt running across the top before going to work on the other. "Two years ago you would've been right. I had an apartment in Chelsea that was basically a nicer version of a frat house. Two other players lived in the building, and if I didn't answer my door, they would knock it down. I had to replace the front door four times."

I laughed. "What made you make the change?"

He shrugged. "I don't know. I guess I grew up. I wanted to be able to come home and relax. I play hard all day long. Coming home to a place that was peaceful became important. Though...I do still have the big-screen TV. Stay put. I'll show you."

He finished taking off my other shoe and walked into the living room to grab the remote. As he pressed a button, the wall of windows started to disappear as a large shade slid down. Once it finished, Max pushed another button, and a panel I hadn't noticed in the living room ceiling opened, and a projector dropped down.

"It's a blackout shade and projection screen in one," he said. "It's eighteen feet long. It feels like you're *in* the game when I watch on this thing."

"Wow." I laughed. "Now that's more like I thought."

Max walked back over to where I was still sitting on the counter. He nudged open my knees and stood between them. "There's a gym in the building, so I got rid of my spare room full of weights, and I have a cleaning lady who stocks the fridge and keeps the place from looking like a bachelor pad. So you weren't wrong; I just hide it better in my old age."

With the blackout shades down, the room had gotten dark. The only light came from the entryway, making the moment feel more intimate. Max swept hair from my shoulder and leaned in to kiss my neck.

"Is this okay?" he whispered.

I nodded.

He ran his nose from my chin down to my collarbone, then sucked his way back up with a groan. "You smell so fucking good. We better go sit in the living room before I get myself in trouble."

I really wanted to stay right here with his lips on my skin, but considering I was the one who'd told him I wanted to go slow, it didn't seem fair to do that. So I nodded, and Max lifted me from the counter and set me back on my feet. He held my hand and guided me to the couch, where he tossed a throw pillow against one end and gestured for me to sit with my back against it. When I did, he lifted my legs and set my feet on his lap, then began to rub the sole of my foot with his thumbs.

My eyes almost rolled back in my head. "Oh my God. That feels so good."

"Between all the physical therapists and massage therapists who have worked on me over the years, I might've picked up a thing or two."

He worked his knuckles into the ball of my foot, and I let my head loll back for a few minutes.

When I opened my eyes, Max was watching me. "What?"

He shook his head. "I just like seeing your face when you're relaxed."

"You might want to take a picture. Rumor has it that doesn't happen very often."

"We'll fix that this summer. I'll make sure of it."

I smiled.

"So this taking-it-slow thing. How slow are we talking?"

I laughed. "Are you asking because you want to push right up against whatever line I draw?"

He grinned. "What if we pretend we're in ninth grade, studying in your bedroom with the door open because your mom is downstairs?"

I snorted. "What does that even mean?"

"It means I get to make out with you and cop a quick feel, but I can't push it too far because your mom is right in the other room."

"I don't think our ninth-grade experiences were exactly the same."

Max crooked his finger. "Come here."

"Where?"

He patted his lap. "Right here. It involves dry humping, too."

It was absolutely impossible to resist this man's grin. So when he held out his hand, I took it and followed his lead to straddle his lap.

He smiled. "Scooch your ass up a little."

I did and felt a prominent bulge press between my legs.

Max closed his eyes. "Oh yeah. Much better."

"You're crazy."

He held one finger to his lips. "Shhh. Your mom might hear."

For the next half hour, we sat on the couch and made out like two horny teenagers. At one point, he began to move my hips back and forth over what had become a full-fledged erection. I was so worked up, and the friction felt so good, I started to worry I might come, so I pulled back the reins.

Max groaned. “Did you hear Mom coming?”

“No, but I thought I might...you know.”

He raised a brow. “Would that have been so terrible?”

“I’m just trying to play fair.”

“Don’t worry about fair with me. Just take what you want. We won’t be keeping score.”

Things stayed calmer after that. Probably because I shifted off of his lap and was no longer grinding on his dick. We talked for a long time, never having an uncomfortable lull in the conversation. Eventually, I said I needed to get going. Max called an Uber and insisted on walking me down and making eye contact with the driver. But he stopped short of threatening harm if he didn’t see me home safely.

Max opened the car door and kissed my forehead. “I’ll call you tomorrow.”

“Okay.”

“And don’t forget to send me your list.”

“List?”

“The things you’ve been putting off that you want to do this summer.”

“Oh, that’s right. I’ll send it to you, but then you should add some things, too.”

He leaned in and whispered in my ear. “No problem. But my list of what I want to do this summer is short—*just you.*”

— Eleven —

Max

Three days after our date, Georgia finally texted me the list of things she wanted to do this summer. Most of it was stuff she'd talked about:

Unplug more

Be more spontaneous

Red hair

Volunteer

Watch the sunrise from the Highline

Go to an after-hours club

Stay out all night

Take a staycation and see the landmarks I've never seen

Leave work by five every day

Take two full weeks of vacation

Then there were a few we hadn't discussed:

Get over my fear of public speaking

Join 23andMe and learn about my ancestors

The fear of public speaking one surprised me. But everything else was pretty much what I'd expected. Rather than text back, I hit *Call*.

Georgia answered on the first ring.

"So when do we get to start?"

"Boy, you sound anxious," she chided. "You must be dying to see the Statue of Liberty."

I chuckled. "Yeah, that's what it is."

"I don't know. I guess we can start whenever."

"Okay. A week from today then. This week is crazy, but my last game is Saturday afternoon, and then I'm a free man. Can you take off?"

"Monday?"

"Nope. For the next two weeks. You have *take two weeks off* on your list. Why not start there?"

"Hmmm... I'm not sure that's a good idea, Max."

"Why not?"

"Well, my new operations director has only been here a few months, and we have a lot going on, and—"

I interrupted her. "Has there been any time since you started the company that you didn't have a lot going on?"

"No, but—"

"We'll stay here in the city while you're off. If anything goes wrong, you'll be able to shoot back to the office in no time."

"I don't know, Max..."

"I'll make all the plans. I promise you'll have a good time."

She sighed. "Alright. Though you can't get mad if I need to come back to the office."

"You got it."

"I can't believe I'm agreeing to this. But I suppose I better get going since I'll have to be at the office until midnight the next few days to be ready to take off for two whole weeks."

"I'll leave you alone to do what you gotta do. But my last game is Saturday afternoon. It's home. Will you come?"

"Yeah, I'd love to."

"I'll messenger the tickets over to your office."

"Thanks, Max."

After we hung up, I sat thinking about what I could plan for the next two weeks. I wasn't sure of the specifics, but I knew one thing: a staycation needed a hotel.

• • •

Monday seemed to take forever to get here. On Saturday, Georgia had come to my game as promised. But she didn't stick around after since she had to go to her office and wrap up some things before she started her time off today. I had a feeling she was probably stressing right about now, but I'd made some plans to help alleviate that as much as possible.

I arrived at her building at noon and went up to help her with her bag.

"Hey." Her forehead was creased with worry lines. "I'm not done packing. I have no idea what to bring, since you won't tell me any of our plans or where we're staying."

"Just bring comfortable clothes. Maybe something nice to go out at night once in a while."

"You can't just say 'something nice to go out at night' to a woman. We need more than that. Are we going to a fancy place? Casual? Will there be walking involved? We have heels that are for being dropped off at the door, and heels for walking a few blocks. But if it's going to be more than that, I might need flats." She shook her head. "Shoot. I didn't pack flats. Only sneakers. Which reminds me—will there be exercising? Because I brought leggings and casual things, but they're not the leggings I'd wear to the gym. I like moisture wicking for that. Oh, should I bring towels? What about rain gear? Did you bring an umbrella? Shoot. I didn't bring ponytail holders—"

She was on the verge of losing it. So I spoke over her. "Georgia..."

Her eyes flashed to mine.

I set my hands on her shoulders. "Whatever you're missing, we'll buy it. We're staying in the city, not going to the wilderness where we're fucked if you forget the bear spray. Or if you don't want to go shopping, we can come back here and pick up something if you need it. Take a deep breath."

She did, but then stalked away two seconds later.

I followed her into her bedroom. When I saw the piles of shit on her bed, I got a little concerned. There had to be a few hundred hangers of crap. "You're not planning on bringing all that, are you?"

She shook her head. "I couldn't find a green sweater I wanted to bring. So I took half the stuff out of my closet."

Jesus, that's only half? "Did you find the sweater?"

"I think I might've loaned it to Maggie."

"Do you want to stop over there and get it?"

"Maybe this isn't a good idea."

My brows shot up. "Because you don't have your sweater?"

Georgia avoided making eye contact and rummaged through the piles on her bed. After moving things around for a while, she let out a big sigh and looked up at me. "I'm nervous."

I couldn't have stopped my smile if I'd tried. "Really? I never would've been able to tell."

She picked up a sweatshirt from the top of a pile and threw it at me.

I caught it and set it back down. Then I moved another pile to the floor and sat on the bed, holding my hand out to her. "Come here."

She hesitated, but eventually she took my hand, and I used it to pull her onto my lap. "Talk to me." Georgia looked down, and I pushed a lock of hair behind her ear. "What are you nervous about?"

"Everything."

I nodded. "Okay. Let's take them one at a time. Tell me all the things that are freaking you out."

"Not being in the office."

"You're bringing your laptop and cell, right?"

"Yes."

I shrugged. "So if there's a problem, they know how to reach you. And we'll be right here in the city, so you can get back if something important comes up. You go out of the office for meetings sometimes, right?"

"Yes, but that's different."

"Why?"

"I don't know. It just is. This is two weeks, not an afternoon."

"Okay. So the amount of time is what's bothering you. Why don't we cut our trip from two weeks to two days? You can decide after two days if you need to go back or want to keep going with our staycation."

"But...you said you made plans."

"I'll change them, if need be."

"Really?"

I nodded. "Not a problem. But you should know, you're not the only one who's competitive. I'm going to do everything I can to make you have such a good time that you won't want to go back."

For the first time, a smile peeked through the stress on her face. "Okay."

"Anything else?"

She looked down and twisted her fingers. "I'm nervous about...us."

I lifted her chin so our eyes met. "I booked us two rooms. They're adjoining. There's no pressure there."

"You did?"

I nodded. "I did."

Her shoulders relaxed, and she let out a rush of air. "Okay."

I smiled. "We're doing great. What else you got?"

"Those are really the two biggest things."

"That wasn't so bad."

"For you..." She laughed.

"You know what will make you feel even better?"

"What?"

I slid my hand up from her back to her neck and pulled her close. "Kissing me hello."

Georgia sank into me. I could feel the sigh roll through her body, taking the tension with it as she opened and let my tongue in. By the time we separated, I'd almost forgotten my name. So if it was half as good for her, I'd done my job, and she'd be okay today.

I cupped her cheek. "Feel better?"

She nodded. "I should've called you last night to come do that. Maybe I would've had a better night's sleep."

"Well, I'll be right next door tonight if you start to stress." I looked around the room. "Think you feel up to finishing packing?"

"Yeah. Just give me a few minutes. I'm going to change, too. Why don't you go have some coffee while I get done?"

Twenty minutes later, Georgia emerged from the bedroom wheeling a suitcase. She had on a pair of tight jeans and a Wolverines T-shirt.

"What do you think?" She pushed her hair behind her shoulders so I could see the full logo and held her hands out.

"Very nice tits," I managed to say with a straight face.

She laughed and pointed. "I'm showing you the Wolverines T-shirt. I bought it on my way out of the game on Saturday."

"I'm teasing. I love it."

She turned and showed me her back, lifting her long hair. Now *that* I hadn't been expecting. I didn't even know they made T-shirts with a logo on the front and my name and number on the back. But I fucking loved it on her.

"*Nice.*" My brain quickly conjured an image of what she might look like wearing it with nothing else—just the T-shirt with my name across the back and her long, sexy, bare legs sticking out the bottom.

Georgia turned back around. She took one look at my face and squinted. "What's going on in that head of yours?"

I smirked and walked over to her. "You don't want to know. We just got you calm." I took the suitcase from her hand. "Do you have more bags?"

"I jammed everything in the one. I might be back in a few days anyway, right?"

"Sure." *Though, not if I have anything to say about it.*

Twelve

Georgia

Max surprised me with an entire day planned. When we finally left my apartment, a car was waiting at the curb. It whisked us off to the Four Seasons Hotel downtown, where we handed our bags to the concierge and told him we'd be back to check in later. Then we headed to Battery Park to catch the ferry to the Statue of Liberty. We stayed outside on the deck, taking in the gorgeous spring day from the railing as we crossed the Hudson River.

"Have you ever been to Liberty or Ellis Island?" I asked.

"Yep, with my brother Austin when we were in college. I was in my first year and had an exhibition game here in the city. He came with me, and we stuck around for an extra few days. Austin was really into buildings and history, so he wanted to come see it." Max looked out at the water reflectively and smiled. "I got smacked while we were waiting to get in to the statue."

"By Austin?"

Max shook his head. "No, by a woman a couple of people ahead of us in line. I was an idiot back then—basically checked out anything with legs. I motioned to a woman I thought had a nice ass, wanting Austin to check her out, too. When he did, he didn't agree with me, so we debated the subject a little. I thought I'd kept my voice low, but apparently Austin was louder than he intended as he explained how her ass wasn't symmetrical."

I covered my mouth. "Oh my God."

He nodded. "Yeah. She overheard and figured out we were talking about her, but she didn't let on until we'd made it up to the pedestal. Then she walked over and asked which one of us was the pig. I raised my hand, and she reared back and slapped me. A security guard came over, and the woman told him we'd been harassing her, and he asked us to leave. So we didn't get to climb up to the torch."

I chuckled. "Well, hopefully you can keep your eyes where they belong, and we won't get kicked out today. Cross your fingers you can make it up to the top."

Max wrapped his arms around my waist. "My eyes have no interest in wandering anywhere."

"I bet you say that to all the girls." I smiled.

Max's face turned serious. "You know I'm not seeing anyone else, right?"

I hadn't given that subject any thought. I guess between me working so much and his hockey schedule, it never occurred to me that either of us would have time to go out with anyone else. But Max was off for the summer now. And technically I was still in a relationship, so that didn't seem fair.

"You could, if you want..."

Max frowned. "I don't want."

"But I'm in a relationship still."

"I get that. Though he's not here. And you aren't seeing him until at least after the summer is over, so it's easy to put it out of my mind." His brows pulled together. "Are you planning on dating other people this summer?"

"God, no. I didn't even date more than one person at a time before Gabriel, when I was single. I've always looked at dating like trying on shoes. You try on different ones to see what feels right and is comfortable, but if you try on two different shoes, you never really know if either of them is any good."

Max smiled. "So it's settled. Our summer will be just that—*our* summer."

"Are you sure?"

He held my eyes. "Very sure."

"Okay."

The boat pulled into the dock at Liberty Island. After we disembarked, the line to go into the statue was long, so Max and I wandered around for a bit, walking along the paved path. Max held my hand, and the simple gesture meant a lot to me. For all of the self-deprecating stories he'd shared—commenting on a woman's ass, telling his friends about getting to second base at the movies—he seemed like he would make a good boyfriend. He was attentive and thoughtful. The fact that we were here at all proved that. A man who looked like him and had his celebrity didn't have to work this hard to get laid. So when we came up to a big tree, I tugged his arm and led us behind it, then wrapped my hands around his neck, pushed up on my toes, and pressed my lips to his.

Max smiled when our kiss broke. "What was that for?"

I shrugged. "Just for being you. For making me take this time off, for not wanting to be with other women this summer, and..." I grinned. "You're also kind of hot, and I just wanted to kiss you."

Max's dimples deepened. "Keep going. My ego's taken a beating lately. A certain brunette had to be coaxed into even going out with me."

I laughed. "Come on. We better go. I think our tickets are only good between certain times."

The rest of the afternoon was so much fun. We climbed three-hundred-and-fifty-four crammed steps to reach the crown—a reminder of how much I needed to get back into exercising. But the view at the top made it all worth it. After that, we went to Ellis Island, and I was able to find my great-great grandfather's name on a passenger manifest from a hundred years ago. By the time we took the ferry back and an Uber to the hotel, it was already six o'clock.

Not surprisingly, the young girl at the reception desk recognized Max and batted her eyelashes at him. Then she only took his credit card when I'd held mine out to her, too.

"You really need to let me pay for this," I told him. "I'm sure it was a fortune."

"Does it offend you when I insist?"

"Offend me? No. But it's not your job to pay for things."

"It doesn't feel like a job. It makes me happy to do it. So can you just let me?"

I hesitated. "You know I can afford it, right? I might not have a big, fancy apartment like you, but I do well for myself."

Max smiled. "I think it's sexy as shit that you make a lot of money. But I still want to do it. Okay?"

How could I say no when he put it like that? "Fine."

Once we'd checked in, a bellman showed us to our rooms, which were on the top floor. He unlocked the door between the suites and told us complimentary champagne and fruit would be sent up momentarily. Both rooms had terraces looking out over the city, and Max and I walked out on his to take in the view.

Someone knocked at the door to my suite.

"I'll get it," Max said. "It's probably the champagne. It was part of a package that came with the room."

"Okay."

I stayed on the balcony, enjoying the last of the sunny day, while room service wheeled in a cart. When I heard the cork pop, I went back inside.

"That sound is like Pavlov and his bell for me."

Max poured two glasses and handed me one before extending his in a toast. "To wearing matching shoes."

It took a few seconds for me to remember our conversation earlier. I smiled as I did, and happily clinked to that. "I'm a lucky girl. Mine are really cute shoes, too."

Max winked. "So are you ready for your big evening plans?"

"Big plans? I hope you're referring to soaking in that ginormous tub I saw in the bathroom."

"Nope. Better."

"I'm not sure much could be better than that after a long day of walking around."

Max looked at his watch. "Well, you're going to find out in about fifteen minutes. So drink up."

"Fifteen minutes? I need to take a shower before we go anywhere."

"Not for this you don't."

"What are we doing?"

He kissed my forehead. "You'll find out soon enough. I'm going to put on ESPN for a few minutes before we go—see what they're saying about all the trades going on."

"Okay." He walked through our adjoining door, and I yelled after him. "Wait! What should I wear?"

"Just leave on what you're wearing."

"Really?"

"Yeah." He wiggled his brows. "You won't be needing your clothes for very long for what I have planned next, anyway."

• • •

I hadn't paid attention to the button Max had pushed, but when we stopped on the third floor and he put his hand at the small of my back to guide me, I shook my head. "This isn't the lobby, Max."

"I know." He gave me a little nudge to keep walking. "We aren't going to the lobby."

"Where are we going?"

That answer became clear as we turned the corner from the elevator. *The Four Seasons Spa.*

"Oh my God, did you book us massages?"

"I did. And a little something extra for you."

"What?"

He opened the door. "You'll see."

Inside, the pretty woman at the front desk did a double take and immediately turned pink when she got a load of the man next to me. She put her hand over her heart. "Mr. Yearwood, I'm sorry. We're not supposed to make a big deal when celebrities come in. But I'm a huge hockey fan. I grew up in Minnesota."

"Oh yeah? I went to high school in St. Paul, at Mounds Park Academy."

"I know!" She squealed. "I'm from Bloomington. It's only about twenty minutes away."

I had to work at not rolling my eyes. I was pretty sure she hadn't even noticed me standing here.

"We have two massage appointments." Max motioned to me. "I wasn't sure what kind she would want. Would you happen to have a list of the different types you offer so she can take a look?"

"Of course." The woman pulled out an oversized menu and held it in my direction, still batting her eyelashes at Max.

"Also," he said. "She's getting another service after the massage. But she doesn't know what it is. So, if you could keep that under wraps for now."

"Oh, how fun! Of course." She pointed over her shoulder. "Why don't I let your therapists know you're here, and that will give you a few minutes to make your massage choices."

"Thank you."

Little Miss Enamored disappeared down a hall, and Max and I took seats in the waiting area a few feet away.

"She was nice," he said.

That time I couldn't hold back my eye roll. "Would you like to bet that she asks you for an autograph when she gets back...on her breast?"

Max looked amused. "Do I detect a hint of jealousy, Ms. Delaney?"

"*Pfft*. No."

His smile grew wider. "Don't worry. She's not my type."

I stared down at the menu and mumbled, "I wasn't worried."

After a minute, Max asked, "So what are you thinking?"

"About what?"

He pointed to the salon services menu I'd been staring at. "Which massage are you going to get? I thought about booking us a couple's massage, but I didn't know how you'd feel about that. So I went with two private ones."

Once again, his thoughtfulness softened me. "Thank you. I think I'm going with the deep tissue massage. How about you?"

"That's what I already picked."

The young woman returned. "Your therapists will be right out."

"Thank you."

"By the way..." I tilted my head and lowered my voice. "You said she wasn't your type. What *is* your usual type?"

Max shrugged. "Not sure I have a usual type. But I can tell you what I really like in a woman."

"Okay..."

He leaned forward and hooked a big hand around my neck, pulling me to meet his lips. "You. *You're* what I really like in a woman."

Good answer.

"Mr. Yearwood? Ms. Delaney?" the woman from the desk called. Another woman stood beside her wearing all white. "This is Cynthia. I'm sorry—I didn't ask if either of you had a preference for a male or a female therapist. We have both available."

Max shrugged. "Whatever. I don't care."

"Me neither."

Just then, a guy walked out from the back—a *very* good-looking one. He was a different kind of handsome than Max, but nonetheless gorgeous in his own right. Tall, lean but muscular, clean cut—he sort of reminded me of a younger version of Gabriel. "This is Marcus," the receptionist said. "He'll be your other massage therapist today."

Marcus slipped his hands into his pockets and bounced back and forth on his heels. "Which one of you is my victim?" He smiled, and dimples popped out.

They weren't Max level, but still adorable.

Max frowned. He glanced over at me and quickly raised his hand. "Me. I'm your victim."

"Right this way," Marcus said. "Cynthia and I will show you to the locker rooms."

As we followed, I leaned over to Max and whispered with a grin, "What if I wanted Marcus?"

"No shot, sweetheart."

I raised a brow. "Who's jealous now?"

"Me. But at least I'll admit it. If I don't have my hands all over that body, that dude definitely isn't going to either." He leaned down as we arrived at the locker rooms and brushed his lips with mine. "Enjoy your massage. You have another treatment after this. I'll find you when you're done."

"Okay."

• • •

"You guys work really late," I said to Kara, the stylist. After my amazing massage, I took a shower in the locker room and was shown into the salon, which was now completely empty except for the two of us.

"We actually closed about twenty minutes ago."

"Oh, I'm sorry. I didn't realize that. Cynthia just brought me in after we were done." I started to get up, but Kara put her hand on my shoulder.

"Your boyfriend made special arrangements for me to stay late." She smiled at me in the mirror. "Don't give it any thought. He made it very worth my while. Plus, I think we close too early. People don't even go out until eleven in the city. If we were open later, we might get a younger crowd like you. We tend to get an older clientele."

"Well, thank you for staying."

She played with my hair as she stood behind me in the chair. "So, how red are we going?"

"Red? I thought I was just here for a blowout."

The woman's brows furrowed. "I'm a colorist. You were booked for color and a blowout. The notes said you wanted to go red. Did they get that wrong?"

"No." I shook my head. "No, they didn't. That sounds like something Max would do."

"Did you not want to get color?"

"I do want to try red. I just didn't realize it was going to be today. I mentioned that I've always wanted to go red to the person who made the appointment."

She tossed my hair around some more. "I think you'd look great with red. What were you thinking? Like a Lindsay Lohan, Nicole Kidman, or like an Amy Adams with some golden-blond hues?"

"I actually have a picture on my phone. Let me see if I can find it." It took me a few minutes to locate the photo because it was so old. I looked at the date at the top before holding the phone up to her. "God, I took this photo more than three years ago. I guess I've been meaning to do it for longer than I thought."

"Sometimes it takes a while to pull the trigger on a big change like this." She pointed to the phone. "But this is exactly the color I would have recommended for you with your skin tone. A deep auburn. It'll look gorgeous with your green eyes—very natural."

Kara looked at me. She must've read the nerves on my face.

"I'll tell you what. Why don't we do a semi-permanent color? I won't use any ammonia, so the color won't penetrate your hair shaft. It'll give you a chance to see if you like it without having to go through the pain of trying to recreate your natural color if you don't. It'll wash out within four to six weeks. If you really hate it, I can give you the names of some heavy-duty shampoos that can get it out quicker with extra washes over the next few days."

I nodded. "That sounds absolutely perfect."

"Okay." She smiled. "I'm just going to dry you quick, and then I'll go whip up some potion, and we can get started."

"Thank you."

She handed me back my phone, and I realized this had been the first time I'd had it in my hand since Max picked me up this morning. He'd managed to accomplish four things on my list in one day—start my staycation, go red, see the Statue of Liberty, and unplug more. My natural inclination was to start scrolling, but I somehow resisted the temptation and only perused my missed calls to make sure neither Maggie nor my director of operations had called. Then I tossed it back into my bag.

After the stylist began applying the color, I felt my excitement building as I watched.

"So, your boyfriend seems like a great guy," Kara said. "He surprised you with a massage and also color you'd only mentioned that you wanted."

"He is."

"How long have you guys been together?"

"It's new. We only met three or four weeks ago."

"Are you serious? Does he have a brother? I think the nicest thing a guy I just met has ever done for me is bring me chocolate. And I get hives from chocolate."

I smiled. "Yeah, Max is a great guy."

Forty minutes later, my color was done, and Kara started to blow out my hair. I loved it already and couldn't wait to see it fully dry. Max came in just as she was finishing up. He stood a few feet away, off to the side, but I still saw him in the mirror.

Kara caught my eye in the reflection and pointed over her shoulder. “I take it this is Max?”

I nodded. She turned to him. “I’ll be done in five minutes.”

“Take your time.”

After the stylist finished drying, she grabbed a curling wand and threw in a few loose waves, then swiveled my chair to face Max. “Well, what do you think?”

He flashed his dimples. “I think it looks incredible. She was gorgeous before, but damn...I really like it.”

Kara smiled at me. “He’s right. How about you, Georgia?”

“I love it. I’ll admit, I was super nervous when you started, but I’m so glad I went through with it.” I smiled at each of them. “Thank you, both of you, for getting me to finally do this.”

When we returned to our rooms upstairs, I stopped Max before going in. “This day was one of the most fun I’ve had in a long time. You are so thoughtful and generous, Max.”

“You’re welcome, but I really didn’t do anything but make a few phone calls.”

“Maybe, but you pay attention, and you care about making me happy, and that means a lot.”

Max gazed into my eyes before nodding.

“How was your massage?” I asked.

“It was great. I hit the steam room for a while after. But I’m freaking starving. You want to go out to eat or order in?”

It had been a long day, and I wasn't in the mood to share Max. "Do you mind if we just order room service or something?"

He smiled. "Not at all. I was hoping you'd say that."

He opened the door, and we went in through his room. We lounged a moment as we checked out the menu, and then Max phoned the order in to room service. While he did that, I poured two glasses of champagne and set one beside him before wandering back to my own room to check out my new look in the bright lights of the bathroom.

I looked so different, but I wasn't entirely sure the change was just my hair. There was a giant smile on my face, my eyes seemed more sparkly than usual, and my skin had a glow. The happiness I saw in my reflection wasn't just coming from my lips.

"I'm going to jump in the shower," Max yelled from somewhere behind me.

"Okay!"

"Room service said about a half hour. I won't be more than fifteen minutes." He stepped into the bathroom and tilted his head with a playful grin. "What are you smiling about in here?"

"Nothing." I laughed. "I guess I'm just happy."

"I'm glad."

I turned around to face him. "Do you know I haven't checked my phone messages or texts since you got to my apartment this morning?"

"Really?"

I nodded. "When I was at the salon, I scanned to make sure I didn't have any messages from work. I know Maggie would call me if anything urgent came up. But it's a workday, and I didn't check email or texts."

"We were out for most of the day, but why didn't you while you were getting your hair done?"

I shrugged. "I'm not sure. I guess I didn't want to burst the bubble it feels like we're in."

"Except...this is reality. We're only a few miles from our apartments, and all we did is stay in the city."

That was true, but something about the day felt magical.

Max held my eyes another minute, then knocked on the doorjamb. "Well, I'm glad you didn't. Gonna hit the rain locker. I'll be back."

I decided to get changed while Max was in the shower. I'd been in the same clothes since this morning, and I wanted to put on something comfortable, but also look nice. So I dug out my favorite pair of Lululemon leggings and paired them with a simple top that was soft, but also clung to my curves nicely. It had a low, scooped neck, and a demi-cup push-up bra underneath made my small Cs look more like full ones. The door to our adjoining room had been open since we arrived, so when someone knocked at Max's door, I heard it. It had only been ten or fifteen minutes since we'd ordered, but I figured it must be room service. A uniformed hotel employee stood on the other side when I opened the door, but he didn't have a food cart. He held out a black leather wallet.

"Mrs. Yearwood?"

"No, but if you're looking for Max, he's in the shower."

The guy nodded. "This was left behind at the spa. It has Mr. Yearwood's license and credit card inside."

"Oh. Yes, we were at the spa until just a little while ago." I took the wallet. "Thank you very much. I'll make sure he gets it."

The man turned to walk away, but I stopped him. "Oh—hang on a second."

I figured Max would do the same, so I opened his wallet and fished out some cash, which I handed to the guy. “Thank you.”

Max opened the bathroom door as I was about to pass on the way back to my room. He had only a plush, white towel around his narrow waist, and a cloud of steam billowed out from behind him. My eyes lined up with his pectoral muscles, which were sculpted to perfection, and two lucky water droplets sluiced toward an eight-pack of honed abs. I couldn’t take my eyes off them as they raced to the finish line, which seemed to be at some point between the super-sexy V muscles of his pelvis.

After a period of time most definitely longer than it should have been, I blinked myself out of my stupor and cleared my throat. “Umm...” But I couldn’t for the life of me remember what I was going to say or why I was even in his room.

“Did you...need me?” Max lifted a brow, a slight smirk on his face.

I tried to look anywhere but at his gorgeous body. Yet he was just so *right there* and vividly beautiful. It seemed a waste not to enjoy the view. Plus, I didn’t think he’d mind. Nevertheless, while I was busy trying to find a safe landing place for my eyes, I saw the leather wallet in my hand.

“Oh!” I held it up. “The spa sent up your wallet. You must’ve left it there. That’s why I was in your room. I heard the knock at the door.”

“Damn, and here I thought maybe you’d come to help me dry off.”

“Uhh... Our food will be here soon.”

Max moved closer. He ran his knuckles along my throat. “We could skip it, and I’ll eat something else.”

Oh my.

The large suite suddenly felt small as Max watched me. I *really* wanted to just rip the towel off the man. But then another knock came at the door.

I shook my head and cleared my throat. "I'll get it. It's probably dinner."

Max smiled ruefully. "Shame. My idea sounded much better."

Thirteen

Max

"If I'd known dinner was going to be this fancy, I would've dressed a little nicer," I said stepping back out of the bathroom in sweats and a T-shirt.

"I kind of liked your outfit before." Georgia smiled.

"Oh yeah?" I thumbed toward the bathroom. "I'd be happy to change back."

She laughed. "I'm sure you would. But come on, let's eat. I didn't realize how hungry I was until I saw the food. It looks delicious, and how beautiful is this table? Bone china, sterling silver, crystal–it's nicer than most restaurants." Georgia pointed to the middle of the table. "They even brought candles."

There was a small box of wooden matches next to them. I walked over and picked them up. "Mind if I light these and lose the lights?"

"No, I think that would be perfect."

Georgia looked gorgeous lit by only the flame from the candle. I'd ordered two bottles of wine, so I poured us each a glass and settled in. She'd ordered ravioli, and I got the steak, but we wound up sharing our plates again.

"I know I said this earlier, but I had such a good time today," she said. "Thank you again for planning everything. I still can't get over that my hair is red right now."

"I had a good time, too. But considering I enjoyed myself when I came over while you were sick, I'm pretty sure it's the company rather than the plans that I like."

She smiled. "Can I ask you something?"

I shrugged. "Whatever you want."

Georgia shook her head. "Why in the world are you single? I mean, you're attentive, thoughtful, funny—and you can clearly wear the hell out of a white towel."

I smiled. "Thank you. But I'm not always so attentive. In fact, I've been accused of being just the opposite on more than one occasion. My last girlfriend told me I made her feel neglected, that she was never a priority. It was probably our biggest issue during the time we were together."

"Really?"

I nodded.

"Were you...always like that with her? Or did things just sort of wane a bit?"

"I'm not sure. I don't think I was any different in the beginning. But she might have a different opinion if you asked her what went wrong."

Georgia was quiet for a moment.

I could see she wanted to say something. "What are you thinking about right now?" I asked.

She shook her head. "You're really good at reading me. I was wondering if things changed...you know, after you slept together?"

I shook my head. "We slept together on the first date, so I don't think so. I take it you're worried that if we sleep together, you'll wake up to a different guy the next morning?"

"I guess I'm just trying to figure out what the catch is. How you can be this great and yet you're single?"

I looked into her eyes. "Maybe I just didn't find the right woman yet."

Georgia chewed that bottom lip of hers. I wanted to bite it in the worst way. "What else are you thinking about right now, Georgia?"

"Honestly?"

"Of course."

She lifted her wine and drank half the glass, then took a deep breath in and let it out. "I don't want to go back to my room tonight. I really want to be with you, Max."

"You sure?"

She nodded. "Very."

"Then get your ass over here."

Georgia smiled. "But you're not done with your dinner."

"You're right." I tossed my napkin on the table, crooked a finger, and stood. "I haven't even gotten started yet."

Her words had been bold, yet I still sensed hesitance on Georgia's face as she walked over to my side of the table. So I figured I should slow things down a little. "Do you want to take the wine out on the balc—"

Georgia collided with me, jumping up and wrapping herself around me like a koala. I stumbled back a few steps.

She crushed her lips to mine. "No wine," she breathed. "Just you."

I'd been looking for her to take a baby step so I knew she was ready, but this... This was so much fucking better. There was nothing sexier than a woman who knew what she wanted and decided to take it. I carried her to the bedroom and set her down.

"You went to so much trouble, ordering wine and having the table set with romantic candles, and here I am attacking you," she said. "You didn't even get to finish eating."

"No problem, sweetheart. I'm happy to fuck you full of romance instead." I dropped to my knees. "And I'm about to eat until I'm finished..."

Five minutes ago, I'd been perfectly fine taking things slow, but now I couldn't get my mouth on her fast enough. I stripped her out of her leggings and practically ripped the thong from her body. Guiding her to lie back on the bed, I pulled her ass to the edge and salivated as I got a look at her beautiful pussy. She was mostly bare, except for a thin strip of hair, and when I spread her legs wide, her feminine smell made me want to dive in and never come out.

Georgia's back arched off the bed as I lapped at her, flattening my tongue and licking her one end to the other, then teasing her clit with tiny circles. When she moaned, any hope of trying to go slow went to hell. It wasn't enough for just my tongue to be on her, I needed to bury my entire face—cheeks, jaw, nose, and tongue—into her sweetness. She began wiggling around as she moaned, so I reached up and held her in place with one hand while my other slipped two fingers inside.

"Oh...Max...*oh*!"

She was tight; the wall of her muscles gripped my fingers, as she said my name over and over. The more she moaned, the faster I pumped. Georgia reached down and grabbed my hair, yanking and digging her fingernails into my scalp. When her voice started to get thready, and I knew she was on the edge, I sucked harder on her clit until I felt her pulsating around my fingers. After her body went slack, and she released her death grip on my hair.

Wiping my face on the back of my hand, I dragged myself up and over her. I was hard as a rock, more turned on than I'd been in ages, and she hadn't even laid a finger on me yet.

"Wow." A goofy smile crossed her face as she blinked her eyes open. "Now I feel like an idiot."

My brows dipped together. "Why?"

"For making you wait when you could've been doing *that* the last month?"

I chuckled. "I'll just have to make up for lost time."

"Can I tell you a secret?"

"What?"

"I'm dying to see you completely naked. I have been since the night we met."

I laughed. "I think that can be arranged."

She shook her head. "No, I like...want at least a full minute of leering time."

I kissed her lips. "You want the light on for your show?"

Her eyes grew wide, and the biggest smile stretched across her face. "That would be awesome."

Let's face it, if this woman told me she wanted me to cluck like a damn chicken, I'd be doing it. So I reached over her head, gathered all the pillows into one tall pile, and then dragged her up the bed and propped her against them. "Comfy for your show?"

She grinned and nodded.

I reached over to the nightstand and flicked on the light before climbing off the bed. Once we were both naked, there was no way I was going to waste any time, so I went to my suitcase and pulled out a strip of condoms from the hopeful box I'd brought. Tossing them next to her, I stood at the end of the bed and started my little striptease by reaching up and behind me to tug my shirt over my head.

Georgia rubbed her hands together. "Eeep. I wish I had some dollar bills to tuck into your pants."

"Would be a waste. They aren't staying on for that long." I yanked my sweats down, stepped out, and kicked them to the side. Standing in just my boxer briefs, I looked up to find Georgia's playful smile gone, replaced by something I recognized very well at this moment—need. She swallowed, and my eyes moved to her throat. I loved my hands wrapped around it, but I couldn't wait to be inside it, too. Her eyes dropped to the outline of my cock, so I fisted it through my underwear, sliding my hand up and down a few times. When she licked her lips, I gave it a good, firm squeeze before hooking my thumb into the corners and bending to peel the last layer of clothing off.

Standing, my cock bobbed against my stomach at full attention, proud and ready for action. Even I was a little impressed with the showing. But the look on Georgia's face was priceless. Her eyes bulged, and she lifted her hand to her mouth and spoke with it covered. "Oh, God. That thing looks like it might hurt."

I wrapped my hands around it and pumped once for good measure. "Maybe you need a closer look."

She took a deep breath and nodded. "Yes, please."

I tugged her down to the middle of the bed and climbed up to straddle her hips. Leaning over, I sucked one of her pebbled nipples into my mouth. When she started to squirm, I moved to the other, not stopping until she dug her nails into my back and whimpered.

"Please...Max, I want you."

I grabbed the strip of condoms, tore one off, and sheathed myself in record time. Then I hovered over her, taking her mouth in a kiss before pulling back so I could watch her face as I sank inside.

Absolutely fucking beautiful. Our eyes locked, and I pushed my hips forward, little by little, feeling her stretch around me. She was so damn snug, and I didn't want to hurt her, so I only went a few inches in before easing back. The next time I pushed in a little farther. It was torture to go so slow, yet the most blissful kind of pain. When I was finally buried deep inside her, my arms started to shake.

"You good?" I groaned.

She smiled. "Very."

Georgia lifted her legs and wrapped them around my back, allowing me to sink even deeper. My eyes practically rolled to the back of my head when my balls slapped against her ass.

"Fuck," I groaned. "You feel so good."

Georgia reached up and pulled me down to her mouth for a kiss before moving her lips to my ear. "Don't be gentle. Make me sore tomorrow."

That she definitely didn't have to ask twice. I set myself free, fucking her hard and deep, with no restraint left. Georgia's hips lifted to meet each of my thrusts, and we kept at it until the sound of our sweat-soaked bodies slapping against each other became the backdrop for all our groans and grunts.

"*Max*!" Georgia cried. She clamped down around me and started to throb, milking every last ounce of self-control from my body. I held off for as long as I could, wanting to keep her going as long as possible. When the muscles in her face started to go slack and her legs fell from my waist like dead weight, I finally let go.

After, I needed to collapse. But two-hundred-and-twenty pounds might've suffocated her, so I rolled to my back, taking her with me.

She yelped as we flipped around, but there was a smile on her face as she settled into the crook of my shoulder.

I wrapped my arms around her and kissed the top of her head. "I feel kind of bad."

"Why?"

"Because I told you about all these plans I made for us, but after that, you're not going to be able to get me to leave this hotel room."

Georgia giggled. "I don't think I'll mind one bit."

• • •

I could definitely become addicted to this.

Georgia laid her head over my heart, curled on top of me, as I stroked her hair. We'd just had sex for the third time in twelve hours, this time with her on top, riding me slowly, as the sun came up and streaks of light cut golden rays across her beautiful face.

"I need to pee," she said. "But I'm too lazy to get up. It's one of my superpowers, you know. I can hold it for hours, despite having to go."

"Why would you want to do that?"

She shrugged. "Sometimes I get busy at work and don't want to stop what I'm doing."

"Can you hold it in if I do this?" I slid my hand down to her waist and tickled her.

"Oh my God! No! Stop." She giggled. "Don't do that!"

I laughed. But just in case tickling was the kryptonite to her superpower, I also stopped.

Georgia turned and propped her head on her fist on top of my chest. "What's the most times you've ever had sex in a day?"

I shrugged. "No idea. Three, maybe four at most? You?"

Her eyes danced. "Sadly, two. So we've already beaten my lame record. But we can beat yours!"

I laughed. "Finally your incessant need to compete lands on a challenge with a solid cause. What time did we start last night?"

"I'm not sure...about nine, I guess?"

"What time is it now?"

"Six thirty. So we have like another fourteen-and-a-half hours to do it once more. Think you're up for it?"

"Once? What kind of a wuss do you think I am? We need to smash that record, not beat it."

She smiled wide. "Okay!"

"As long as we're at it, I don't think I've ever received more than six blowjobs in a day."

She slapped my stomach and laughed. "I think you'll be keeping that record. But I better go to the bathroom, or we're going to start a new competition for you—number of times you've been peed on." Georgia got up from the bed and yanked the sheet that had been covering both of us to wrap it around her.

While she was gone, I got two bottles of water from the mini fridge and grabbed the room service menu. I'd worked up a damn big appetite. Sitting down on the bed, I started to take mental notes on all the shit I planned to order when a phone buzzed on the nightstand. Out of habit, I picked it up. But it only took the name flashing on the screen to confirm it wasn't mine. *Gabriel.*

It might've been the first time since last night that my dick fully deflated. When Georgia padded back, I held it up. "Phone's ringing."

She took it, read the name on the screen, and frowned.

I tilted my head. "Not going to get it?"

"No."

"Why not?"

"Umm...because that would be rude."

"Would that be because we're both naked, or because your pussy is still sore from riding me ten minutes ago? I'm not sure what the proper etiquette is here."

Georgia's lips twisted. "Eww. You don't have to be a jerk about it."

At the moment, I felt like I did. So I got out of bed. "I'm going to go take a shower. You can take that call if you want."

It didn't even take the whole shower to realize what a dick I'd been. I was jealous, plain and simple, and I'd taken it out on her when she'd done nothing wrong. So as soon as I dried off, I went to apologize.

Georgia wasn't in the bedroom anymore, but her phone was still plugged in on the nightstand, exactly how I'd left it. I went into the adjoining room and found her staring out the window.

Walking up behind her, I kissed her shoulder. "I'm sorry. I was an asshole."

She turned and her face softened a little. "I was upfront about everything with Gabriel."

"I know you were." I shook my head. "I just got jealous. Maybe I shouldn't have, but it happened. That's on me. But I put it on you, which was wrong. So I apologize." I reached out and took her hand. "Forgive me for being a jealous dick?"

She smiled sadly. "Yes."

"Thank you." I grinned. "Because I really want to win that competition. I heard there's a booby prize."

She cracked and laughed. "You're such a jerk."

"I am. But you like me anyway. So what's that say about you?"

Georgia rolled her eyes.

I lifted her hand to my lips and kissed her knuckles. "Can I ask you something?"

"What?"

"Do you want to call him back?"

"I didn't."

"That's not what I'm asking. I'm asking if you *want* to call him back. Like, do you feel the need to talk to him?"

She shook her head. "Not really."

"Do you talk to him every day?"

"No, I don't. When he first left we spoke every two or three days. But now, maybe it's once every week or week and a half."

I nodded. "Are you going to tell him you're seeing someone?"

"I'm not sure. To be honest, he's never asked. Even when we were in Paris, and I asked him, he never asked me. I think he just assumes I'm not, or maybe he doesn't want to know if I am. I'm not sure." When I was quiet, she added, "Would it make you feel better if I did?"

The truth was, it didn't make a shit of difference if he knew. I was jealous because he'd had her, and in some ways he still did—and I didn't. Not really anyway. Plus, I didn't want to make things more complicated for her. "No, I don't think it would make me feel better. Don't do anything for my sake. You do whatever you think is best for you."

Georgia nodded.

"Are you hungry?" I asked.

"I'm starving."

I tugged at her hair. "Come back to the room and look at the menu. I'll order us some food."

After we ate breakfast, Georgia said she needed to check in with the office and shower, so I gave her some privacy and hit the gym downstairs. When I returned, I heard her talking next door. She hadn't shut the adjoining door.

"Oh my God, Maggie," she laughed. "Do not do that. How old is he?"

Quiet.

"I'm pretty sure you can find a man who can do it more than once a night who was eligible to vote in the last election."

Quiet.

She laughed again. "He definitely can. Honestly, it's nothing like with Gabriel, and I can't even put all that blame on Gabriel. Even at the beginning, I didn't want him the same way I want Max. I can't explain it, but there's just so much more sexual chemistry than we ever had."

Quiet.

"Alright. Well, thank you for holding down the fort. I'm glad everything is going smoothly. Though you know a part of me feels a little sad I'm not as needed as I thought."

Quiet.

"Okay. Thanks, Mags. Love you."

I waited a minute, then walked into her room. I'd picked up two more coffees in the hotel lobby. Holding one cup out, I dangled it from my fingers. "Caffe latte."

"Oooh...my favorite. Did I tell you that?"

I nodded.

She looked me up and down. "Did you shower already?"

"Downstairs, after I worked out."

Georgia puffed out her lower lip in a pout. "I was looking forward to seeing you all sweaty and then in your after-shower towel."

I tugged her to me, running my nose along her neck. "I'm happy to get all sweaty again."

"I'll definitely take you up on that. Just a little bit later. I made plans for us. Did you have anything on the agenda today? It will only take an hour or two, but we have to be somewhere at one."

"If we're in the neighborhood, I'd like to stop by the Garden for a few minutes to check in on my friend Otto. His health isn't great, and I haven't seen him in a few weeks."

"Oh, I'm sorry to hear your friend's sick. We can definitely do that."

I nodded. "Great. So what is it you have planned?"

She smiled. "You'll see."

"Alright. Unlike you, I like surprises. So I won't be trying to figure it out and asking for hints." I kissed her. "Everything okay at the office?"

"Yeah. Well, except for Maggie considering seducing a nineteen-year-old."

"What happened to her ex's lawyer?"

"They finished the last conference and have all the terms of the divorce agreed to finally. There's no more chance that Aaron will walk in on them, so I guess she got bored. Plus, the nineteen-year-old is apparently her neighbor's little brother—the neighbor she used to be friends with who slept with her husband. So this is a new and exciting way of getting back at them."

"Remind me never to get on Maggie's bad side."

"You're not kidding." She laughed. "So the place we're going today is a long walk, but it's nice out, and the Garden is on the way. Why don't we stop by to see your friend and then if we have time, I'd love to also stop by my flower shop that's right near there. It's the first one I opened. I like to pop in from time to time. Would you mind if we left a little early and did both?"

"Not at all. I'd love to see your shop. We just need to be back by seven."

"Oh, okay. Do we have plans tonight?"

"Only me. Doing you. I want to make sure we break that record."

Georgia bit down on her bottom lip. "We could...bank one now with a quickie before we go?"

"Oh yeah?" I grinned. "What's the fastest you've ever come?"

Georgia's eyes lit up. "I don't know. But I'm sure we can beat it."

I lifted her off her feet and tossed her over my shoulder. "Damn right we can."

Fourteen

Georgia

"This used to be the prep room, where we dipped the flowers and put them through the preservation process." I pointed to an area that was now wall-to-wall refrigeration. "We had folding tables I'd bought at garage sales lined up against this wall, and thick plastic bags laid out over flattened cardboard boxes under them to catch any leaking chemicals. Now I have big, fancy machines that were custom made to do what I did by hand."

I was showing Max around one of my flower showrooms. Back when we'd started, this was my first expansion—taking Eternity Roses from my apartment to this little shop.

"Where are the machines now?"

"In our production facilities. I have one in Jersey City and one out on the West Coast. None of the flowers are made here anymore. These refrigerators just keep the humidity out and keep premade pieces at optimal temperature. We sell stock pieces from the showrooms and take orders for anything customers want custom made. New deliveries come in from the distribution center every day, and all of the orders that are made online, which is the majority of them, are processed from whichever warehouse is closest."

"Wow. You really grew this from mom and pop to something big."

"Yeah, we did. It wasn't just me. Maggie helped a lot. When I first started, she was working as a marketing manager for a cosmetics company. I didn't have the money to pay her for a long time, but I gave her twenty-five percent equity in the company as compensation. It could have amounted to nothing, of course. Eventually, when I could afford a salary, she quit her job to work with me full time. But she took a risk, and I'm glad it paid off for her, too." I looked around and smiled. "We had a lot of good times here, even when things started to take off and we were working eighteen hours a day." I laughed, remembering the shit we used to do. "One afternoon, we had a customer come in and place two flower orders. I asked him what he wanted to spend on the first order, and he said there was no limit—he just wanted them to be really nice. When I asked what color he wanted, he said whichever I liked best. I told him I favored a mix of bright colors because they're so vibrant, and they made me smile. He said that's what he needed, because the woman he was sending them to hadn't exactly been smiling when he'd left her earlier. I still remember, the woman's name was Amanda, but he'd told us he'd accidentally called her Chloe at an inopportune time. When we got to the card, he filled it out, and I saw that he'd written, *I'm sorry, Amanda*. I suggested that if he'd left his girlfriend thinking he had another person on his mind, that maybe his note should let her know that wasn't the case. I thought something a little more romantic might be in order, but the guy rewrote the card to say something like, *I'm sorry for today, Amanda. I can't stop thinking of you in that red teddy.*" I shook my head, still remembering what the guy had looked like.

"Anyway, he gave me Amanda's address, and when he was done, I'd almost forgotten he'd said he wanted to send two arrangements. Turned out, the second one was for Chloe. He picked out the least-expensive piece we sold and one color. You know what that card said?"

"What?"

"*Happy 10th wedding anniversary, Chloe.*"

"Shit." Max chuckled. "I had a feeling that's where this was going."

"The guy wasn't even embarrassed to be sending flowers to his wife and mistress from the same shop. And it really pissed me off that he was so cheap about what he picked out for his wife, yet the sky was the limit for his girlfriend. So I...accidentally delivered the wrong card with the arrangements."

Max's brows shot up. "Accidentally?"

I grinned. "Well, as far as he knew it was an accident. He was *not* happy about it. He came in the next day, demanding a full refund. I was out, but he got Maggie. She told him we'd be happy to refund him, but that we'd mail the check payable to Chloe."

Max laughed. "You two are some team."

"We do work well together. She takes my ideas, multiplies them a hundred times, and creates unique marketing plans from them. Like when I opened my first store, I used to keep a few annotated books I loved by the register. If someone struggled with what to write on the card to send with the flowers, I'd show them passages that were relevant for the occasion. F. Scott Fitzgerald was my favorite. I could find a million simple quotes in his books. When Maggie worked with the designer on our website, she surprised me by adding all the annotated quotes from those books to our website, plus hundreds more from different authors. So when customers get to the card, they're asked if they need assistance, and if they do, a database selects quotes based on their responses. So many people have used the quotes I picked that she added a feature where the customer can buy a special edition of the book the quote is from to be delivered with their flower order. It's done really well."

Max smiled. "Your eyes light up when you talk about your business. It's sexy."

Gabriel had always had a problem with me working too much. In fact, I'd come to question my own priorities because he made me feel flawed for being as dedicated as I was. I suppose Max understood dedication more, since he'd had to give up so much for his own career.

I smiled back. "Do you ever regret the things you might've missed out on for your career?"

He shook his head. "Regret? No. Have I missed out on things because I spend half my life at the rink? Yeah, of course. But it's easy for me to say I don't have regret because the things I did, the chances I took, have paid off. Not everyone is so lucky. If I were standing here today having given up so much over the years only to not make the cut, maybe my answer would be different. But I had to try, because while I might have regrets if things hadn't worked out the way they did, the one thing I know for sure is that I would definitely regret not having taken the chance to go for it."

"Yeah, that makes sense." I moved closer and wrapped my arms around his neck. "By the way, do you know what *I* find sexy?"

"What?"

"A sweet man, and that's what you are."

"Oh yeah? Why is that?"

"I love your friendship with Otto. When you said you wanted to stop by and check on a friend, I didn't realize it was an older man who worked there."

"Not sure you'd think our friendship was sweet if you heard the way we usually talk to each other. He was just on his best behavior this morning because you were with me."

"How did you two become friends?"

Max shrugged. "He called me out about the chip I had on my shoulder when I first joined the team. I'd never tell him, but he actually reminds me a lot of my dad. He has the ability to see through clutter and simplify things, if that makes any sense. He's grounded and gives good advice. But if you ever tell him I said that, I'll deny it."

I smiled. "Your secret's safe with me."

Susanna, the store manager, walked into the back. "Sorry to interrupt. But we're going to order some lunch. Do you want us to order you guys something?"

"No, I think we're okay. But thank you." Though the mention of lunch made me check the time on my phone. "I didn't realize it was so late." I looked over at Max. "We should get going."

He held his hand out for me to walk first. "Lead the way."

The place I was taking Max was only a block away. When I stopped at the storefront, he looked up at the sign. *Lift Aerial Yoga.*

"Shit," he chuckled. "This is gonna be ugly."

I laughed. "I got us a private class, so you don't have to worry about pictures of you getting out. Though I might snap some photos and use them to blackmail you into servitude as my sex slave later."

Max opened the door, but when I went to pass, he hooked an arm around my waist and pulled me flush against him, planting a kiss on my lips. "No blackmail needed. I voluntarily accept the position."

• • •

I couldn't remember the last time I'd laughed so hard. Max was absolutely a disaster at aerial yoga. At the moment, he'd gotten himself tangled in the silks for the third time and was hanging with one leg suspended in the air, holding his weight in a handstand as the instructor tried to unravel him. I shouldn't have been laughing. Lord knows I wasn't moving gracefully in this contraption either, but I couldn't help myself. It wasn't his inability to get into positions that amused me, it was how frustrated he got when he couldn't conquer something.

"I'm going to kick your ass if you don't stop laughing," he grumbled.

His threat only made me cackle harder. I actually snorted. "You'd have to be able to get out of that lock the silks have you in."

"Why don't you give the swan another try?" the yoga instructor said to Max as she untangled him. "You're very good at that one." Considering the swan was the most basic position—leaning forward and balancing across the fabric, without any twisting or turning—I thought that was a good idea.

"Yeah," I said grinning. "You do a mean swan, Yearwood."

He pointed at me. "You just wait."

By the end of the class, Max did start to get the hang of it. The instructor had said he needed to *make friends* with the silks, instead of fighting them. And I had no doubt that given another class or two, he'd surpass the people who'd been practicing for years. His determination made him unstoppable.

I wiped sweat from my neck as I walked over to the instructor, who was cleaning up at the front of the room.

"Excuse me, Eden."

"Yes?"

"I just want to confirm," I glanced over at Max to make sure he was paying attention. "I did better than Max, correct?"

She frowned. "It's not really about who did better."

"Oh, it is to us. We're a little bit...competitive."

Eden still seemed troubled as she looked over at Max.

He rolled his eyes but nodded. "Just tell her she won."

"No," I said. "She shouldn't *just tell me* I won. She should provide her honest opinion."

Eden shook her head. "You both did very well. Max obviously struggled at the beginning, but he got the hang of it. He's very strong, and that's important as you move on to the more complicated poses."

"But today—just solely based on how we did today—who did better?"

Max walked over. He slung his arm around my neck. "We're going to work on getting her a counselor for her obsessiveness. But just so I don't have to debate it with her all day, would you mind telling us who was better?"

Eden sighed. "Georgia was able to pick up the poses more easily."

I fist pumped, which made Max chuckle.

We thanked Eden and told her we'd definitely be back for more classes. Outside on the street, Max still had his arm around my neck.

"You're gloating," he said. "Nobody likes a gloater."

"Really, is that a *saying*? Because I thought it was nobody likes a *loser*."

We were both laughing, and I almost completely forgot we were walking on the busy New York street, until...

"Georgia?"

The voice was familiar. I looked up to find a man who had been walking in the opposite direction had stopped on the street. He looked back and forth between Max and me.

"Josh Zelman," he said. "I'm an English professor with..." He glanced at Max's arm around my shoulder and changed course. "...over at NYU."

Shoot. That's right. I'd met him a few times at parties. I just couldn't place him out of context. I forced a smile. "Yes, of course. Hi, Josh. It's good to see you."

"You, too." He turned his attention to Max. "You look very familiar. Have we met?"

Max's face was stern. "Nope."

Josh kept staring. It looked like he was going through his mental Rolodex, trying to figure it out. Eventually, he shifted his eyes back to me. "Ellen was just talking about you the other day. We were at the spring mixer, and she said she was bored without you there."

I forced a smile. "Please tell her I said hello."

He nodded. "Will do. I'm actually running late for class. I wasn't sure if it was you, but I figured I'd say hello."

"Nice seeing you."

Max slipped his hand from around my shoulder and stayed quiet as we started to walk again.

"That was... Josh is an English professor at NYU."

"So he said."

"He works with Gabriel. They're good friends, actually."

"Okay."

I wasn't sure what Gabriel had told his friends, or if he'd told them anything at all. So that might've explained the awkwardness. Regardless, I wasn't sure what else needed to be said, so I let it go, hoping Max would, too.

"So...I think a late lunch is on you since I beat you at aerial yoga."

Max smiled, though the playfulness that had been there a few minutes ago was gone. "You got it."

We stopped at a sushi place. The waitress came over with a little girl who was probably about five and set waters on the table. Both of them had black, pocketed aprons wrapped around their waists, and when the woman slipped a small pad and pencil out, the little girl watched her and did the same thing.

"It's bring-your-daughter-to-work day. I hope you don't mind."

"Of course not." I leaned over to the little girl. "What's your name?"

"Grace."

"It's nice to meet you, Grace. I like your apron."

The girl reached into her pocket again. This time, she pulled out two small action figures. I thought they might be from a Disney movie. She held the one of a girl with long, brown, wavy hair out to me.

I took her. "Who is this?"

"Moana."

"Oh. Is she a princess?"

The little girl nodded and held out another figure. This one was a crab. "Tamatoa."

"Tamatoa, huh?" I glanced over at Max. "Are these lucky? Is that why you carry these around?"

She shook her head.

I grinned. "Of course not, because you're a big girl." I leaned closer. "You want to know a secret?"

She nodded.

I pulled Max's plastic Yoda from my purse. "This little guy." I pointed to Max. "Belongs to this big guy."

The little girl covered her mouth and giggled.

I nodded. "I know, right?"

The waitress laughed. "What can I get you?"

I ordered soup and one roll, and Max ordered *four* rolls. The little girl waved to me before following her mother away.

I set Yoda in the middle of the table.

"I didn't know you carried him on you," Max said.

"It's probably why I did so well at aerial yoga, and you, well, *sucked*."

Max laughed. "She was cute."

"Do you want kids someday?"

Max sipped his water and shrugged. "I'm not sure. If you had asked me that five or ten years ago, I would have said no. But now I'm not sure."

"How come you would have said no?"

"I watched what my mother went through when Austin died."

"That's right. I'm sorry. I wasn't thinking. Of course that would have an effect on you."

He shrugged. "Since my nieces were born, I guess it's made me a little more open. Or maybe it's that I'm getting older now. What about you?"

"I definitely would like to have kids. A few, actually. I had a nice childhood, but it was just my mom and me, and I was always a little bit envious of my friends who have big families." I paused. "Maggie and I always said we wanted to have our kids at the same time so they could grow up together. I remember when we were thirteen, saying we wanted to have three kids each and be done by thirty so we were young moms. I guess that's not happening, considering she's in the middle of a divorce and I'm...no longer engaged."

Max looked away. "Life doesn't always go as planned."

Fifteen

Max

Ten years ago

"This is different than what I expected."

"What did you expect, *Animal House*?"

I'd taken Teagan to a party tonight, just not one I'd normally go to. All of my friends were a few blocks over, probably making *Animal House* look tame. Instead, I'd taken her to a party thrown by the architectural club my brother belonged to. He had said he'd be here, though he was nowhere to be found as of yet.

Teagan sipped her beer and watched me. It felt like she was trying to put her finger on something that felt off, so I lifted my chin to a guy walking by. "Hey, what's up? How ya been?"

The guy looked over his shoulder to see who I could have been greeting. Teagan caught the exchange and narrowed her eyes.

"Do you even know anyone here?"

"Sure." I pointed to a random guy across the room. "That's Chandler over there." I scanned the room and pointed to another guy. "That's Joey." A woman I'd never seen passed by and smiled at me. I offered a friendly wave. "Hey, Monica."

"Really, Max?"

"What?"

She pointed to a blond girl. "Is that Phoebe? I've seen *Friends*, too, you know."

I grinned. "Sorry. Do I at least get an E for effort?"

She shook her head. "You get a D for dimples, and they are the only reason I'm still standing here. What's the deal? Why did you bring me to a dull party where you don't know anyone?"

"You want the truth?"

She rolled her eyes. "Max..."

"Okay, okay..." I huffed. "These are my brother's friends. Mine are at a different party."

"Did you just want to hang out with your brother?"

"I thought his friends would make a better impression."

"Why?"

"Because hanging out with my buddies ends one of two ways on a Saturday night: someone gets arrested, and occasionally that's me, or someone starts a fight, which is also occasionally me, and then the entire hockey team jumps in. You said you could tell a lot about a person by the company they keep. I figured it would be safer to have you fall for me *before* bringing you around those clowns."

She raised a brow. "Oh, that's the plan? Tell me, exactly how are you going to make me fall for you?"

I smiled and pointed to my cheeks.

Teagan laughed. "They are adorable. I'll give you that. Though I think you're going to need more than a great smile. How about we go to the other party, and I promise not to hold your friends against you? Believe it or not, I was in a sorority and went to a fraternity party or two."

"Thank fuck." I dropped my head. "This party sucks."

We were both laughing as we headed to the door. I waved at the two guys I'd pretended to know. "Later, Joey. Later, Chandler."

They both looked at me like I was nuts.

Out on the porch, I saw my brother walking up the path.

"Hey, there he is. It's about damn time." I thumbed over my shoulder. "We almost died from boredom waiting around in there."

Austin smiled and shook his head. He looked to Teagan and extended his hand. "I'm this bonehead's brother, Austin."

"Teagan. Nice to meet you." She tilted her head. "Have we met before?"

My brother shrugged. "Not that I know of."

"Probably just saw you around campus. I've been living here for so long, everyone is starting to look familiar." She glanced between the two of us. "You guys don't look alike."

I bounced on my heels with a grin. "Such a shame... for him."

Austin chuckled. "He might've gotten the looks, but I got the brains. Someday he'll be bald and fat, and I'll still be smart. You sure you don't want to go out with me instead?"

Teagan laughed. "Well, you do share the same wit."

"Are you guys heading out already?" Austin asked.

"Yeah. No offense, but this party sucks. You want to come with us? We're going over to the hockey team party."

Austin shook his head. "No thanks. They're a little much for me off the ice. Besides, my back's been killing me all day. I'm just going to sit around and have a couple of beers and call it a night."

"Again with the backache? What could possibly make it hurt? There isn't even any checking in your sport."

Austin looked at Teagan, shaking his head. "I run track. This mo-mo thinks you can't get injured unless you play a contact sport."

"You know, if they'd let people try to tackle the runners as they ran, it would be a much better time."

Austin chuckled. "You two have fun."

I slapped my brother on the shoulder. "Don't do anything I wouldn't do."

"Yeah, there would have to *be* something you wouldn't do for that to be advice."

I grabbed Teagan's hand. "Ready?"

"Sure." She turned to my brother. "Bye, Austin. It was nice meeting you."

"You, too."

As we walked away, Teagan turned to look back again.

"Did you forget something?"

"No. I just...I feel like I know your brother from somewhere, but I can't place it."

"As long as you didn't go out with him before me. Because that would just be weird."

She smiled. "I think I'd remember if I went out with a guy."

"I don't know. They say memory is one of the first things to go. You are pretty old."

She bumped her shoulder to mine as we walked. "God, you're lucky you're cute, because you can be sort of obnoxious."

I grinned. "Oh yeah, you think I'm cute?"

Her eyes dropped to my lips, and she sighed. "Yeah, I guess that makes two of us who know you're cute."

• • •

"I can't find my earring. Have you seen it?"

I rolled over on my back and threw my arm over my eyes to block the sun. "I didn't even notice you had ears."

A pillow whacked me in the abs. "Jerk." Teagan pouted. "You didn't know I had ears? Do you remember my name?"

I squinted one eye open. "Brandy, right?"

She pretended to be pissed but couldn't hide her smile. "I'm serious about my earring. My grandmother gave them to me. She died last year."

"Okay, sorry." I rubbed sleep from my eyes and crawled out of bed, wearing only my boxer briefs. "Where did you look so far?"

"Only in the bathroom. I just noticed it missing. It's got to be in the bed somewhere."

I grinned, remembering us stumbling back to my room last night after the party. "Or near that door. Or over there on that chair."

She whacked me with the pillow again, this time not hiding her smile. "Just look for it."

"Yes, ma'am."

While she searched the floor, I shook out the pillows and blankets, moved the mattress to see if it had fallen behind, and rustled my clothes from last night to see if anything fell out. But we both came up empty.

"Damn it. Maybe I lost it at the party last night. Do you think they cleaned up yet?"

I looked at her. "There's still six weeks left in the semester."

She laughed as she zipped up her leather boots. "Alright. I have to run because I have a shift at the hospital today. Will anyone be up if I stop over on my way to see if it fell out there?"

I grabbed a box of Cheerios and dug inside for a handful, shoving them into my mouth dry. "There isn't even a lock on the door. Just let yourself in if no one answers."

"Okay."

She pushed up on her toes and kissed me while I chewed. "I had fun last night."

"Me too."

"You want to hang out next weekend?"

"Can't," I said. "Games Friday and Saturday night and then Sunday I'm heading down to New York to go ice skating with a bunch of the guys from the team."

"All the way to New York to skate?"

"Yeah, it's some sort of tradition. The hockey team goes to Wollman Rink, where they have the big Christmas tree in Central Park, to skate on the last day and then to the Irish pub a few blocks away."

"Well, I have either class or rotations Tuesday through Friday this week."

I shrugged. "Want to meet up after your shift ends later?"

Teagan smiled and stuck her hand into the Cheerios box. "Yeah, maybe. Text me." She turned around at the door and ate some of the cereal from her hand. "And this doesn't count as you buying my breakfast. So you're buying me food next time."

"No problem." I held up the Cheerios. "I'll bring the box. They're good any time of the day."

She chuckled. "See you later."

That afternoon, Teagan texted to say she hadn't found the earring at the house where the party had been last night. She asked if I could go by the place my brother's party had been. Since I had practice, I told her I'd stop by afterward and pick her up at the library where she was meeting someone to swap notes after her shift at the hospital.

She was waiting outside wearing blue scrubs when I pulled up at the front of the library.

"Any luck finding my earring?" She climbed into the car and pulled the door closed.

I shook my head. "I looked myself and asked two of the guys if anyone found it. By the way, Chandler's name is actually Rene. I think Chandler works better for him."

Teagan sighed. "I can't believe I lost that earring. It's only the second time I wore them out. Would you mind driving to the house we went to for the first party, and we can walk the path we took to the second party before it gets dark? Maybe we'll get lucky."

"Sure."

Parking in Boston was a bitch sometimes, so I had to leave the car a block away before we could trace our path to the other house and back. We didn't find the earring, but when we were almost to the car again, Teagan pointed up ahead to a guy getting out of a car. "Is that your brother?"

I squinted. "Yeah, I think it is... Austin!"

He turned and waited. "Do you work at a hospital?" he asked Teagan as we approached.

"I'm a med student." Teagan snapped her fingers. "That's where I know you from. You were a patient."

"You were in the hospital?" I said.

Austin shook his head. "No, I wasn't."

Teagan's brows furrowed. "Yes, you came into Boston Medical Center a week ago, right?"

Austin's eyes flashed to mine and back to Teagan. His tone was stern. "No, I didn't. But if I did, wouldn't you be bound by doctor-patient privilege or something?"

Teagan's face fell. "Uh...yeah... Sorry."

"Jesus, lighten up, bro. She's a student."

Austin frowned and put his hands on his hips. "What are you guys doing here anyway?"

I pointed to Teagan. "She lost an earring somewhere last night. So we were retracing the walk from here to the party we went to after."

He nodded. "Any luck?"

"No, but we're going to go grab something to eat. Want to third wheel?"

Austin shook his head. "I gotta study."

"Alright, later. But look around the living room for her earring when you go in. I checked earlier, but it can't hurt to look again."

"You got it. Have fun."

Maybe it was me, but it felt like my brother couldn't wait to get the hell out of here. He was already at the front door before Teagan and I finished saying goodbye.

I looked at her. "Sorry. Not sure what's up his ass."

She looked back at the house as Austin walked inside. "Maybe he just has something on his mind."

—Sixteen—

Max

We stumbled back into my suite, still laughing.

Ice skating today had gone about as well for Georgia as aerial yoga had for me yesterday. I was sure her ass was pretty sore right now from how many times she'd bounced on it. Not surprisingly, she didn't take her loss well. Since the score from the last two days had been 1-1, she'd insisted on a tiebreaker competition. Still cocky from showing off my skills on the ice, I'd agreed and let her pick.

In the Uber on the way home, she'd decided on a speed math competition, asking the driver to give us numbers to add in our head, before checking them with her phone. Of course, she was a business major with an MBA, and I was a hockey player, so she'd assumed it was a slam-dunk. But she'd never asked what my major had been in college—*math*. It served her right for assuming I'd studied beer pong. So I upped the ante—winner gets head.

After I kicked her ass, I let her in on my college major. We were still laughing and arguing about whether I'd played fair when we got back to the hotel room.

"Didn't take you for a welcher, Delaney."

She grabbed my shirt and fisted it in her hand, backing me against the wall.

"I'm no welcher. But *you're* a cheater."

Smiling, I put my hands on her shoulders and gave her a gentle shove down. "On your knees, sweetheart."

Georgia's eyes sparked, and she flashed an evil grin. "We're even if I can make you come in less than three minutes."

I can definitely hold out for three minutes.

Before I could even respond, she sank to her knees. Looking up from under thick lashes, Georgia ran her tongue along her top lip. And fuck if it wasn't the sexiest thing I'd ever seen. I watched as she unbuttoned my pants, and the sound of the zipper coming down made the hair on my arms stand up. She tugged off my jeans and boxers in one swoop and looked back up at me with the wickedest grin I'd ever seen.

"Three minutes—deal?"

I answered by digging one hand into her hair and winding it around my fist, and grabbing my cock with the other.

"You got a deal. Now stop talking and open wide."

Her beautiful, plump lips opened, and I guided myself into her hot mouth. She sucked as I pushed in, going slow and feeding her a few inches, then pulling back out an inch or two, and pushing back in for more. After a few times, I hit that sink-or-swim spot—the place where most women gagged if you drove farther, and I was about to pull back again when she looked up at me. It took everything I had in me not to ram myself down her throat.

"*Fuck*, Georgia. *Fuuuck*. Take more."

Her eyes gleamed, and in that instant, I realized I'd just taken a sucker's bet I was about to lose. Georgia adjusted her jaw, opening wider, and surged forward, not waiting for me to push the limits as she swallowed me down her throat.

My eyes rolled back in my head.

Her throat squeezed me like a vise, warm and tight. I hadn't even been in her mouth for thirty seconds, yet I could already imagine what my cock would look like as it erupted down her throat.

I groaned.

She moaned.

And something within me went from playful to fucking *carnal*. It became a frantic race for me to feel what I'd just imagined happening. Somehow I joined *her* freaking team and wanted her to win this one more than anything. I began to pump faster. Using my hands in her hair to steady her head, I took over. She'd bet I couldn't hold out for three minutes while she gave me head, but she hadn't mentioned anything about fucking her face. This was a whole different ballgame, and my release came barreling down like a runaway freight train. *Fuck her wager. Losing this is way better than winning anything else.*

"Georgia..." I slowed down. Even though she could deep throat better than a damn porn star, I wasn't going to make assumptions. "Babe..." I loosened my grip on her hair. "I'm going to come."

Georgia looked up at me, letting me know she'd heard my warning, then sucked me in deeper again.

"Fuck. Fuck. *Fuuuuck.*"

So I dug my hands into her hair one more time, pushing in as deep as I could, and released. The pulsating stream seemed to go on forever. At the risk of sounding like a wuss, I was completely out of breath and felt a little lightheaded after.

Georgia wiped her mouth as she got up and grinned. "I win."

I blew out a hiss of breath. "If that's losing, I'm a damn moron for spending my entire life competing to win."

• • •

We slept pretty late the next morning and were still in bed playing around at eleven when Georgia's phone rang. Maggie's name flashed on the screen, so she swiped to answer while I sucked on her neck.

"Hey."

"I think Gabriel is losing his shit."

I hadn't meant to listen, but I heard the words loud and clear since I was currently on top of her with our heads so close. Pulling back, my eyes met Georgia's. She frowned.

I got up. "I'm going to take a shower."

I heard half the conversation as I walked to the bathroom.

"What do you mean?" And then a pause before, "Why would the receptionist tell him that?"

I probably could've heard the rest of it from the bathroom, but rather than eavesdrop and ruin my mood more, I took an extra-long, hot shower. When Georgia had first told me about her open relationship, I figured it was the perfect arrangement. We could enjoy each other for a few months, and then, probably when things between us started to wane anyway, I wouldn't feel bad leaving her high and dry when I left for California. Besides, the other guy wasn't even in the country, so that would make it easy not to remember he existed. But the more I got to know Georgia, the more the other guy who wasn't even in the country was still somehow too close. I was starting to understand how the women I'd dated the last few years felt. Two people agreed to a physical-only relationship, some light fun without strings attached, yet one ends up wanting more. Only this time, it was me holding the short stick. And it royally sucked.

My fingers were pruney by the time I finally came back out of the bathroom. Georgia had put on a T-shirt and looked lost as she stood at the window staring at the city below.

When she heard me, she turned. "Sorry about that."

I rubbed my wet hair with a towel. "Nothing to be sorry about."

"Maybe not technically, but it still feels wrong to discuss another man on the phone while I'm here with you."

I said nothing.

She frowned. "Gabriel texted me a few times yesterday. When I didn't respond, and I wasn't answering my office phone, he called the main number at my office. Apparently, the receptionist told him I was on vacation for two weeks and asked if he'd like to speak to Maggie. When they transferred him, he gave Maggie the third degree. She told him she'd pass along his message, but that was all she would say."

I nodded.

"Should I call him and tell him I'm seeing someone?" she asked.

"I don't know, Georgia. I don't think I'm the right person to give you advice on how to manage things with your ex-fiancé. I'd probably tell the guy to go fuck himself. You don't try to track him down while he's busy fucking other women, do you?"

Georgia frowned again.

"Yeah, like I said, not sure I'm the right person to ask."

I headed back to the bathroom to brush my teeth. When I came out again, she was still at the window. I walked up behind her and rubbed her shoulders.

"I'm not trying to be a dick, Georgia. It's just...I know this is supposed to be only a summer of fun, yet I can't help but feel territorial when it comes to you, whether that's right or wrong. I also care about you, and I don't like the idea of some asswipe stringing you along and then suddenly showing some interest when you start to pay less attention to him. He sounds like he's just playing games."

She turned around. "I do understand it's weird to talk to you about it. Do you think we can pretend Maggie never called and enjoy our day? The last thing I want is to put a damper on our fun. I can't remember the last time I didn't want to go to work, or even check in with the office. I love being in this little bubble with you, and I don't want it to end."

I forced a smile and leaned in to kiss her. "What phone call?"

The smile that spread across her face made my chest hurt. "Thank you. Actually, I'd like to thank you properly." She reached for the towel tucked at my waist and gave it a quick tug. It fell to the floor, and suddenly I really couldn't remember any phone call.

Seventeen

Georgia

The next week flew by way too fast. Max and I did just about every touristy thing in New York, and then some. It made me sad to think that in just a couple of days, I'd be going back to work. Tonight we were venturing out of the city—not too far, only to New Jersey—to watch a hockey playoff game with his teammate Tomasso and Jenna, his wife, whom I'd sat next to a few times watching their games.

"Hey!" Jenna stood when we got down to our seats. They weren't as good as the ones at the Garden, but close. She gave me a hug while Tomasso and Max did some one-armed shoulder hug thing. The game hadn't started yet, and people around us started to whisper. A few took out their phones and snapped pictures. Max had only been recognized a few times while we were out during our staycation, but I guess it was impossible for it not to happen when we were in an arena full of hockey fans. A girl from the row behind us asked him to sign her jersey.

"You want me to sign a jersey for a team I'm not on?"

She twisted a bracelet on her wrist. "I'm sorry. It's all I have."

"I'm teasing." Max grinned. "I don't give a shit. I'll sign it."

She handed him a Sharpie, and he leaned down to sign her jersey, but he stopped before he'd finished, putting his hand up in front of her friend.

"No, she's off limits," he said.

I then realized her friend had been aiming her camera at me. She apologized and put the phone down.

"Sit here," Jenna said. "I don't need to sit next to my husband. He's been home two weeks, and I'm already ready for him to go back to practice. The other day I told him to take some initiative, because unless I tell him to do something, he will spend an entire day lying on the couch like a lump. I meant for him to maybe load the dishwasher or start a load of laundry. When I came home that night, he'd gutted our bedroom—removed two windows and there was no sheetrock on two of the walls anymore. He said I'd complained about the window having a leak last winter. Umm...caulk around the window, don't gut the room." She shook her head. "When I asked him what the hell he was doing, he said he was taking initiative. The man has an off and on switch and no in between."

I laughed.

"Anyway...enough about me. How are things with you and Max? I was so excited to hear you two were still going strong. You know when you just have a feeling about two people? Your gut just thinks they're right for each other?"

I smiled. "Things are good. I took some time off from work, and we've just been doing stuff in the city."

"I'm happy for you. Though my auction total is going to take a hit without Pretty Boy in the lineup."

"Auction?"

"I run a charity auction every fall. We raise funds for kids who can't afford to go to hockey camps all over the country. People donate things for us to auction off, but the highlight of the night is always when we auction off dates with some of the single players. Last year we got thirty-five thousand for Max—the most we've ever raised on an item."

Max finished signing autographs and sat down next to me. He took my hand and weaved my fingers with his.

"You were auctioned off?" I asked.

He groaned. "They made me do it."

Jenna laughed. "Yeah, we *made* him do it. But we didn't make him take off his shirt and start flexing when the bidding started."

Max hung his head. "I got into it. I wanted to get the bidding higher."

I grinned. "You wanted to make sure you pulled the biggest price tag ever, didn't you?"

He raised an eyebrow. "Like you would've done any differently."

"Thirty-five thousand, huh? You must be a hot commodity. I hope I don't get a big fat bill later."

Max leaned to me and lowered his voice. "I'll take it in trade."

The game started, and within the first five minutes, I saw a side of Max I'd never seen before. He and Tomasso yelled and screamed. They jumped up out of their seats a hundred times, and when they did sit, they sat on the edge. They were completely focused on the game. Max had started with his hand resting on my thigh, but I had to ask him to remove it, because every time something happened in the game, he squeezed so hard I was definitely going to have finger bruises. He'd had no clue he was even doing it. But I found his intensity and passion kind of sexy.

I leaned over to Jenna when the two of them jumped to their feet to yell at the ref during the second period. "These two are hysterical. I've never seen Max like this."

"Is this the first game you've been to with him?"

I nodded. "Why do I find it kind of hot?"

Jenna wiggled her brows. "Wait until you get home later. They need an outlet for all that adrenaline coursing through their veins. Unlike with their own games, it doesn't matter if their team wins or loses. So it's a win-win for us."

When the buzzer sounded at the end of the period, the guys practically collapsed into their seats. Max suddenly seemed to remember I was there.

He leaned over. "You good?"

I smiled. "I'm great."

"Oh my God!" Jenna tapped me on the shoulder. When I looked over, she was pointing at the Jumbotron. My eyes widened upon finding my own face plastered on it. The camera zoomed in closer on Max and me. While I tried to figure out what the heck was going on, *Kiss Cam* started to flash on the bottom of the screen.

"You have to kiss!" Jenna laughed.

I turned to Max, who shrugged. "Works for me."

Rather than lean over and brush his lips with mine, he stood and yanked me from my seat. He wrapped an arm around my back and proceeded to dip me dramatically before planting one hell of a kiss. People were hooting and hollering all around us, and when he pulled me back to standing, we were both laughing and smiling from ear to ear.

"Always the showman," I said.

"Can't help it. These days I have something worth showing off." He winked.

• • •

The following day was the last full day of our staycation. Tomorrow morning we'd be checking out and going back to our respective apartments, and then Monday was back to work for me. Even though we had the rest of the summer to have fun, a feeling of melancholy set in. Max's agent had texted him last night and said he wanted to get together to go over the terms of the contract he'd been negotiating. Max had tried to push it off until next week, but his agent had said it needed to be done this weekend because of some meeting the owner of the other team had on Monday. Max told him he could only give him an hour and asked him to meet him for breakfast in the lobby of the hotel.

"Are you sure you don't want to come?" he asked. "You could at least eat while we talk?"

I was still lying in bed, naked with a sheet draped over me, enjoying the view while Max got dressed. "I'm good. I'm going to answer some emails while you go to your meeting."

Max walked over and pulled the sheet off, then smacked my ass before leaning down and pressing his lips to mine. "Alright but stay naked."

"I'll think about it."

Once he was gone, I propped some pillows behind me and scanned through my messages. Ten minutes in, my phone buzzed. The name I saw made my chest heavy.

Gabriel.

I sighed. Over the last week, I hadn't thought about him too much. When Max was around, it was hard to think about anything else, especially another man. The morning Gabriel had called the office, I'd sent him a long text telling him I was fine but taking a much-needed break from work and I would call him when I had time. But even though I'd spent plenty of hours lounging around each morning and evening since then, that *time* had never seemed to come.

Now there really wasn't a reason not to answer since Max would be gone for a while. So I sat up a little straighter and swiped.

"Hello?"

"God, I missed your voice," he said.

I sighed heavily. "It has been a while, hasn't it?"

"Longer than we should have let it go."

"How are things?"

"The same. Teaching, writing...one day just rolls into the other."

"How's the book coming along?"

"I write four or five pages, throw away three, so I guess it's progress."

"I suppose it's better than not writing," I said.

"What about you? Tell me about this time you took off of work. I never thought I'd see the day. When your office told me you were out for two weeks, I got worried. I don't remember you taking two *days* since you started your company."

"Yeah, I know. I guess it was time."

"So what have you been up to?"

"Mostly doing things around the city that I've always wanted to do and never made time for, like go to the Statue of Liberty and the Empire State Building."

"By yourself?"

I shut my eyes. This was the moment of truth I'd been avoiding. I could lie and say yes, but why? I wasn't doing anything wrong, and Gabriel had been honest with me when I'd asked. Plus, it felt wrong to hide Max.

So I took a deep breath and came clean. "No, not by myself."

Again Gabriel was quiet. His voice was lower when he spoke. "With the guy Josh saw you with?"

I blinked a few times. Of course Josh had called Gabriel to tell him he'd run into me with another man. If I'd seen Maggie's ex with someone, I would have gone straight to her with the information. But I guess I was surprised by how Gabriel was handling the news.

"Yes, his name is Max."

"Was it just a date or...more?"

"We've been seeing each other."

There was another long pause. "How long?"

"I guess we met about a month ago, maybe a little more."

"You like him?"

"I do."

A rush of air blew into the phone. I pictured Gabriel dragging his hand through his neatly groomed hair. "I know I have no right to say a word, as this was all my idea, but I gotta tell you, it hurts. I guess when I imagined how things would be, I was imagining what things have been for me—a hookup now and then, some companionship for dinner or something. But that was dumb of me. I know you better than that. You weren't going to do some random hookup."

"I tried. I even joined Tinder. But it didn't feel right."

"My sister sent me a link to a news story—a kiss at a hockey game. It said he was a player."

Oh, God. I was devastated that Gabriel had *told* me he'd been with other people. I couldn't imagine if I'd had to see it on a Jumbotron. That kiss had been all over the news. I had an ache in my chest. "I can't believe you saw that."

"Victoria didn't know things had changed between us... So she thought..."

"Oh my God. She thought she was catching me cheating on you?"

"Yeah. I hadn't told my family anything."

"I hope you set the record straight so your family doesn't think I'm horrible."

"Yes, of course I did."

"Why hadn't you told them?"

"I don't know. I guess I just figured it would be hard to explain things. My family adores you. Plus, once I got home and we were back together, it would make no difference." He paused. "Is it serious? Things between you and this guy?"

Once he was home and we were back together—as if it were a foregone conclusion. Which I suppose I'd been desperately trying to make sure it was. But in this moment, I wasn't sure how to answer that. Things between me and Max felt serious. We'd spent every waking moment for the last two weeks with each other. And I had feelings for him, strong ones even. But we also had an expiration date, so how serious could we really be?

"He's moving at the end of the summer."

"Oh."

"Can I ask you something, Gabriel?"

"Of course."

"What if I'd just said yes, that things between me and Max are serious? How would that make you feel?"

"How do you think it would make me feel? I haven't slept for a week, ever since I heard you were dating someone. It fucking sucks. I love you, and you're with another man."

"But you don't love me enough to be faithful while you're gone. You do know we could have visited each other and made it work long distance." I felt a lump in my throat. "If you love me, how could you let me go?"

"It was never about not loving you, Georgia. I told you that. It was about not liking myself. I felt like a failure—my career, my life, everything. And at the same time, everything was falling into place for you—your career was soaring, you were ready to move on to the next phase of your life… You're a shining star. I knew something needed to change when I started to resent your success." His voice cracked. "I didn't feel worthy of your love."

Tears slid down my cheeks. I'd heard Gabriel say some version of those words before, but this was the first time they'd made much sense. Our breakup had come as such a shock to me. Until now, all I'd felt was my own pain. At this point I could better comprehend Gabriel's need for space to get himself in a better place, but I still couldn't understand loving someone, yet wanting to *be* with someone else.

I took a breath. "I'm sorry you felt unworthy. And I'm sorry I didn't realize how much pain you were in."

"None of this is your fault, Georgia. I'm not trying to make you feel bad. But you asked how I could let you go, and it was never because I didn't love you enough, it was because I *do* love you enough to let go so I can try to fix me. I want to be the man you deserve."

I was about to remind him that fixing himself didn't need to include seeing other people, but the sound of his crying on the other end of the phone broke me. My tears fell faster. I don't know what I'd expected to happen when I admitted I was seeing someone else, too, but it certainly wasn't this. It would have been easier if he'd been angry and given me attitude—yelled at me and picked a fight. But this… Him breaking down just made my heart sink. We'd spent years together, and even if he'd hurt me, I didn't wish that back on him.

I wiped tears from my cheeks and took a deep breath. We talked for a few minutes after that, but couldn't move past the heaviness of the conversation we'd just had. We left off saying we'd talk soon, but neither of us committed to when that might be. After, I jumped in the shower, hoping to clear my head and change my mood. But I couldn't shake the melancholy feeling that had set in.

Max came back just as I was getting dressed. My back was to the door as I clipped on my bra, and he came up behind me and wrapped his hands around my waist.

"You have the sexiest bras and underwear, you know that?"

I smiled. "It makes me feel good to have something lacy on, even when it's hidden under sweatpants at home. How did your meeting go?"

Max turned me around, and his face fell. "What's the matter?"

"Nothing."

His brows pulled together. "Bullshit. It looks like you were crying."

I was so damn emotional, and I knew if I talked about it I'd break down. And I didn't want to cry to Max about Gabriel. So I took a deep breath and steadied myself, hoping he would let it go if I gave him something. "I spoke to Gabriel."

Max's jaw tightened. "Did he upset you?"

"No." I shook my head. "Well, yes. But he didn't do anything. It was just...a hard conversation to have. He knows I've been seeing someone."

Max looked into my eyes. "Do you want to talk about it?"

I smiled sadly. "No. But thank you for asking. I'd really just like to enjoy our last day here."

He looked down for a minute before nodding.

"Tell me about your meeting with your agent," I pressed. "Were you happy with what he had to say?"

He nodded. "It went well. Hockey contract negotiations aren't just agreeing on a number. The structure of payments can take longer to finalize than coming to the total because of the team's salary-cap limits."

"I didn't realize they couldn't just pay people what they want."

"They also want me to fly out to California next week—meet with the owner and general manager."

"Are you going to?"

He brushed his hand over my hair. "Why don't you come with me?"

"I wish I could," I sighed. "But I need to go back to work. I have a lot of things waiting for me."

Max tilted his head. "Are you sure it's not because of the conversation that upset you earlier?"

I shook my head. "No, it's really not."

He nodded. "So what do you want to do for our last day?"

"Honestly, I'd love to just go to the park for a little while and then come back here and snuggle."

Max smiled. "Done."

• • •

The next morning I woke to find Max staring at me.

"What are you doing?" I asked groggily.

He stroked my cheek with his knuckles. "Looking at you."

"While I sleep? That's creepy, Pretty Boy."

"You were snoring pretty good."

"I do not snore."

"Oh yeah, I forgot." He smiled. "Can I ask you something about...him?"

"Gabriel?"

Max nodded.

"Of course."

"What if he hadn't broken things off, but still went to go teach in London for the year or however long he signed up for?"

"What do you mean?"

"Do you think it would've worked out? Him being in London and you being in New York for that long?"

"And him not sleeping with anyone else? He would be faithful?"

"Yeah."

I shrugged. "I guess so. I can't think of a reason it wouldn't have. But I didn't know he was planning on going to London until a few days before he broke things off. I suppose we could have worked out a travel schedule and taken turns visiting on weekends and stuff. I mean, we didn't see each other most weekdays anyway because I worked late."

Max nodded.

"Why do you ask?"

"I don't know." He shook his head. "Just thinking, I guess."

He was talking about Gabriel, but I felt a flutter of hope in my belly that maybe, just maybe, he was asking because the flying time to London was about the same as a trip to California.

"What time is it?" I asked.

"It's almost ten."

"Oh wow. Is checkout at eleven?"

Max nodded.

"I guess I should get my lazy ass out of bed and shower."

"I have a better idea."

"What's that?"

He slid his hand down my body and dipped between my legs with a grin. "Let's get you wet. But you can shower later."

— Eighteen —

Georgia

"Alright, that's it. We're leaving." Maggie stood from the guest chair on the other side of my desk.

My forehead wrinkled. "What? Where are we going?"

"To get some answers."

I laughed. "What are you talking about, crazy lady?"

"We're going to that cute wine bar two blocks down, the one next to the questionable foot-massage place that only ever has men walk in and the massages are in private rooms."

"I still have work to do."

I'd been back in the office for four days but had barely dug out of the backlog of emails to answer, reports to review, and calls to return.

"It will all be here tomorrow. I want to hear about your time with Max."

"I told you all about my time with Max on Monday morning. Remember, you were in my office waiting for me at six thirty in the morning with coffee you'd spiked with RumChata?"

"Yes, but you told me what you *wanted* to talk about. Now I want to hear what you don't want to talk about. And don't even tell me there's nothing else on your mind. Because you're three for three on the Georgia scale of something's bugging you. Your hair is up in a bun by nine AM. You only do that when you have a problem you can't solve. You're checking the time on your phone like you're waiting for someone to flip the switch on the electric chair, and you have that upward inflection when speaking."

"What upward inflection?"

"At the end of every sentence you raise your voice like you're asking a question, when you're not."

"There's no way that *I do that*?" I covered my mouth. "Oh my God, I just did it."

Maggie laughed. "You only do those things when you have a problem you can't solve."

"Maybe I have a work problem that's bothering me."

Maggie folded her arms across her chest. "Okay. What is it?"

"I, uh..." Drawing a complete blank, I shook my head, pulled open my desk drawer, and yanked out my purse. "Fine. But we can't overdo it. I'll have to get in extra early tomorrow to make up for all the things I should be doing now."

Maggie grinned. "Of course."

• • •

"I wasn't supposed to grow feelings for Max. He was only supposed to be my distraction." *Hiccup.*

Maggie smirked. "I knew you were lying when I asked you on Monday if you were falling for him. You oversold the '*Nah, we're just having a good time.*' If you had debated my question for thirty-six hours and then answered, I might've believed it."

"But I love Gabriel. I'd decided to marry him."

"You can love someone but not be *in love* with them. I love you, but I don't want to wake up to you every morning."

"That's different."

She shrugged. "Not really. You want to know what I think?"

I pouted. "No."

"That's a shame. Because you're going to hear it anyway. I think you spend so much time analyzing every decision that you've forgotten to listen to your heart. Things in your life have changed—and those changes were started by Gabriel. Let's not forget that."

I dropped my head into my hands. "I'm so confused. And Max is moving at the end of the summer."

"So? He's a professional athlete. He's probably on the road for most of the hockey season anyway. He has to live near his team to practice and go to work, but why couldn't he be bicoastal and spend the offseason here, if things worked out? You have a shop in Long Beach, California. You could work out of that, if you wanted, at least for some of the season. You're self-employed, Georgia. Hell, you could move the entire damn operation to wherever he is."

"You're making my head spin."

Maggie smiled. "I'm not saying you need to do any of those things. I just mean that him leaving doesn't have to mean the end."

"But that's what we agreed to."

"And Aaron agreed to love me forever and not covet thy neighbor." She shrugged. "Shit changes."

"I don't even know if Max would want more."

"He hasn't given you any indication that he might be interested in something longer than a summer fling?"

"Well...on the last morning of our mini vacation, he asked me if I thought things between me and Gabriel would've worked out long distance, if he hadn't broken things off before he left. For some reason, I thought he might be asking because he was moving to California. But that could just have been wishful thinking."

"Hmmm..." Maggie sipped her wine. "I bet he was. With men, our first instinct is usually right. I know that's hard for someone like you to believe, because you analyze problems from fifty different angles, but usually our intuition sees things right in front of us pretty clearly."

"Even if I was right, and somehow we were able to work it out and try the long distance thing. What about Gabriel?"

"What about him?"

"He's going to come home in six months. What if he comes home and says he wants to be together, that his time away made him realize what he really wants in life?"

"What about what *you* really want in life? Let me ask you something. Tomorrow morning, you wake up and find out you won the lottery. You grab your cell phone and you call...who? Who are you calling? I mean, after me, of course."

"I don't play the lotto."

Maggie shook her head. "Work with me here. *Pretend* you played the lotto. Close your eyes for a minute."

I took a deep breath before shutting them.

"Okay... You climb out of bed. You flick on the news while you're getting ready, and you hear the anchorman say there was only one winning ticket for the billion-dollar lottery—the largest in history. And it was purchased at the same store you purchased yours. Then he reads the numbers: five, fourteen, one, thirty-one, three, twenty-five. You run and get your ticket to double check, but you know those are the numbers you played because it's my birthday, your birthday, and your mom's birthday. Your hand is shaking while you confirm you're the winner. You grab your cell phone and you call..."

I squeezed my eyes shut, trying to imagine the entire thing. I could see exactly what she'd described—the TV on, running to my purse to fish out my ticket, even grabbing my cell phone to call someone. But...then I stare down at my phone. I'm not sure who to call first.

I opened my eyes. "I don't know. I don't know who I'd call!"

"Welp, that's what you need to figure out. You know what we need to help us do that?"

"A pros and cons list?"

Maggie guzzled the last of her wine. "Nope. More wine. I'll be right back." She pointed to my glass, which was still half full. "Finish that before I return."

While she was at the bar, my phone started to jump around on the table. I picked it up and smiled seeing Max's name. Since Maggie was talking to the cute bartender who hadn't yet filled our glasses, I figured I had a few minutes. So I swiped to answer.

"Hey."

"What's up, beautiful? You know what I was thinking about earlier?"

"What?" I sipped my wine.

"Eating you out while you're sitting at your desk."

I inhaled sharply. Unfortunately, I hadn't swallowed the wine all the way yet, so it went down the wrong pipe. I started to cough.

"Are you okay?"

I patted my chest and spoke with a strained voice. "No! You made me choke on my wine."

"I wish I was there to make you choke on something else."

I felt my cheeks heat, and it had nothing to do with swallowing down the wrong pipe. "Someone is in a mood today."

"I can't help it. I had that meeting with the general manager. He was running a few minutes late, so they showed me into his office. He had this big desk with all these awards hanging on the walls and stuff. It just looked like the office of a guy who was in charge. That got me thinking what you might look like sitting behind your desk—all powerful and sexy. It makes me want to make you beg."

"Let me get this straight. You envision me being powerful, and that turns you on and makes you want to... make me beg?"

I obviously couldn't see him, but I heard his smile in just two words. "Fuck yeah."

I laughed. "You're bad."

"Why don't you go lock the door to your office and let me tell you the things I want to do to you while you slip your hand down into those lacy panties I know you have on."

Damn, I kind of wished I were still at the office now. "Tempting...but no can do. I'm not at the office."

"Where are you?"

"At a bar a few blocks away with Maggie. She's trying to get me drunk."

"Nice. I'm glad you left the office at a decent hour tonight."

"I still have a lot of catching up to do."

"Well, get it done. Because once I'm back, I'll come carry your ass out if you're working too late. You promised me a summer, and I'm not taking just weekends."

I smiled. "I'll try."

"Alright. I'll let you go so you can enjoy your time with your friend."

"You're flying home tomorrow, right?"

"Shit—no. That's what I called for. You made me forget by telling me you wanted me to eat you while you sat at your desk."

I laughed. "I did not say that."

"I heard it in your voice. But anyway, I called to tell you my dinner with the owner was rescheduled to Saturday night. His daughter had a baby a few weeks early, so he flew out to wherever she lives. He's coming back Saturday, so I had to change my flight to Sunday. I have to cancel our plans for Saturday. I'm sorry."

"Oh, okay."

"Unless you want to get your ass on a plane after work tomorrow. There's a desk in my suite. I can make due."

"Tempting. But I really can't."

Maggie returned, carrying two glasses of wine and a phone number scribbled on a napkin. I shook my head, pointed to the phone, and mouthed *Max*.

He was quiet for a bit. "I miss waking up to you."

My heart squeezed. "I miss waking up to you, too."

"There's a simple way we could both be out of our misery..."

I smiled. "I know. I just have too much to catch up on at work to jump on a flight tomorrow afternoon."

"Okay. But if you change your mind, let me know. I'll get you a ticket."

"Thanks, Max."

"Have a good night. Stay safe."

"You, too."

I pulled the phone away from my ear to swipe, and Maggie grabbed it from my hand.

"Max? Are you still there? It's Maggie." She grinned at me. "Oh, hey. Listen, buy the ticket. I'll get her ass on that plane."

"Give me that phone," I said.

She leaned back, as if that would keep me from reaching.

"That's a good idea. Thanks, Max." She wiggled her fingers at the phone even though he obviously couldn't see her. "*Toodle-oo*."

Maggie swiped to end the call and held my phone against her chest, looking all dreamy-eyed. "He told you he missed waking up to you. You have to go."

I shook my head. "I wish I could, but I can't. I have so much to do at the office."

"Let me ask you something... Is this man as sweet as he seems from the little I've been around him?"

I sighed. "He really is. Under that tough-guy, hockey-player-who-hits-people-with-a-stick exterior is a real softie."

"And how's the sex?"

I smiled just thinking about it. "He checks that sweetness at the bedroom door. And when he kisses me, he wraps his big hand around my throat. It's very dominant and probably should scare me a little, but I kind of love it."

"How long is he gone?"

"He was supposed to come back tomorrow afternoon. But something came up, and now he won't be back until Sunday."

My phone chimed from Maggie's hand. She held it out to check the screen and then looked to the two glasses of wine in front of me on the table. "You better finish that wine and get started on the next one."

My brows furrowed. "Why?"

She turned my phone around and showed me the screen. "Because Max just sent you a ticket. I need to get you drunk enough to talk you into getting on the plane tomorrow afternoon."

• • •

"I'm going to jump in the shower," Max said to my reflection in the bathroom mirror. "Breakfast should be here in a few minutes."

I set the blow dryer down. "Okay. I'm done. The bathroom is all yours."

He flashed his dimples and pulled down his boxer briefs. "Or you can stay and watch." He kissed my shoulder. "Better yet, join me."

Just then, someone knocked on the door to the suite.

"Looks like it's a shower for one." I grinned.

Max pouted.

Back in the bedroom, I grabbed my purse to dig out a tip before answering. But the only thing I had was a hundred-dollar bill. So I popped my head back into the bathroom.

"Hey. Do you have any small bills for a tip? I only have a hundred."

Max was already in the shower. "Yeah, I should. I think my wallet might still be in my pants pocket. Help yourself."

"Thanks."

I looked around the bedroom to find his pants, but they weren't there. Then I remembered they were probably still right near the door—where he'd pulled them down as he held me against the wall about two seconds after I arrived last night. I smiled at the memory as I picked them up and found his wallet. He had a ten, so I slipped it out and answered the door.

Room service wheeled in a cart, and I chuckled at the full-size box of Cheerios and big, glass carafe of milk. I handed the attendant the tip and walked him to the door.

Just before it shut, he turned back. "Miss?"

"Yes?"

He held out a business card. "This was inside the bill you just gave me."

"Oh. Sorry." I took the card. "Thank you."

Back in the room, I went to return the card to Max's wallet. As I slipped it in, I couldn't help but notice the words printed on the top: *Cedars Sinai Neurology & Neurosurgery*. There was an address underneath, and a handwritten date and time on the appointment line for two days ago. Rather than put it back in his wallet, I left it on the room service tray so I wouldn't forget to ask him about it.

Then Maggie called, and just as Max got out of the shower, his phone rang. So it wasn't until we were half done with breakfast that I noticed it again.

I lifted the card. "This was tucked into the bill I took out of your wallet to give the room service person. I didn't notice it, but the guy handed it back to me as he was leaving."

Max looked down at the card and then up at me. He said nothing.

"Did you go to a neurologist the other day?" I asked.

He took the card and shoved it into his pocket. "Yeah. Just a checkup."

"A checkup? I've never been to a neurologist."

Max shoveled a heaping spoonful of Cheerios into his mouth and shrugged.

"Is there a reason you get checked?"

I don't think I'd ever realized Max usually made good eye contact when he spoke—until now, when he avoided making any at all. He pushed the Cheerios in his bowl around with his spoon. "I get migraines. So I get checked once in a while."

"Oh. You never mentioned migraines."

He shrugged again. "Guess it never came up."

"Your doctor is out here, in California?" My forehead wrinkled. "So you come all the way out here to get your checkups?"

"He's a good doctor."

Something seemed odd about this exchange... "Did everything at your appointment go okay this time?"

"Yep. You want his number to check for yourself?"

I shook my head. "Sorry. I'm being nosy."

"Not a problem." His phone buzzed on the table. He picked it up and read. "You have anything you want to do today?"

I shrugged. "Not really."

"Would you want to go check out some houses with me?"

"Houses?"

"Yeah. The team operations manager hooked me up with a real estate agent, and she asked if I wanted to see a few houses this afternoon."

"Oh...I didn't realize you'd planned to buy a place."

"I hadn't. But my finance guy has been pushing me to invest in property for the last year. He says it's the right time to buy. I figured it couldn't hurt to get an idea of what you get for your money in different areas. I agreed to it before I knew you were coming, so if you aren't up for it, it's no big deal. I can cancel."

"No, that's fine. It sounds like fun."

"Alright. I'll tell her to give us an hour."

• • •

"What's going on with you?" Max came up behind me as I stared out at downtown Los Angeles from the third-floor-bedroom balcony of one of the houses we were looking at. He put one hand on either side of me on the railing.

"What do you mean?"

He pushed my hair to the side and gently kissed my neck. "You're being too quiet."

"I guess I'm just taking it all in." It was the fourth house we'd visited this afternoon, each nicer than the last. Though with the price tags the real estate agent had mentioned, they definitely should've been. I turned around to face Max. He made no attempt to back up, keeping me locked between his thick arms. "These places are beautiful, but a little overwhelming, I guess."

"Yeah."

Each of the places we'd visited had at least four bedrooms. But the overall living space was just so wide open and grand. "Why is she taking you to see such large homes? Is that what you asked to see?"

"I told her at least a few bedrooms. My family likes to come visit. And my financial manager said I should be prepared to hang onto anything I buy for seven to ten years. So I figured..." Max shrugged. "You know...down the road I might need more space."

Down the road. He meant in a few years when he'd probably have a family to fill all this empty space. Of course, it made sense to buy a house you could grow into, but the idea that he'd be growing with someone else hit hard. There was a difference between renting a one- or two-bedroom bachelor-pad apartment like he had now and buying a multimillion-dollar home. That meant permanency, planting roots *three-thousand miles* away.

The real estate agent wandered into the bedroom. "What do you think?"

"It's great," Max said. "Would you mind giving us maybe ten minutes to talk in private?"

"Of course." She thumbed over her shoulder. "I have some phone calls to return. Why don't I go outside and give you some time to talk? I'll be in the front when you're ready."

"Thank you."

Once the real estate agent was out of earshot, I asked, "Are you interested in this one?"

Max shook his head. "Nah. It's nice, but I feel like I'm in a doctor's office. Too modern and sterile."

I laughed. "So why did you tell her we needed to talk in private?"

"Because you're not smiling anymore." One of his hands dropped to the hem of my sundress and dipped underneath, slipping between my thighs. "I'm going to put that smile back on your face."

My eyes widened. "I am not having sex with you on someone else's balcony."

"Of course not." He gripped my waist and guided me to turn back around before his lips moved to my ear. "I'm just going to make you come with my hand. I'll fuck you properly when we get back to the hotel. We'll just take the edge off."

"Max..."

I'd started to protest, but he fisted a hand full of my hair and tugged my head back. "I won't let anyone see you," he groaned in my ear. "You're totally covered from behind, and no one can see my hand under your dress." Without giving me time to respond, he slid his hand up, pulled my panties to the side, and rubbed gentle circles around my clit. "Spread your legs a little wider."

When I didn't immediately respond, he tugged harder on my hair, and my body sparked to life. "Open and hold onto the railing with two hands. Don't let go."

Whatever trepidation I had disappeared, right along with my shame. I spread my legs and grabbed the rail.

Max's voice was gruff as he ran his fingers up and down the length of me. "You're so wet for me already." He slipped one finger inside and glided in and out a few times before adding a second. "Someday soon, I want to watch you do this to yourself. Lie on my bed, legs spread wide apart, and put your fingers inside yourself. Will you do that for me?"

I nodded. In the moment, I would have told him I'd do anything he asked. My body was climbing so fast and furious, I just needed another minute. Max pulled his fingers all the way out and plunged back in with three. And suddenly I didn't need those sixty seconds after all. He pumped once, then twice, and then I was falling over the edge. I hadn't even realized I'd made a sound until a hand covered my mouth.

After, I'd barely caught my breath when Max turned me around.

He smiled. "Better?"

When I didn't respond, he chuckled. "Come on. Let me clean you up in the bathroom before the agent comes looking for us."

Two hours later, we were back in Max's hotel suite and had sex for the second time today. I laid with my head on his chest while he stroked my hair.

"Will you come back with me next month to help find an apartment?" he asked.

"If I can. Can I get back to you about it?"

He chuckled. "Sure."

"What are you laughing about?"

"You should've been a man. You've perfected the art of not committing to anything."

I sighed. "Sorry."

"It's fine. I'll keep working on you. Do you like California?"

I propped my chin on top of my hands to answer. "I do. The weather is great, and I love the canyons and all the different topography. But I also love the four seasons of New York and all its energy. And I hate to drive. What about you? Are you going to miss New York?"

Max stroked my hair. "I'll miss three of the four seasons. And the pizza. But I prefer to drive than take public transportation. How often do you come out here for business?"

"Two or three times a year."

Max nodded. He stared into my eyes for a long time. "I'll also miss *you*."

Being out here was a stark reminder of what was coming at the end of the summer. If it made me feel this emotional now, how would I feel then? Refusing to get upset, I turned my head and kissed his heart. "I'll miss you, too."

Nineteen

Max

"What can I get you to drink, Max?" Celia Gibson walked over to the bar on the covered patio in her backyard. "Would you like more wine, or do you prefer an after-dinner drink?"

"More wine would be great." I looked around at the sprawling landscape, which included a large, glass greenhouse at the far corner. The lights were on, and I could see her husband and Georgia talking inside.

Celia came to stand next to me, passing me a glass of wine. "So I know you're not officially on our roster yet, but can I solicit you for a charity event that's near and dear to my heart anyway?"

"Of course."

"In early August, before practices start, I run a charity exhibition hockey game. This will be my eighth year. Since we're the team in the celebrity mecca of the universe, it's Hollywood stars vs. pros. People get a kick out of it, and you'd be surprised how many celebrities are die-hard hockey fans and get into it. All of the money from ticket sales and advertising revenue goes to the National Alzheimer's Foundation. Both my mother and Miles's father had the horrible disease."

"I'm sorry to hear that. I'd love to be part of it."

"Good. I'll have my assistant send you the dates and some free tickets for Georgia or anyone you want to invite."

"Sounds good."

We looked back over to the greenhouse. Celia sipped her wine and smiled. "I'm afraid you won't be seeing your Georgia for a while. People always assume the flower garden is mine, not my husband's. I guess it's a strange combination. His passions are his beloved hockey team and flowers. Once Miles gets someone into his greenhouse, he talks their ear off for at least a half hour."

I smiled. "Roses are Georgia's thing. She won't mind."

Celia motioned to the furniture behind us. "Why don't we have a seat?" After we got comfortable, she smiled. "I hope you don't mind me saying so, but it's nice that Georgia has a thing. I've seen a lot of wives and girlfriends move out here with their significant others. Some give up their career, and some are young and didn't establish their own career before jumping into the hockey lifestyle with their partner. But the ones that last, at least from what I've seen, are the ones where the partner has something important of their own to tend to. As you know, players are on the road half the year. Many start out with their partner following along to every city, and that's fun for a while. But it starts to lose its luster, or kids come and the constant travel isn't feasible anymore. Don't get me wrong, kids are a full-time job. But a woman who has her own thing, something she's passionate about, that helps them keep their identity. Trust me, it's very easy to become a Mrs. Gibson or Mrs. Yearwood and forget you're also a Celia or a Georgia."

I nodded. "I get it."

"Georgia's headquarters are on the East Coast, right?"

"New York."

"Is she planning on moving out here with you?"

"No, she's not."

"When Miles and I first met, I'd just opened my own real estate brokerage firm in Chicago. I'd worked for a company for six years and wanted to expand into property management, which my old company didn't do. I took three of my real estate agent friends with me and hung out a shingle with only enough money to pay my rent and their salaries for three months. So it was sink or swim, but I loved every minute of the hustle." She smiled. "I met Miles at a party. We went out a few times when he was in town, but he was a busy man, so it wasn't that often. At some point, he asked me if I'd consider moving to California where his business was located, in order to give things a real shot. I asked him if he would consider moving to Chicago, where mine was located. Needless to say, we hit a stalemate."

"How did you work it out?"

"We didn't at first. We split up for six months. Eventually he showed up at my office and asked me where I did my negotiating. I showed him into the conference room, and we brokered a deal. He bought an apartment in Chicago, and we split our time—four days a week in one city and three in the other. It was doable because I could shift all my showings and in-person things to fill up a few days and save my office work for the days I was in California."

"How long did that last?"

She sipped her wine. "A few years. I actually fell in love with Southern California. There's no comparison in December, that's for sure. So I decided to move, but I didn't give up my Chicago office. I just promoted an agent to manage the day-to-day things there and expanded into California. I only sold the brokerage a few years back." She smiled. "It was my thing."

Too bad long distance was the least of the problems with Georgia and me. I liked Celia, but I wasn't about to go into detail and explain the rest of the shit we had going on. She actually reminded me of Georgia in some ways, which was why I knew the best way to manage this conversation was to agree and steer it away from a debate of any sort.

So I nodded. "We both have a lot to think about in the coming months."

• • •

"Fifty-Seventh Street?" The driver looked in the rearview mirror.

Georgia and I hadn't talked about our plans once we landed back in New York. But I wanted her in my bed—that wasn't a question for me. So I turned to her. "My place?"

"I think I need to go home. I have an early meeting tomorrow that I need to prep for, and I don't even have my laptop with me. You're welcome to stay at my place."

"Can't. I didn't book the dog sitters for tonight. Plus, I've been neglecting them."

Georgia nodded. "We could both use some actual sleep anyway. Neither of us tends to get much when we share a bed."

I grinned. "I'll take fucking you and being tired over sleeping alone any day."

The driver was still waiting for an answer. Georgia gave me the wide-eyed, silent shut-up warning. I chuckled and leaned forward to give him her address.

"Thanks for coming this weekend." I leaned back and took her hand.

"I'm glad I came. I had fun. And I can check *be spontaneous* off my list of things to work on."

"Maggie had to get you liquored up and talk you into it." I shrugged. "But yeah, let's go with spontaneous."

She laughed. "Well, it's spontaneous for me. What are your plans for this week?"

"I have a meeting with my business manager tomorrow, I think. Tuesday I have to go up to Providence, Rhode Island, for a photo shoot."

"More underwear that you'll have to fluff up your bulge with a contraption?" She grinned.

"No, thank God. It's a cologne ad. Depending on how late it goes, I might go by my brother's in Boston for a quick visit. I haven't decided if I'm flying or driving yet. What about you?"

"The usual...tons of meetings, emails, production scheduling. I also have to take a ride out to our distribution center in Jersey City this week. We're getting our first shipment of inventory for some new products, so I want to go make sure everything comes in at the quality we ordered. We're also having some billboards put up the next day along the Jersey Turnpike, so I might ask Maggie to come and take a ride to see how those look after."

"Will you have time for dinner one night?"

Her face softened. "I'll make time."

When we pulled up at her apartment, I told the driver to give me fifteen minutes so I could walk her up. I grabbed both our bags from the trunk and started to follow her, but after seeing her ass in those yoga pants, I asked her to give me a minute and jogged back to the driver.

"Do you have to pick up someone else?"

He shook his head. "You're my last ride of the day."

"Good." I pulled my wallet from my pocket, peeled off a few bills, and held them out to him. "Is it a problem if I'm more than fifteen minutes?"

The driver looked down at the Benjamins and shook his head. "Not a problem at all."

"Thanks." I jogged back to Georgia.

"What was that all about?"

"Did I mention your ass looks spectacular in those pants? It almost makes me want to do that dumb yoga class with you again. *Almost*."

She laughed. "What does my ass have to do with the driver?"

"I paid him to stay in case you let me in to tap it."

Georgia's nose wrinkled. "Tap it?"

"What? Not eloquent enough for you? How about in case you let me bang you?"

"Yuck."

"Put the bread in the oven?"

She laughed.

I opened the door to her building. "Pork you?"

She shook her head.

"Slap skins? Shag? Boink? Bump uglies? How about raw-dogging it?"

"Keep going." She pushed the elevator button, but smiled. "The only thing you're going to be bumping is your palm."

"Ah. You want something more mature sounding. Make whoopie? Copulate? Fornicate? Do the hanky-panky?"

We stepped off the elevator, and she laughed as she dug out her keys. "I think you may have wasted that money asking the driver to wait."

I grabbed a handful of her ass as she unlocked the door. It opened, and we fell inside, both laughing. "How about *fuck*? That's a classic. I'd like to fuck the shit out of you, Georgia."

I dropped her bag on the floor and wrapped my hands around her waist, ready to peel those sexy-as-shit yoga pants off her body.

But Georgia froze. Her laughing abruptly stopped.

"Gabriel? What are you doing here?"

• • •

"I'm sorry." The asswipe rubbed the back of his neck. "I texted you, but you didn't answer."

Georgia shook her head. "My phone was on airplane mode. I must've forgotten to turn it back on. But why are you here?"

"I came to talk to you. You weren't home, and I still have my key. I didn't have anywhere else to go."

My eyes zeroed in on a suitcase. I folded my arms across my chest. "It's New York City. There are hotels on every corner."

He looked at Georgia. "I just want to talk to you. I'll go to a hotel after if that's what you want."

If that's what you want. This fucker walked out on her months ago and had the balls to let himself in? He apologized, yet his territorial stance told me he felt like he had every right to come back.

He was taller than I'd expected from the picture I'd seen, and in better shape. But I'd crush him without breaking a sweat, if it came to that. At the moment, I kind of hoped it did.

But instead, the guy took a step toward me and extended his hand. "I'm Gabriel Alessi. I'm sorry if I've interrupted your evening."

I made no attempt to move.

Georgia sized up the situation and put her hand on my arm. "Max, do you think we can talk for a moment?"

I looked over at her, but said nothing. She nodded toward her bedroom. "In my room. Do you think we can talk in there?"

I glared at the guy for a good, long while before nodding. I was pissed. It felt like smoke should be coming from my nose. But when I followed Georgia in and she looked up at me with tears welling in her eyes, the ache in my chest made me bend. I couldn't handle any woman crying, but especially not Georgia when she hadn't done anything wrong.

"I don't know what to do," she said.

I blew out a rush of air and nodded. "What do you want to do?"

"Honestly, I want to curl up in my bed and just go to sleep."

"Do you want to talk to him?"

She looked down for a long time. "I'd like to know why he's here."

To me, it was obvious. The fucker wanted to put her on ice for more than a year and have his fun. But the minute he found out she was putting herself out there and not sitting at home crying, he'd hopped on the first plane to New York. "Do you want me to leave?"

She was quiet again. "I don't think I'm in the right frame of mind to be with either of you. You have been nothing but good to me since the moment we met, and I'm not going to disrespect you by having you walk out of my apartment while another man is sitting in my living room, a man you know I have a past with. I'd also rather not spend time with you while my head is spinning and I'm emotional over Gabriel coming back. So I think it's best if I tell Gabriel I'll meet him tomorrow somewhere, and he and I can talk."

While I would have preferred to have her tell me to toss the guy out on his ass, her solution was fair. I'd come into this knowing he was on the sidelines and would come back into play at some point. I just didn't expect it to be today, that was for sure. But I respected Georgia's decision, and I also hated that she looked like she was going to break if I did anything but agree.

So I nodded and opened my arms to her. "Okay. Come here."

She melted into me. I held her tightly for as long as I could, then kissed the top of her head. "Call me if you want to talk, okay?"

She forced a smile and nodded. "Thank you, Max."

"I'm going to walk out first. But I'm going to wait downstairs to make sure he doesn't give you a hard time before I leave."

"He won't. But I know that will make you feel better. Thank you for being so protective of me."

Georgia took a deep breath before we walked out of the bedroom. I waited until I got to the door before turning back and pointing to Gabriel. "Don't make me regret walking out this door first. Be respectful."

My heart pounded as I left. I knew leaving without a scene was the right thing to do, but that didn't make it suck any less. Outside, I told the driver we needed to stay a little while, and then I leaned against the car and waited. Not quite five minutes had passed before the door to her building opened again, and Gabriel walked out, wheeling his bag. He took a few steps and faltered, finding me leaning against the car. Our eyes locked, and we continued to stare until he reached the sidewalk. Then he turned without a word and walked on down the block. Guess he was smarter than he looked.

Twenty

Georgia

Nervous was sort of a pass-through stage for me.

I hated the churning that happened in my stomach whenever I was anxious about something. I hated not being able to focus on anything other than whatever was freaking me out, and most of all, I hated that no matter how hard I analyzed things, I couldn't come up with a solution. All of this made me angry—and that was the stage I'd just entered as I sat in the restaurant at eleven fifty-eight the next day and watched Gabriel walk to the table for our noon lunch.

He smiled, but I didn't reciprocate.

"I hope I didn't keep you waiting long," he said, pulling out the chair across from me. "I walked out of my room without my wallet and then realized the key was in my wallet, and the front desk didn't want to give me a new one because I didn't have any ID."

"It's fine."

Gabriel sat and folded his hands. "You look nice. The lighting in here makes your hair have a red highlight to it."

"It is red. I dyed it. I finally decided to try it."

"I didn't realize that was something you'd wanted to do."

I sighed. "What are you doing here, Gabriel?"

He lifted the napkin from the table and laid it across his lap. "I came to talk to you."

"You should have told me you were coming. And you definitely shouldn't have let yourself into my apartment last night."

"I know." He looked down. "I've handled this all wrong, and I'm very sorry."

The waitress came over and poured us waters, then asked if we were ready to order. I hadn't even looked at the menu, nor did I have much of an appetite. "Do you have Caesar salad?"

She nodded. "We do. Would you like blackened chicken in that? It's really good. I eat it all the time."

I held out the menu to her. "Sure. Thank you."

She looked to Gabriel, who handed her his menu, too. "I'll have the same."

Once she was gone, Gabriel shook his head. "I practiced what I was going to say to you a dozen times on the flight over. But I can't seem to remember where to start now."

"How about starting with what you're doing here? I thought you weren't planning on coming back until after your sabbatical."

"I wasn't. I came back to talk to you." He picked up his water and gulped. Then he took a deep breath. "I made such a big mistake, Georgia."

"Coming here?"

He shook his head. "No, not at all. I made a mistake leaving."

I had on a long-sleeve, fitted shirt, and suddenly the arms felt too tight. It was like my clothes had shrunk two sizes and were trying to suffocate me. When I said nothing, Gabriel reached across the table and covered my hand with his.

I pulled mine away.

He frowned. "You're the best thing that's ever happened to me, Georgia. And I ran away when things got tough. I love you, and I was a complete idiot. I made a mistake, and I'm here to try to fix it."

"You made a mistake?" I don't know why, but his word choice pissed me off. *Mistake.* It was just so cavalier. I shook my head. "No. A mistake is when you eat the salmon even though it looked a little funny and then you're sick the next day. A mistake is when you read the SparkNotes rather than the actual book and then show up for the test and can't answer a single question. A mistake is *not* when you tell the woman you proposed to that you're moving to Europe and want to sleep with other people. That's a *choice*."

Gabriel held up his hands. "Okay. Okay. I get it. It was a poor choice of words. I've made some bad decisions. But I'm here, and I want to make all my wrongs right."

"Why?"

"Because I love you."

I shook my head. "No, why *now*?"

Gabriel dragged a hand through his hair. "I don't know. Because I'm stubborn, and it took me this long to pull my head out of my ass."

I felt my face heat. "Bullshit, Gabriel. You're here because of Max. It was okay for you to sleep around and date other people. But as soon as you found out I'm seeing someone, suddenly you change your mind."

At least he had the decency to look ashamed.

Gabriel shook his head, looking down. "Maybe. Maybe that's what ultimately woke me up. But does the reason really matter?" He lifted his gaze. "Sometimes it takes losing what you have to realize how much it means to you."

"I think it's more like you knew exactly what you had, but you never thought you'd actually lose it."

Gabriel swallowed. "Have I? Have I lost you already?"

I wasn't sure of the answer to that question anymore. "Are you back from London for good?"

He shook his head. "I signed a contract for the entire year. I can't just up and leave before December."

"So what's changed then?"

"I have. I'm committed to you."

"What does that mean?"

"It means you're all I want. All I need. You have my word that I will be faithful."

"Even if I keep seeing other people?"

Gabriel's spine straightened. He blinked a few times. "Is that what you want?"

I wasn't sure I knew up from down at the moment, but I didn't feel like just giving in. I shook my head. "I don't know what I want, Gabriel."

He let out a jagged breath. "God, I really screwed up."

The waitress came with our salads. Both of us were quiet long after she left, neither touching our food. My head was way too much of a jumbled mess to eat, let alone understand where this left me.

Gabriel's voice was low when he spoke again. "Are you in love with him?"

That question made me feel like throwing up. It made me realize how far in I'd gotten with Max.

"I don't know," I whispered.

For the next half hour, I pushed my food around my plate with my fork. I couldn't eat. I couldn't think straight. It was hard to even hear over the thoughts swirling in my head. Gabriel tried to make small talk, but when they came to take our plates, I couldn't have told you one thing we'd spoken about.

"I'm flying out on the redeye tonight. Today was a public holiday in England, so the university is closed, but I need to make it back by the time class starts tomorrow."

I nodded. "Okay."

"Do you think we could have dinner tonight?"

I felt a little bad that he'd come all this way, but I shook my head. "I need some time to absorb everything."

He tried to force a smile as he nodded, but failed miserably. After he paid the check, we stood outside the restaurant awkwardly.

Gabriel took my hand. "I need to say a few more things, because they need to be said in person, and I'm not sure when we'll see each other again."

"Okay..."

"I was lost for a while. Losing Jason, finding out my parents weren't my parents, finally getting my book published only to realize I don't have what it takes—even watching your career take off like a rocket. I let it all make me feel unworthy, and I sought validation from the wrong places—a new job, dating again, even moving to another country. I was ashamed of who I was, but also afraid to let you know what I was feeling. I never stopped loving you, Georgia. I just hated myself more." His eyes brimmed with tears, and I had to swallow to keep my own at bay.

I squeezed his hand. None of that made me feel any better. "I'm sorry I didn't see how much you were hurting."

"It's not your fault. I hid it behind my big ego pretty well." He forced a smile. "Would it be okay to hug you goodbye?"

I nodded. "Of course."

Gabriel held me tight for a long time before letting go. I could feel his reluctance to leave, and it reminded me how I'd felt saying goodbye to him before he left for London.

"I'll give you some time before I call. Unless you want to talk before that."

"Thank you. Take care, Gabriel."

• • •

I'd stared out the window for so long that the motion-sensor light in my office flicked off. Though I didn't notice until Maggie screeched.

"Shit!" She held her hand over her heart when the lights turned back on. "I didn't think you were in here because it was dark. I just came to leave these samples on your desk."

"Sorry."

She zoned in on my face. "What's the matter? Was your trip not good? When we texted over the weekend, it sounded like you were having a great time."

"No, my trip was fine."

"Is something wrong here at work?"

I shook my head. "Gabriel's here."

Maggie's eyes widened. "Here, as in New York?"

I nodded.

"Have you seen him?"

"He was in my apartment last night when I got home. Waiting for me. Max was with me."

Her jaw dropped. "Do you need help burying the body Max murdered?"

I shook my head. "I thought it might be touch and go for a moment there. I could feel the anger radiating from Max. But he was the man he's been from the start—thoughtful and considerate. We talked in private. I didn't want to ask Max to leave with Gabriel in my apartment, so I had them both leave, and I met Gabriel at a restaurant for lunch today."

"Why didn't you call me?"

"You were in a meeting when I came in, and I wasn't even sure why he was here."

"Well, what did he want?"

"He wants to close our open relationship."

Maggie rolled her eyes. "Of course he does. Because *open relationship* meant other women opened their legs for him, but you kept yours closed."

I sighed. "Of course that's the reason for his change of heart. But the choices Gabriel has made lately... Even if I want them to, they don't erase what we had together when things were good. He's hurt me, there's no doubt about that, but I was in love with him, Mags. I'd decided he was it for me."

"What did you tell him?"

"I said I needed some time. Gabriel and I have a long history. And most of that was good. I care about him."

"I know you do."

I shook my head. "But then there's Max, who I'm crazy about. I don't know what it is about him, but he makes me want to live *more*. Like I want to go to the park and have sex while looking at five-million-dollar houses in the Hollywood Hills with the realtor waiting outside, and hide away in a hotel giving myself a time-out from the world. He makes me feel *alive*."

"Umm...can we go back to the sex with the realtor waiting outside?"

I smiled sadly. "But Max is temporary. He's leaving at the end of the summer. I suppose long-distance relationships are hard, not impossible, but he only signed on for what we have."

"If Max was not leaving and wanted an exclusive relationship with you, what would you do?"

How could I be sure about anything at this point? I needed time to think. I dropped my head to my hands. "Oh, God. I can't even figure out what to do with Gabriel. You can't ask me that."

Maggie laughed. "Sorry. I thought I was helping."

"I feel like the decision with Gabriel shouldn't be dependent on Max. I either want to be with Gabriel or I don't. Like, if I went to Max and asked him if he wanted to try a long-distance relationship and he said no. And then I went back to Gabriel and said yes, let's get back together, I'd only be staying with Gabriel because Max wasn't an option. I should want to be with the person I love regardless of what opportunities I might have out there, you know?"

Maggie nodded. "It makes a lot of sense... But let's keep playing this out. What if you decide you don't want to be with Gabriel because you have feelings for Max, without knowing what Max wants. So you break things off with him, only to find out Max doesn't want to keep things going after he leaves. Then where does that leave you?"

I took a deep breath. "Obviously that would suck. But if I was willing to end things with Gabriel to take that chance, my relationship with him was doomed anyway."

"Is it an all-or-nothing with Gabriel? Is he giving you an ultimatum—stop seeing other people or it's over?"

I shrugged. "I didn't ask that question. But I guess if I don't want to go back to being exclusive and he breaks it off completely, it is what it is."

Maggie shook her head. "In a weird way, it was easier that Aaron cheated on me. He made the decision for us. All I had to think about was which of his friends and business partners to fuck first."

That might've been the first time I'd smiled for real since last night. But then my phone buzzed on my desk. I stared at it like it might blow up if I touched it. Maggie saw my face and chuckled, right before leaning forward and picking it up.

She looked down for a moment, then turned the phone to face me.

"It's Max. He wants to know how you are."

Twenty-One

Max

"Are you staying in Rhode Island tonight?" Breena, the makeup artist, dabbed more shit on my forehead.

"I have family in Boston, so I'm going there after we're done."

My phone buzzed from my pocket. I pulled it out to check if it was Georgia, only to find a California area code calling. Again. Though this one was a different number than the doctor's office that had called a few times. The neurologist I'd gone to in LA last week had left me a few messages, but I hadn't gotten around to calling him back. I sent the current call to voicemail and checked my call log to see if maybe I'd missed Georgia. Of course, I hadn't.

Breena caught my eye in the mirror and smiled. "That's too bad. I could've showed you around the city."

She was pretty, but I had zero interest in any woman except the one who'd been avoiding me the last two days. "Thanks. Maybe another time."

I'd been getting my picture taken since ten o'clock this morning. We'd just finished lunch, and the photographer had said it shouldn't be more than another hour or two once we restarted. It was a good thing they hadn't wanted me to smile for this campaign and instead wanted *brooding*, because brooding was the only damn mood I'd been in since I'd walked into Georgia's apartment Sunday night.

I knew she'd had lunch with her ex yesterday—that much she'd told me. And he was back in London by now. But I had no idea what was going on in that head of hers. No doubt she was overanalyzing everything to death. Which I didn't think would work in my favor, since we had an expiration date. It sucked, but I had no right to fight for her when I wasn't sure what I could offer her long term.

Lyle, the photographer, walked in and interrupted my ruminations. He had Four in his arms, like he had practically since I'd walked in with the dogs this morning. "How would you feel about shooting with this little guy?"

I spoke to his reflection, since Breena was still putting crap on my face. "He'll probably lick off whatever she's painting on my skin right now." I shrugged. "But sure, if that's what you want. I appreciate you letting me bring them today."

"Great. I think we got everything the client wanted in the can this morning. Usually, I spend half the time doing what they *think* they want, then the other half shooting what I think would work better. Nine times out of ten, they go with something I improvised." He held up his free hand and motioned like he could see writing in the air. "Irresistible, even to the savage beast," he said. "I think it would make a fun ad. And with your face, it'll still ooze sexy."

I shrugged. "If you say so."

"Tell me, does he have a favorite food? I'd like to shoot some of you lying on a plush rug and the dog licking you. It might work best if we hide some bait behind your neck. There's a supermarket up the block I can send my assistant to."

"He likes Cheerios."

"Perfect! I'll grab us a box."

Two hours later, my dogs and I were finally done being photographed. Breena gave me some makeup wipes to remove the shit she'd splattered all over my face. When I was done, she handed me her phone. "I took some pictures of you and the dogs from behind Lyle. They came out adorable. Take a look."

I swiped through and smiled. They were actually really good. It did look like Four was trying to smell my neck. "Would you mind sending me one or two of them? My nieces would love it."

"Sure, put your number in, and I'll text them."

"Thanks."

After I said goodbye and set my dogs up in their safety hammocks in the back of my car, my phone pinged with an incoming text. It was Breena, who had sent me a shitload of photos, along with a message at the bottom:

Breena: If you have time on your way back through, give me a call. I'll show you around Providence. Or... you could just come to my place.

She ended the text with a winky face.

Rather than respond, I forwarded one of the pictures of Four licking my face to Georgia.

Max: From the shoot today. I think my mutts might need their own agent.

I waited a few minutes and watched the text go from delivered to read. I got more excited than I'd been in the last forty-eight hours when I saw the dots start jumping around. But disappointment set in when her response chimed.

A smiley face.

Nothing more.

Grumbling, I tossed my phone into the center console and started my drive to Boston.

• • •

"What's going on, Altar Boy?" My brother Tate handed me a beer and held his out to clink.

I was standing on his back porch at the railing, looking out at...the lawn, I guess. "Not much. You?"

"Nursing a bit of a hangover," he said.

"On a Tuesday?"

"I had a few drinks while Cass was out last night. She went to book club. By the way, I'm thinking of starting one of those things."

"You? Read?"

"She leaves with two bottles of wine and a book and comes back drunk. *Book club* is just code for the married woman's girls' night out." He sipped his beer. "I'm thinking my guys' book club will read historical fiction—you know, 1950s *Playboy* magazines that have articles on how to get your woman to give you head after you're married—and our meetings will be at the bar."

I chuckled. "Let me know how that goes over with Cass."

Tate leaned over the railing. "So what's bugging you?"

"Who says something is bugging me?"

"Well, one, I got you in a headlock in less than thirty seconds. That hasn't happened since you were twelve. Two, at dinner, Cassidy brought up that I'd made an appointment to get snipped, and you didn't even joke about my balls being cut off a long time ago, and three, you've checked your phone forty times in the two hours you've been here." He paused. "Girl problems?"

I sighed and nodded.

"Georgia?"

"Can't be anyone else, since I haven't noticed another woman since the day I walked by that bar and saw her smiling."

"What's going on?"

I hadn't filled Tate in on the details of my relationship with Georgia. And I wasn't usually the kind of guy to talk about problems with women I was dating, but looking back, I think that might've been more because I didn't have any than because I didn't want to discuss them.

"Long story short, she was engaged. He broke it off and moved to London for a year. Told her he wanted to have an open relationship. I knew that going in. She was upfront about her situation. I figured it was the perfect scenario. I'm moving in a few months, and she wasn't looking for anything serious because she's not sure where she stands with her ex. And we burned hot, which in my history usually means it burns out pretty fast."

"And...it didn't fizzle out? You've fallen for her?"

I nodded and sucked back my beer. "Her ex showed up unannounced the other day. He told her he wanted her back."

"Shit." Tate shook his head. "I'm sorry, man. I guess she's taking him?"

I shrugged. "I don't know. She said she needed some time to think things over."

"But you told her how you feel about her?"

I shook my head.

"Why the hell not? That's not like you. You usually go five-hundred miles an hour after the thing you want. We're all afraid to get in your way because we'll get run over. What's the rest of the story you're not telling me?"

I caught my brother's eye. "She doesn't know."

Tate's head dropped. "I thought you said you were going to tell her?"

"It just...never seemed like the right time."

My brother was quiet for a long time. Eventually, he nodded. "And now you're thinking you should just bow out—walk away because she deserves more than you can promise her."

I was close with all of my brothers, but Tate knew me best. I nodded.

"Fuck." He blew out a long breath and shook his head. "I get it, man. I really do. I'd do whatever I needed to not hurt Cass. But you gotta know Georgia deserves the truth. We aren't kids anymore. What are you going to do? Walk away every time you get into a relationship that means anything to you?" Tate looked at me. When I said nothing, he shook his head. "Jesus, really? You're shittin' me. That's your plan? You can't be serious."

He stood. "You know what? I'm not going to lecture you because it's your life. But I seem to remember a guy I looked up to once giving some really good advice to someone else. *'If you're not living life the way you want, you're dying anyway.'*"

I shook my head. "Yeah, and look what that got him."

Twenty-Two

Max

Ten years ago

"What the hell?" I handed my brother a red Solo cup. "Do you not like my girlfriend or something?"

"What are you talking about?"

I thumbed over my shoulder. "Teagan just left. She seemed upset. I saw you guys together while I was stuck talking to Coach. It looked like you were arguing."

It was the BU end-of-the-hockey-season barbeque, and I'd invited both Austin and Teagan. She had to be at the hospital later, but she'd said she could hang out for an hour or two before her shift started. Yet she'd disappeared twenty minutes in, after my brother got done talking to her.

He drank his beer. "We weren't arguing."

"Then what were you talking about?"

"What were we talking about?"

I looked around. "Is there an echo in here? Yeah. What was the topic of your conversation?"

Austin looked away and shrugged. "Nothing."

"Well, your mouths were moving, so I'm pretty sure there were *some* words spoken."

My brother shook his head. "I don't know. I guess we were talking about school."

"What about it?"

"I don't remember. And why am I getting the third degree?" My brother raised his arms in the air. "You're just in a bad mood because you lost your last game this morning."

"Don't do that."

"Do what?"

"Try to make this about me. We had a great season. It was just an off game with a lot of guys out hurt at the end of the year. I shook it off. I was actually in a good mood—thought it would be nice to get to hang with my brother, who seems to have avoided me the last six weeks. Which is funny, because six weeks *also* happens to be the amount of time I've been seeing my new girlfriend—you know, the one I just saw him yelling at but he's trying to pretend never happened."

Austin looked back and forth between my eyes. "It was nothing, okay?"

"Then why the hell can't you tell me what nothing was?"

Austin rubbed the back of his neck. "I don't know. I guess we also were talking about politics."

"Politics?"

"Yeah, I'm for universal healthcare, and she's against it. It lowers the salaries for doctors."

I searched his face. "Seriously? Why wouldn't you just say that then?"

"I don't know. It slipped my mind."

"It slipped your mind?"

"Yeah. Can you please stop repeating everything I say?"

I searched Austin's face. Something was weird, but maybe he was just grumpy in general lately and the problem wasn't with Teagan. "Is something else going on, bro? You seem off."

"I'm fine. Just a lot of pressure. The dual architecture and architectural engineering program is a lot to handle, especially at the end of the year with finals coming up and projects due."

I nodded. "Alright. Sorry. It's beautiful out, the food is free, and the beer is cold. Let's just have a good time."

Austin smiled, but I still felt something odd between us. Nevertheless, we managed to move past it and enjoy the afternoon. Later that night, I went home, and Teagan came over after her shift ended. She liked to shower right away, so she hopped in mine since she'd come directly here. We talked through the open door.

"How was the barbeque?" she asked.

"Good. My brother managed to lighten up. Sorry if he's been a dick to you lately. He said he's just stressed."

"Did he...say about what?"

"Classes."

Teagan paused. "Oh...okay."

Again, that weird feeling was back—like something was going on between the two of them. But I knew my brother would never do that to me. That wasn't a question in my mind. Still...something was there.

I stood in the doorway, listening to the shower water hit the tub. "So...uh, what were you and Austin talking about before you left? It looked like things were getting a little heated."

"We, um, were talking about sports. You know how us native New Englanders get about our teams."

"Sports?"

"Yeah... Go Pats."

What the fuck? I left the bathroom and sat down on my bed. I'd chalked a lot of odd moments up to my imagination, but I wasn't imagining that these two were full of shit. When Teagan came out of the bathroom, she had a towel wrapped around her. Normally that would be enough to make me forget everything, but not the way I was feeling.

She tilted her head and smiled. "Should I get dressed?"

"Yeah, you should."

Her face fell. "Oh."

I said nothing while she gathered her clothes and went back into the bathroom to change. When she came out I stood. "Are you *fucking* my brother?"

"What? No!"

I looked her square in the eyes. "Then what the hell is going on, Teagan? Because you two were arguing about something. And it wasn't sports or universal healthcare—like my brother said it was."

She closed her eyes. "We're not sleeping together, and we never have. But you need to talk to him about what's going on."

"What do you mean, *what's going on*? Are you saying you know something I don't?"

She stared at me.

I moved closer. "Teagan, talk to me."

"I can't."

"Why not?"

She took a deep breath. "Think about it. What's the one thing I wouldn't be able to talk to you about?"

"I don't know. Stuff from work? Medical stuff?"

Teagan just kept staring at me.

I closed my eyes. *Fuck*. I was such an idiot. The first time they met, she'd thought he looked familiar and later asked if he'd been in the hospital. He'd been a dick to her ever since. The realization kicked me in the stomach. I opened my eyes.

"Is he okay?"

"Talk to your brother, Max."

• • •

"What the hell?" My brother rubbed his eyes. "Are you drunk? It's two in the morning."

I brushed by him and entered his apartment.

"Tell me what's going on."

He shook his head. "Not this crap again."

"I'm not screwing around, Austin. I know something is going on with you, and Teagan won't tell me, which means it has something to do with your health." I folded my arms across my chest. "I'm not leaving until I get the truth. So you might as well get it over with and start talking."

My brother's face changed to something resigned. "Take a seat."

He walked over to the cabinet and took out a bottle of vodka and two shot glasses. Filling them both, he held his up to me before sucking it back. I followed his lead. Austin poured a second, but only filled his glass this time.

"I had back pain for a while. I figured I'd pulled something. But it didn't get better. Then I started to have trouble running. I'd get winded in half a block when I used to be able to run ten miles without breaking a sweat. One night, I was getting a bottle of water from the fridge, and the next thing I knew I was waking up on the floor. I'd passed out. So I went to the ER."

"Why didn't you call me?"

"You were away for a hockey game. That's the night I met Teagan. I didn't remember her at first. She hadn't said much, just shadowed the doctor as he went from patient to patient. It wasn't until I saw her in scrubs that I remembered. I guess seeing her in context jogged my memory."

"Okay...but what happened at the hospital?"

"They ran some tests, took X-rays, and did an ultrasound. When they came back, the doctor told me I had an abdominal aortic aneurysm."

My eyes widened. "Like Dad?"

Austin nodded. He lifted the shot glass from the table and knocked the second one back.

I dragged a hand through my hair. "What can they do for it?"

"They can take it out surgically. But there's always the risk of it rupturing during the procedure."

Which was exactly what had happened to our father, and he'd died on the table. This time, I poured the shots. After we each drank another, I shook my head.

"Why didn't you tell me?"

"Because you're going to tell me I'm young and healthy, so my chances are better than Dad's were, so I should just have the surgery to reduce the risk of it rupturing itself."

"Is that what the doctor recommends?"

Austin nodded. "He said if I don't get it taken care of soon, walking will probably become difficult. I'm already winded just going from my car to class. I feel like an eighty-year-old man."

"Well, it doesn't sound like you have much choice then. If you're not living life the way you want, you're dying anyway."

"I'm fucking scared, Max."

"Of course you're scared. But you gotta talk about it if you're going to get past that. If you don't deal with it, you're just giving your fears more power. You can't let shit fester."

My brother frowned. "I don't want to fucking die."

"You're not going to die. Have you gotten a second opinion yet?"

He shook his head.

"Alright. That's where we start. Does Mom know?"

"No. And you're not telling her either. She's barely over losing Dad."

"So, what? You just plan on having the surgery and not telling anyone? In that case, you'll definitely die, even if the surgery is a success. Because Tate will kill you."

Austin smiled sadly. "Not yet, okay? I don't want anyone else to know—at least until I figure out what I'm doing."

"But you'll get a second opinion and let me go with you?"

Austin nodded. "Fine. But promise me you aren't going to say anything."

"I'll do you one better. I won't say anything, *and* I promise I'm not going to let you die."

—Twenty-Three—

Georgia

"I'm in love with Max."

Maggie's eyes flashed to me and back to the road. "Well that's nice to know. But where the hell did that come from? We've been together since I picked you up to go to the warehouse at six o'clock this morning. I've tried to prod you into talking about things a half dozen times. And you pick *now* to spring that on me? At nine o'clock at night, after a fifteen-hour day, when we're five minutes away from your apartment?"

I smiled. "Sorry. It's been a long few days, and I haven't slept well. I'm really tired, and normally the only thing I want to do when I'm exhausted is crawl into my own bed and knock out. Gabriel and I have argued over it more than once. Like when we've rolled out new products, and I spent every night working really late? He would tell me to come stay at his place, but I wouldn't because I just wanted to be in my own bed. I'm exhausted right now, but I would rather go over to Max's apartment and snuggle and sleep with him and his two dogs that snore than have my entire bed to myself. And it made me realize that a shitty night of sleep with Max is better than a good night of sleep alone, and that's because I'm in love with him."

"I'm happy for you. I don't know Max well, but I like him a lot, and I've had a good feeling about the two of you from the beginning. You may not understand hockey, and he might not know much about running a company like you do, but you have a lot of the important stuff in common, like self-awareness and ambition. Gabriel always thought he was ambitious, but there's a big difference between wanting things from life and being willing to put yourself out there to make it happen, you know?"

I nodded. "Max would never get upset because I wanted to work sixty hours a week. He'd try his best to distract me, but he'd also be excited to hear what I was working on."

We pulled up in front of my building, and Maggie double-parked. "So where does this leave things with Gabriel?"

I sighed. "I have feelings for him. I can't deny that. We have a long history together, and there was a time I was sure he was right for me. But now I know I'd rather take a chance on Max than be with Gabriel, even if he is willing to commit to me and is coming home in six months, *and* Max is moving three-thousand miles away."

"Welp, you know the old saying. If you love something, set it free. If it comes back, it's yours. If not, go fuck yourself because you were an idiot for letting it go in the first place."

I laughed. "I feel like that should be a new message option on one of our cards."

"Damn straight. I'm poetic." She smiled. "So what's your plan? I know you have one. Because God forbid you make a decision and not have a twelve-page, outlined work plan for how to execute it ready in your head."

"I need to talk to Gabriel first—tell him we aren't on the same page, that I don't want an open or closed relationship with him anymore."

"And Max?"

"I'm praying he and I *are* on the same page. There would obviously be a lot of logistics to figure out. But maybe he can stay with me in the offseason, and we can take turns visiting during."

"I don't want to be a downer, but it's my job as co-pilot to make sure we're ready for takeoff. So what happens if you break things off with Gabriel, and Max says he doesn't think long distance will work?"

I shook my head. "I become a workaholic spinster?"

Maggie smirked. "Good safety net."

I reached for the door handle. "Thank you for driving today. My mind needed the time to wander."

"No worries. Mine wanders while I'm driving. I don't even remember getting on the bridge."

I laughed. "I'll probably be a little late tomorrow so I can call Gabriel from home. It's not going to be an easy conversation."

"Alright. I'll hold down the fort. Stop by my office when you get in to let me know how it goes."

• • •

"What if we keep things the way they have been? Just leave our relationship open and see where we are when I get back? I won't see other people if you don't want me to." Gabriel paused. "*Please*, Georgia. Give me another chance. I know I fucked up."

The emotion in his voice made my insides twist. But I had to remain steadfast to be fair to both of us. It would be so easy to say *sure, let's continue with an open relationship* and then keep Gabriel on ice while I see how things pan out with Max. But I needed to give things with Max my all, and that meant having all of me to give.

"I'm sorry, Gabriel. I really am. But it's best that we make a clean break at this point."

"Do you...not love me anymore?" His voice cracked.

"You'll always have a piece of my heart, because I gave that to you. But love can change."

"God, I really fucked up. If I hadn't left..."

"I'm not sure that's true. I think any love that has the word *if* involved with it may not be the kind of love that lasts. True love should always be *even though* or *in spite of*, never *if I hadn't.*"

"Did that hockey player make you choose?"

"Max doesn't even know I'm making a choice."

Gabriel went quiet. "I don't know what's left to say, but I don't want to say goodbye because I feel like I might never get to speak to you again."

He wasn't wrong. We were breaking up. People always say they'll keep in touch, but it rarely happens. "I'm sorry, Gabriel. I really am."

"Promise me something?"

"What?"

"If you're single when I get back, for whatever reason, you'll let me take you to dinner, even if just as friends."

I sighed. "Sure."

"I love you, Georgia."

"Goodbye, Gabriel."

• • •

I waited until the early afternoon to call Max.

My heart had felt heavy after I'd hung up with Gabriel, and I'd needed some time to shake that gloomy feeling. But as the hours passed, I went from feeling sad to *really* damn nervous. I'd ended things with a man I cared about to take a chance with one I wasn't even sure felt as strongly as I did.

Eventually, I also began to feel excited at the prospect of what might come of things with Max, but it was the kind of excitement I imagined a trapeze artist might feel as he stepped out to walk the tightrope with no safety net.

Still, I felt more alive than I had in years as I picked up the phone to call Max.

"Hey, beautiful." His deep, gravelly voice wrapped around me like a warm blanket.

I sighed. "Would it be weird to ask you to record that so I can play it whenever I'm feeling down?"

"How about you just call and hear it live when you need to? It's been a few days..."

"Yeah, I'm sorry about that. I needed some time to sort things out."

"Did it work? Are you feeling better?"

"Yeah, I am."

"Good. Glad to hear it. Do you want to talk about it?"

"I do. But I was hoping we could talk in person. Are you busy tonight?"

"Actually, I am."

"Oh...alright. Tomorrow maybe?"

"Won't be back by then. I'm going to California for a few days. I leave tonight."

"I didn't realize you had another trip planned so soon."

"It was sort of a last-minute thing."

"When are you back?"

"Saturday."

Normally, Max was an open book. But he wasn't offering any information about this trip. "Is everything okay with your new team?"

"Yeah. Just have a few things to take care of out there."

His vagueness caused an unsettled feeling in my stomach. But I tried to chalk it up to nerves getting the best of me. Plus, I hadn't yet given Max any indication of where things stood between me and Gabriel, so it would make sense if he was a bit pensive himself. That could be it, too.

So I forged ahead. "Do you think you'll be up for dinner when you get back Saturday night?"

"Sure. I have a morning flight, but with the time change, I think I land around four."

"Okay. How about you come over, and I cook? That way we don't have to worry about the time if your flight is late or something."

"Sounds good."

"Perfect. I got to work a little late today, so I have to run. Have a safe trip. I'll see you this weekend."

Twenty-Four

Georgia

These had been the longest few days I could remember. By the time Saturday arrived, my nerves were shot. Max and I had either seen each other or texted almost every day since we'd met, but he'd been radio silent while he was in California. Of course, I'd been the one to say I needed a little time after Gabriel showed up, and Max had been respectful about giving me that. But even then, he'd still sent me a simple text each day to check in. The last few days: crickets.

So eventually, I'd taken the initiative, and yesterday I'd sent him a message asking how his trip was going, hoping to open up things between us. His answer had been polite, but short, leaving me feeling like I shouldn't push to continue the conversation. Now the uneasy feeling I'd had when we spoke on the phone last had blossomed into full-blown anxiety.

At seven, when he knocked at my door, my palms were sweaty.

"Hey."

Max kissed my lips as he entered, which went a long way toward settling my nerves.

"How was your flight?"

"Uneventful."

"Do you want a glass of wine?"

"If you're having some."

Oh, I was definitely having some. At the moment, I didn't much want to share. I felt like chugging straight from the bottle.

Max followed me into the kitchen. He took a seat on a stool at the island while I got glasses down and took the wine out of the fridge.

"Did you get everything accomplished you needed to on your trip?"

"I did."

It bugged the crap out of me that he hadn't volunteered why he'd gone back so soon. For some reason, I really needed to know. But I wasn't usually one to pry, so it felt awkward to push. I filled one of the glasses and moved it across the counter, looking Max in the eyes.

"What did the team need you to do that you had to go back so soon?"

He looked down into the wine. "Nothing. I just had some things to take care of. I found a place to live."

My wine glass froze halfway to my mouth. "You bought a place?"

He shook his head. "No, I decided to rent for a while so I can get to know the area and figure out where I want to live."

When we were in California together, Max had asked if I'd come back with him to help him look next month. Had he changed his mind about wanting my opinion? Maybe looking at places had been unplanned. So yet again, I tried to shake off my unease.

"Tell me about it. Is it an apartment or house?"

"It's a house. It's in the hills. It's nice. It has three bedrooms and a pool with a nice view. It's owned by some actress who's going to work on two films in Europe, so she's renting it fully furnished, and it's only a one-year lease, so I can get something more permanent after that."

More permanent. My neck felt like someone had reached in and tied it in knots. I forced a smile. "That sounds great. When does the lease start?"

"July first."

My stomach dropped. "Oh, wow. That's so soon."

He looked down and nodded. "Yeah."

The stove buzzed, letting me know the preheating was done. I was glad for the momentary distraction and a chance to hide the emotions probably flashing like a neon sign on my face. Turning around, I took the tray of food from the top and popped it into the oven, then fiddled with the knobs on the stove to buy more time before I had to look at Max again. "I made chicken Milanese and risotto," I told him. "The chicken just needs to go in the oven to warm."

When I was all stalled out, I finished my wine and poured a second glass. "Why don't we go sit in the living room while we wait?" I started to walk without waiting for a response, but Max caught my hand.

"Hey." He looked at me carefully. "You okay?"

I nodded.

"The first night we met, you told me you weren't good at lying because your face gives you away. I guess you haven't lied until now, because you really are a shit liar." He pulled me close and brushed a stray piece of hair from my face. "Come here. What's going on?"

"It's just been..." I shook my head. "An emotional week, I guess. And the thought of you leaving so soon... Well, it sucks."

Max smiled warmly. "What happened this week?"

I wasn't sure why it felt awkward to tell him I'd cut ties with Gabriel, but it did. Maybe it was because without that barrier in the way, things between us were different. I hoped it would be a change for the better, but I took a deep breath before answering.

"Gabriel said he made a *mistake*. He wanted to go back to having an exclusive relationship."

"Okay..."

"I told him I didn't want that. Then he offered to keep things the way they have been, but I told him things have changed for me, and I wanted a clean break."

Max's grip around my waist loosened. He looked like I'd caught him off guard. Which maybe I had, but I'd hoped for a happier reaction. There wasn't even the hint of a smile on his face. As I watched, he seemed to grow almost somber.

"Are you sure that's what you want?" he finally asked.

I nodded. "I care about him. But I deserve more than he could offer me. I finally realized something had been missing—even before he did what he did and left for London."

Max was still so damn quiet. He just kept staring at me, which made me freak out inside. I couldn't take tiptoeing around anymore, so I decided to lay all my cards on the table. "*You* made me realize something was missing. This time we've spent together and how much you've grown to mean to me was so unexpected. But sometimes that's how it happens, I guess." I took a deep breath. "I don't want things between us to end when you leave, Max."

His arms, which had been wrapped loosely around me, fell away completely.

Oh my God. He doesn't want the same thing.

I told him I'd fallen for him, and his reaction was to *let go*? My inner self-protection mechanism jumped in before my heart or brain could catch up. I backed up. "Oh God. You don't feel the same way."

"Georgia..." Max reached for me, but I put my hands up.

"It's fine. I understand. Really, it's fine." I scurried to the stove, grabbed an oven mitt, and took out the chicken. Of course, it had only been in there for two minutes, and the timer still had fifteen more to go, but I needed to do *something.*

Max walked up behind me. He put his hands on my shoulders, but I wiggled out of his grip, went to the refrigerator, and started pulling out random crap—a bottle of wine, even though more than half was left in the one on the counter, grated cheese, salad dressing, a head of lettuce, butter—none of which I needed.

Max watched, staying put near the stove where I'd left him standing.

"I didn't make a salad. I should make a salad."

"Georgia, talk to me, sweetheart."

Sweetheart. For some reason, that word pissed me off. I stopped in place. "Don't call me that."

Max ran a hand through his hair. "Can we just talk for a minute?"

"What is there to say? I think your face already said it all."

"No, it didn't. So how about you give me a chance to actually say something?"

"Fine."

He gripped my hips, and the next thing I knew I was in the air and then deposited in a chair at the counter. Max cupped my cheeks, and my emotions took a hard bounce left. Tears threatened.

"I didn't expect you either, Georgia. I like you. A lot. In fact, I can't think of a single thing I don't like about you. The one thing that kept you from being perfect was that dumbass who had you. But now..." He shook his head. "There's *nothing* I can find to dislike. You're smart, beautiful, aware of exactly who you are and what you want, and you have the balls to go for it all. That might be what I find the sexiest about you—you're fearless. Even tonight. You're sexy as shit naked, but you don't have to be naked to be sexy."

While that all sounded great, I knew the other shoe was about to drop.

Max swallowed and looked down. "But this was supposed to be just the summer."

"And I was supposed to be getting married in the spring. Things happen. Things change. What might've been the right answer a few months ago might not be right today. I'm just realizing how important it is to not lock yourself into a decision forever."

"I'm sorry if I led you to believe this was more than it was."

I shook my head. "I don't understand, Max. Why can't it be? If everything you just said is really true, if you have as strong of feelings as you say you do, then why can't it be more than we planned?"

Again, he wouldn't meet my eyes. "I just can't, Georgia."

"Can you look at me, please?"

Max raised his head and met my gaze. I wasn't sure what I'd wanted to find in his eyes, maybe something I'd missed—that he didn't have feelings for me like I did him. But what I saw was just the opposite. His eyes were filled with love, but also sadness, pain, and anger.

Which only confused me more.

"Are you upset with me because I asked you to leave the night Gabriel showed up?"

"No."

"Because nothing happened between us. We had lunch the next day at a restaurant and talked. That's all."

"I'm not upset. I know nothing happened."

"How? How did you know nothing happened?"

He looked into my eyes. "Because how could it?"

That seemed like a non-answer, but it was also exactly the truth. How could something happen between either one of us and someone else when we had what we had? It seemed like a physical impossibility.

"Do you have feelings for me?" I whispered.

"Of course I do."

"So *why*, Max? I need a reason. I feel like I'm missing a piece of a puzzle, and you know how I am. I'll spend forever trying to figure it out."

Max was quiet a long time. Eventually he took a deep breath and shook his head, looking down. "I don't want more than what we have."

"Look at me, Max. Say that again." I reached out and touched his face, making his eyes meet mine.

He held my gaze before finally speaking. "I don't want more, Georgia. I'm sorry."

It felt like I'd been smacked across the face. I jumped out of the chair and stumbled back from the momentum. Max reached out, like he wanted to steady me.

I put my hands up. "*Don't.*"

"Georgia..."

I felt tears brewing like a storm about to hit. But I refused to allow them. Instead, I swallowed and straightened my spine. "It's fine. Just...just go sit down. Let me have a minute, and I'll finish making us dinner."

"Would you rather I go?" Max asked softly.

I shook my head. "I'll be fine. I just need a little space right now."

• • •

Dinner was awkward, to say the least. I responded when Max spoke, but I didn't have the energy to carry on any real conversation. After, we cleaned up in more silence. I stood at the kitchen counter and refilled my glass, while Max declined more wine.

"Thank you for making dinner."

"You're welcome." I stared down into my wine. "Do you still want to see each other until you leave in a few weeks?"

Max frowned. "The selfish asshole in me wants to say yes, but I don't want to make it harder for you. I'll do whatever you want."

I wasn't sure it made a difference if we said goodbye today or in a month. The damage was done. I'd fallen for him. "I think I'd like to enjoy the time we have left."

Max let out a big breath. He looked physically relieved. "Can I hold you?"

I nodded.

He walked over hesitantly, almost as if he was waiting for me to change my mind, and then looked into my eyes, asking silent permission before wrapping me in his arms. My head pressed against his chest, right over his heart. As crazy as it was, being in his arms made everything feel like it would be okay, even when he'd caused the hurt in the first place. For now, I could let him make me feel better, putting off the day that nothing could help because he was no longer here.

Later that evening might've been the first time we climbed into bed like normal people. Typically, we'd fall in, stumbling to rip off each other's clothes as we went. But tonight, Max took off his own clothes, and I changed in the bathroom like I'd do if I were alone. Slipping into bed without that passion actually reminded me a lot of my years with Gabriel.

I turned to my side, giving Max my back, and he curled up behind me. Even though my mind just wanted to drift off to sleep, having Max's hard chest pressed so close made my body betray me. My skin prickled, and my nipples hardened as his warm breath tickled my neck. I stayed still with my eyes shut, trying to ignore the urge to turn and dig my nails into his back. But when I felt Max harden against my ass, it became all but impossible. I took a deep breath in and let out a frustrated rush of air.

"Sorry," he whispered. "I'm not trying anything, I swear. I thought I could control it, but apparently I have as much restraint as a twelve-year-old boy."

I smiled sadly. "It's okay."

Max leaned his forehead against the back of my shoulder. "I'm going to go...take a quick shower. Get things under control."

Great. Now I had a to-die-for body wrapped around me, a lead pipe pushing against my ass, and a vision of Max jerking off in my shower. He might get relief from that, but I certainly wouldn't. "Or..." I pushed my ass back against him. "We could work it out."

Max groaned. "Fuck, Georgia. Are you sure?"

I wasn't. But lying here feeling frustrated didn't make me feel very good either. So I responded by slipping down my pajama pants and underwear.

Max kissed the back of my neck and gently attempted to turn me on my back, but I wasn't having it.

I shook my head. "From behind. Just like this."

He stilled. "Why?"

I didn't want to analyze the reason, or even talk for that matter; I just wanted what I wanted. And it annoyed me that he wasn't taking off his clothes and getting on with it. This was all he wanted from our relationship, wasn't it?

"Can we not talk? Can't you just fuck me the way I want?"

Max didn't move or say a word.

After thirty seconds or so, I thought he might tell me no. But then he took off his pants. He reached around and found my clit and started to rub small circles. But I didn't want that either. I took his hand from between my legs and lifted it to hold my throat. "I'm on the pill, and I don't want foreplay or a condom. I'm clean, and I trust you if you say you are. Okay?"

Again there was a long pause before his grip around my throat tightened. But then I felt his other hand reach between us and guide himself to my opening. "Open your legs," he said sternly. "Put one on top of mine."

I did, and before I had even settled back into place, Max was pushing inside me. My body wanted him, but it hadn't fully prepared, so it burned a little as he drove in. But it was exactly what I wanted–to feel a little pain. Soft and sweet would've killed me right now.

Though Max was still being too gentle. He pushed in a few inches and pulled back out, trying to ease into me when all I wanted was the opposite. So the next time he started to push in, I used all of my might to push back on him as hard as I could, impaling myself to the root.

Max hissed. "*Fuuuck.*"

"Harder."

He pulled out and pushed back in with a little more force.

"More."

We grew wild. Each time he'd pull out, I'd demand more until we were slamming into each other. My chest was tight with emotion, and it felt like the only thing that could release it was an orgasm powerful enough to make my body quiver. The bed shook, I thrashed around, and our bodies grew slick with sweat.

"*More.*"

"Fuck, Georgia. I'm going to come."

"Don't you dare! Not yet."

He growled and pulled out. I thought he was going to stop, but then suddenly, he flipped me over onto my stomach. Max slid a hand under my belly and hoisted my ass in the air. When I raised onto my elbows and attempted to get up on all fours, he splayed his fingers wide and pressed me back down. "No. You don't want me to look at you, so ass in the air and face in the pillow."

Max got up on his knees, gripped my hips, and pounded into me from behind. When he slid a hand around to my clit, it was like a bomb detonated inside of me. My body clenched around him, and I let out a loud moan even though the pillow stifled it.

Max pumped twice more, letting out a ferocious roar as he buried himself inside me and unloaded.

After, he rolled onto his back and laid next to me, panting. I kept my face buried in the pillow so he couldn't see the tears that came when the dam broke.

—Twenty-Five—

Max

"Do you actually work here? Or just come to get away from your wife?"

Otto shook his head and scribbled something into a small notepad. "Checking the seats, Pretty Boy. Every single one of these gets tested twice a year."

"Sure, that's what you're doing."

"Where's your pretty girl today? She smarten up and kick you to the curb already?"

I chuckled. "Glad to see you're in your regular good spirits."

He got up from one seat and sat down at the next. "Go plant your ass in E forty-four," he said, pointing. "The bolts are stripped. When you sit down, you'll wind up on the floor. It'll do you some good to remember the crappy accommodations the people yelling your name are shelling out two-hundred bucks for."

Otto was eight or nine rows away, so I walked up and took the aisle seat on the other side of the stairs to give him room to work.

"How you feeling?" I asked.

"Good. Finished my treatments and getting my strength back." He flexed his hands. "Pins and needles are the same, but I'll deal with it if it means I buy a little more time. I decided to call it quits here, though. Gave a month's notice yesterday."

"You get a job somewhere else?"

"Nope. My wife talked me into taking a road trip we've talked about since before we got married. Her brother has an RV he never uses, so we're going to drive from here to California taking the north route and drive home through the South. Might take three weeks, might take three months. We'll see how it goes."

"Good for you. That sounds awesome."

"I wanted to work as much as I could, bank money for my Dorothy for when I'm gone. But she says she'd rather have time with me than a little extra cash." He shook his head. "I was being stubborn, but when she asked me what I would want if the shoe was on the other foot, I realized the money isn't important." He lifted his chin to me. "What about you? You coming here on a Wednesday when you're off because you got news? Maybe tell me about your trade to the Blades, or do I have to read about it in the *Post* someday?"

I smiled. "Actually, that's why I stopped over. We finalized the deal, so I'm probably going to be heading out to sign the contract next week, and then they'll want to do a press conference."

"You happy? Did you get what you wanted?"

Three months ago, I wouldn't have hesitated to say yes. But the last few weeks, it felt like no amount of money or fame could get me what I wanted in life. Yet I nodded. "It's a great contract."

"Glad to hear it. And how's your smart girl?"

I smiled. "Georgia's good."

"She moving out there with you, or you gonna be one of those fancy bicoastal couples?"

My face answered before I did.

"Oh, Jesus. You're not going to try one of those long-distance things, are you? I might be old fashioned, but a couple should sleep in the same damn bed at night."

I shook my head. "We were just having fun over the summer."

His bushy brows pulled together to form what looked like a caterpillar. "So you're not in love with this girl?"

"It's complicated."

"Oh." He nodded. "Complicated? I get it. That's young people speak for *cop-out.*"

"Sometimes the best thing you can do for a person you love is set them free."

Otto snorted. "Did you read that shit on a Hallmark card? I didn't realize you were so soft."

"Soft? Don't make me get up and kick an old man's ass."

He waved me off and grumbled something I didn't catch.

"So whatta you think about the Radiski trade?" I knew that would change the subject. Otto thought Radiski was the most overrated goalie in the league, and he'd just snagged a huge, multiyear contract.

For the next hour and a half, I followed along, moving row to row as Otto tested out each chair and we bullshitted about the busy trade season. When it was time for him to take lunch, I figured I'd go.

We walked to the door together, and I extended my hand. "I'll stop back again before you leave."

"Sounds good." We shook, but Otto didn't let go of my hand. Instead, he used it to keep my attention and looked me in the eye. "Humor a dying old man and let me give you some advice."

"What's that?"

"Whatever you think is so complicated, isn't. Don't wait until you're seventy and sick to figure out that life is pretty simple. Be with the people you love, and your life will feel full in the end, whenever that time may come."

• • •

Things just weren't the same between Georgia and me after the night we had our talk. We still spent time together, and most people wouldn't have noticed the change from the outside, but I felt it. There was a wall that hadn't been there before, something blocking my ability to feel as close to her. I understood it, of course. But it still wasn't easy to accept. Every part of my body screamed to take back what I'd said and tell her I'd do whatever it took to make us work. Yet I didn't, because deep down, I knew I was doing the right thing for her.

The following Saturday, I picked her up to go out to dinner. Our table wasn't ready, so we waited at the bar and ordered a drink. While we were there, two women who didn't look old enough to drink the alcohol in their hands recognized me.

"Oh my God! You're Max Yearwood, aren't you?" one of them asked.

I smiled politely and nodded.

They got up from their stools on the other side of Georgia and stood in front of me. "I love you so much. *Please* say you're coming to California? We're just visiting New York. We live in Santa Barbara."

The announcement was coming in a few days, but I wasn't about to have it leaked on a fan's social media.

"We're still working on things," I said.

The taller of the two covered her heart with her hand. "God, you're even better looking in person."

My eyes slanted to Georgia and back to the women. "That's very nice of you. But I'm sort of on a date."

For the first time, the women seemed to notice someone sitting next to me. They looked Georgia up and down. "Are you his wife?" one of them asked.

Georgia shook her head.

"Girlfriend?"

My eyes caught with Georgia's again. She frowned and shook her head.

The more aggressive, taller one reached into her purse. She pulled out a business card and handed it to me. "If you do wind up in LA and want someone to show you around, I'd be happy to."

I held up my hand. "I'm good, thanks."

The woman shrugged. "Can I at least get a selfie with you?"

"I'd rather not. Like I said, I'm on a date."

Luckily the hostess walked over and interrupted. "Your table is ready, Mr. Yearwood."

"Thank you." I gave the ladies a curt nod before offering my hand to Georgia. "It was nice meeting you."

After we were seated, Georgia was quiet.

"I'm sorry about that."

She laid her napkin across her lap. "It's fine. You should've taken her number. They were both pretty."

I frowned sharply. "I wouldn't do that."

Georgia drew figure eights in the condensation on her water glass. "Do you remember when we first met, and I told you one of the things I wanted to work on was to stop overanalyzing everything?"

"Yeah, of course."

"Well, I spent this week completely preoccupied about something, and I think I just came to a decision."

Considering where this conversation had started—with two women who lived out in California trying to give me their number—I didn't have a good feeling. "A decision on what?"

She looked up. "I think we need to say our goodbye now, Max."

My heart jumped into my throat. "What? Why? Because of those women?"

Georgia shook her head. "No, I've been thinking about it all week. It's just… It's hard for me, sort of like pulling the Band-Aid off a wound a little at a time. I need to rip it at this point and start to heal."

Fuck. I forced myself to look into her eyes, but I wasn't prepared for what I saw. Her beautiful green eyes swam with heartache, and I don't know how I hadn't seen it until this moment, but they also had dark circles beneath them, coming through a layer of makeup. She didn't normally even wear stuff on her face. I felt like throwing up.

All I wanted was to convince her to stick it out until the end. It was only a few weeks anyway. Maybe it was the giant ego everyone always said I had, but I felt like I could talk her out of it, if I tried hard enough. But…that would be selfish.

Fuck. Fuck. Fuck.

I had no choice but to agree. The very least I could do was make it easier on her. So I gulped down the lump in my throat and nodded. "Okay. I understand." I waited a minute. When she was still quiet, I said, "Do you want to go? We don't have to have dinner."

"No, it's fine. We're here. And I do enjoy your company."

Thank fuck. "Okay."

"Do you think we can just not talk about it and have a nice dinner?"

"Sure."

Over the next hour, we talked about my trip to California, a new line of outdoor products she wanted to look into developing, and how the ladies who watched my dogs were going to use my apartment to bake their dog treats after I left since I still had six months on my lease.

The entire time, I felt like I was standing on a gangplank, waiting to walk off and drown. When the waitress came by and asked if we wanted to look at the dessert menu, we shared a secret smile and both said yes. Neither of us was ready for the evening to end.

But eventually, the restaurant patrons thinned out, and when the waitress came over for the third time to check on us after we'd finished dessert, we finally gave in.

We were only a few blocks from Georgia's apartment, and I was glad she let me walk her home. But in the lobby of her building, she pushed the button for the elevator and turned to face me.

"I think we should say goodbye here."

My stomach dropped to the floor, but I nodded and did my best to smile. "Okay."

Georgia took my hands, her eyes brimming with tears. "I just wanted to say that while right now I'm hurting, I don't regret our time together."

I swallowed the giant lump in my throat as I cupped her cheek. "The only thing I could ever regret about us is the ending, sweetheart."

Tears streamed down Georgia's face as the elevator arrived and the doors slid open. She put her hand over my hand on her face and turned to kiss my palm. "Goodbye, Max."

I bent and brushed my lips with hers. "Goodbye, Georgia."

She stepped into the waiting elevator, but I couldn't turn and walk away. Instead, I shut my eyes and let her go.

Twenty-Six

Max

A lot happened over the next few weeks. I signed a monster of a contract to play for a team with real playoff potential, flew out to California for a live press announcement followed by a two-day media junket, and I packed up my apartment in New York. I still had plenty of time until practices would start, but since there was nothing keeping me here anymore, I said screw it and booked a moving company to come get my stuff. Then I went online and bought a one-way ticket back to California five days from now.

I should've been out-of-my-mind happy with all of my good fortune. Most people worked their entire life to earn what I was going to earn in one year, and everything I'd dreamed about since I'd laced on my first pair of skates was within reach. Yet I was miserable. *So fucking miserable.*

My mother was currently up in Boston to visit my brother and the kids, and I was supposed to go see her. But considering I could barely stand myself, I couldn't expect anyone else to put up with my miserable ass, so I called and told her I had a lot of things to wrap up here, and instead I would come up to Washington once I was settled in on the West Coast next week.

Then I decided to go for a run.

I had no idea how far I'd gone, but I was a mile or two from home when it started to rain. Not just drizzle either, it goddamn poured. But it felt kinda right. On my way back, I passed the Garden. Glenn, one of the security guards I'd been friendly with, happened to be outside under the overhang, smoking a cigarette. He'd been on duty the night I met Georgia. He waved, so I stopped.

"Yearwood, you traitor." He smiled. "Figured you'd be out on the West Coast, hamming it up at parties with movie stars and starlets by now."

"Soon." I put my hands on my knees and bent to catch my breath. "What are you doing here? I thought you only worked nights."

"A day-shift spot finally opened up. You remember Bernie, the guy with the weird, red goatee but has white hair?"

"Yeah, I know Bernie."

"He got a job in operations. Took over Otto's gig." He shook his head. "Such a shame about that guy, huh?"

"Shame about who?"

"Otto. I figured you knew. They sent out an email to the team."

"I'm not on the team anymore. What happened to Otto?"

"Had a cough that started last week. A few days later, he was in the hospital with pneumonia. Yesterday they had to put him on a ventilator. Antibiotics aren't working, and his immune system is shot from the cancer treatments."

Shit. "You know what hospital he's in?"

"St. Luke's."

"Thanks. I gotta go. It was good seeing you, Glenn. Take care."

• • •

"Hi. I'm looking for Otto Wolfman."

The nurse pointed to one of the glass rooms on her left. "He's in bed four."

The intensive care unit was one big space with a nurses' station in the middle and small, individual, fishbowl glass rooms located around the perimeter. The sliding door to Otto's was open, and a woman sat at his bedside. When she saw me, she stood and walked out.

"Hi. Are you Mrs. Wolfman?" I asked.

"I am."

"I'm Max Yearwood, a friend of your husband's from the Garden."

She smiled. "I know who you are. Otto talks about you all the time, and he never misses watching your games. He adores you."

I smiled back. "You sure you got the right guy? He calls me jackass."

Mrs. Wolfman chuckled. "That's how you know he likes you—if he calls you names."

I looked over her shoulder at Otto. He was hooked up to all kinds of monitors and drip bags. "I just heard what happened. How's he doing?"

She shook her head. "Not too well, I'm afraid. He's got sepsis now, likely from the pneumonia."

"I saw him pretty recently. He seemed like he was doing so well."

"He was. The pneumonia took us by surprise. He's got lung cancer, so having a cough isn't unusual. That's what we thought it was until he came down with a high fever. It spread fast because his immune system is compromised from the chemo."

"Would it be alright if I visited him for a few minutes?"

Mrs. Wolfman smiled. "I think he'd love that. I was going to take a walk downstairs to grab some coffee. There's a Starbucks in the lobby. So I'll leave you two alone for a few minutes."

I nodded. "Thank you."

"Would you like me to grab you a cup?"

"No thanks." I smiled. "Otto is so anti-Starbucks."

"Oh, don't I know it. But I really enjoy it. I'll tell you a little secret." She motioned for me to come closer. "I keep a sleeve of plain, white Styrofoam cups in my cupboard. Sometimes I pick up a Starbucks and dump it into one of those so I don't have to listen to him rant for a half hour about how the place is overpriced."

I laughed. "That's classic."

She patted my shoulder. "I'll be back in a few minutes."

After Mrs. Wolfman left, I stood at the doorway, not sure what to say or do. A nurse came by to add another bag of fluids to Otto's IV pole. As she worked, she spoke aloud, telling him what she was doing. I stopped her on her way out.

"Can he hear you?"

She had a kind smile. "Maybe. Many people do wake up remembering conversations visitors had, but it's different on a case-by-case basis. I like to assume they can and just let them know what I'm up to. There have been studies that show patients benefit from the familiar sound of the voices of loved ones. They believe it can help awaken the brain and improve recovery time." She nodded toward Otto. "Go ahead in. It may feel weird at first, but just try telling him about your day."

I nodded. "Okay, thank you."

I took a seat beside Otto's bed and looked up at all the wires and monitors.

"Hey, old man." I smiled sadly. "I was going to come visit and say goodbye before I left. You didn't have to go and do all this just to get my ass in gear. The nurse says you might recognize voices. I figure if I'm too nice, you might get confused, so I'll just be my regular charming self."

I paused and thought back to the first time Otto and I met, seven years ago. "I'm going to tell you something, but if you remember it when you wake up, I'll deny I ever said it. Anyway...I looked forward to seeing you every day after practice. You always reminded me of my dad. He was my biggest supporter, but never afraid to dish out a dose of reality. My rookie year, I walked in with a chip on my shoulder. I thought the team would be excited to land me, that I'd proven my worth by my stats in college and the price tag of the big contract I'd signed. I didn't understand that some of the guys had put in ten or fifteen years and watched more than one big-name rookie turn out to be a disappointment. There was a guy named Sikorski who rode me hard that first year, and we started to go at it on the ice. One day after practice, I was sitting around in the penalty box, stewing over us getting into it yet again. You were pushing a broom and asked me if I planned on marrying Sikorski. I looked at you like you were crazy and said he wasn't my type. And then you said something that's stuck with me to this day: '*Not every battle is worth the fight.*' You told me to stop wasting my time on shit that comes between my destiny and me." I shook my head. "Something just clicked. I was funneling all of my energy into a fight I didn't have to win. And that just took focus away from the things that really mattered, like improving my game."

I stared up at the numbers on the monitor for a while, watching Otto's heartbeat. "By the way, I finally met Mrs. Wolfman a little while ago. I don't think I have to tell you she's too pretty and nice for your grumpy ass."

I heard a chuckle behind me and turned to find Otto's wife standing at the door.

She had two coffee cups in her hands. "Thank you. I can see why you two are friends now. That sounded just like something he would say."

"Sorry. I didn't mean for you to hear that."

She smiled. "It's fine. That's exactly what Otto would want—people being real." She walked into the room and handed me a coffee. "I know you said you didn't want one, but you always brought him coffee, so it felt right to return the favor."

I nodded. "Thank you."

Over the next two hours, Mrs. Wolfman and I shared funny stories about Otto. She told me the only person who ever got the soft side of her husband was their daughter. Apparently, she had him wrapped around her finger and could get him to do anything. Like the time in seventh grade she was struggling in algebra, and Mrs. Wolfman told Otto their daughter couldn't go out and play until she did all her homework. He got home earlier than his wife and had to enforce the rules. It had seemed like he was, until one day when the teacher called with concerns because their daughter's homework had gone downhill in quality. Even her handwriting had become sloppier. Turned out, Otto was doing her math homework, while she went out to play. And he was even worse at algebra than their daughter.

I was really glad I'd come. Mrs. Wolfman seemed to enjoy sharing stories. But when the nurse asked if we would step out so she could wash Otto, I figured it was time for me to get going.

"Would you mind if I gave you my number so you can let me know if anything changes?" I asked her. "I'm moving in a few days, but I'll pop back in again before then, if that's okay with you."

"I'd love that. Thank you, Max."

After I entered my number in her phone, I said goodbye, but then turned back. "Mrs. Wolfman?"

"Yes?"

"The other day when he told me he was leaving the Garden to drive cross country with you, he told me his life always felt full because he was with the person he loved. It wasn't only your daughter Otto had that soft spot for."

She smiled. "I think there may have been a certain hockey player in that category, too. He just would never let you know it."

• • •

Two days later, Mrs. Wolfman called to tell me Otto had passed.

Twenty-Seven

Georgia

Friday night, Maggie made me go out. It had been at least three weeks since I'd seen Max, and I still had zero desire to do anything. But my best friend was not a person who took no for an answer. She'd told me we were going to an art exhibit, which was far better than a singles bar in my mind, but when we arrived at The Gallery, I realized I'd been duped.

There was art on the walls, but the place was also a bar—one filled with wall-to-wall people. "I thought you said this was an art gallery."

Maggie held her hands out. "It is. They rotate the exhibition every month. Now what do you want to drink?"

I frowned. "Just a water."

"One lemon drop martini coming up. Good choice." She winked and disappeared.

I sighed. Since there was actual art around the perimeter of the room, I stepped closer to the piece right in front of me. It was an abstract painting of a woman. While I studied it, a guy walked up next to me.

He tilted a beer toward the canvas. "So...what do you think?"

"I'm not very good with art."

He smiled. "Well, how does looking at that make you feel?"

I stared at it some more. "Sad, I guess."

He nodded and pointed to the one next to it. "How about that one?"

"The same."

"Damn." He chuckled. "That one is titled *Happiness*." He extended his hand. "I'm Scott Sheridan, and those are my paintings."

"Oh my gosh, I'm sorry. I didn't mean to insult your work. It's probably just my mood. I've been sort of down lately."

He laughed. "I'm not insulted. Art makes people feel different things. As long as I made you feel something, I've done my job." He thumbed toward the bar. "Can I buy you a drink? Full disclosure, one of the perks of showing your art here is that all the alcohol is free, so I won't have to pay for it."

I smiled. "No, thanks. My friend actually just went to get me one."

"So, let's see. So far I've asked you if you like my art and offered to buy you a drink. Should I go for the cliché trifecta and ask you if you're from around here?"

"I live here in the city. How about you?"

"LA. I'm just in town visiting."

My face dropped. *LA*. I'd managed to not think about Max for two or three whole minutes at least. Luckily, Maggie came back carrying our drinks, and I didn't have to continue the conversation unassisted.

"Who's this?" She passed me a cocktail and nodded toward Scott.

"Scott's one of the artists being featured tonight."

"Nice to meet you, Scott." Maggie tilted her head and smiled wolfishly. "The helpful bartender actually just pointed you out and warned me to keep away. She said you come in all the time pretending to be one of the artists who lives out of town, but you're actually a barista over at Café Europa on Sixty-Eighth Street."

The guy scowled and turned on his heel to walk away.

My mouth hung open. "Seriously? What the heck?"

Maggie shook her head. "Creep. I don't get some men. Haven't they ever heard of Tinder? There are women looking for nothing more than a hookup. So why do they need to play games like that?"

I shook my head. "I'm never dating again. I wasn't even slightly interested in that guy, yet I totally believed he was the artist and lived in LA. Am I that gullible?"

"No, he's just that big of a jerk."

I sighed and sipped my drink. "I miss Max."

"I know you do, honey."

"Maybe I made a mistake telling him I needed to stop seeing him before he left at the end of the summer. I should get loaded and booty-call him."

Maggie grimaced. "He's actually gone. I'm pretty sure he left this morning."

My brows drew together. "How do you know?"

She chewed her bottom lip. "I wasn't going to say anything, because you seemed to be doing a little better each day, but I saw him yesterday."

"Saw him? Where?"

"Across the street from our office."

"What was he doing across the street?"

Maggie sipped her drink. "Staring at our building."

"What are you talking about?"

She heaved a loud sigh. "I left to go to the printer at eleven, remember?"

"Yeah?"

"Well, when I walked out, I noticed a guy across the street. He was wearing a baseball hat and sunglasses, but I thought it looked like Max. I figured it was my imagination. I came back a half hour later, and when I turned the corner, I looked over and the guy was still standing there, just sort of watching our building. So I crossed over before he saw me and went to take a closer look. Sure enough, it was Max."

"I don't understand. He was just standing there?"

She nodded. "I said hello and asked him what he was doing. I think he considered lying, but then he said he was waiting for you to come out for lunch. I said he should go in and see you, because we'd ordered in. But he said he didn't want to bother you, that he hadn't planned on saying anything to you when you eventually came out. He just wanted to see you again before he left."

"So he was just going to stand there and what? Look at me silently like a stalker?"

Maggie nodded.

The story made no sense. "That's all he said?"

"I asked him why he wouldn't just go in and say goodbye in person, and he said it would just make it harder for you. Honestly, I thought he was right, so I didn't say anything because you'd just started to come to work without puffy eyes the last few days."

I shook my head. "This is exactly what I don't understand. If he cares about me enough to stand outside our building for hours just to see me from a distance, how could he not want to at least *try* to make things work?"

"I don't know. I wish I had that answer for you."

"Was that it? He didn't say anything else?"

"I asked him when he was leaving, and he said today. He'd pushed up his moving date and mumbled something about some charity game he'd agreed to play in that was in a few weeks—as if that was the reason he was leaving." She shook her head. "So I told him he was a coward with his head up his ass, and I left."

I smiled sadly. That sounded about right.

"Are you mad I didn't say anything?"

"No. I get why you didn't. I know you always have my back."

She slung her arm around my shoulder. "Good. Then drink up. Because tonight we are getting sloshed and blowing off any man who tries to come near us."

Three hours later, it was mission accomplished. It was barely midnight—most young people were only starting to go out now—yet I was slurring and ready for bed. Maggie came home with me to make sure I got in okay, and she decided to crash on my couch rather than go across town to her apartment. She pulled my favorite sweats and T-shirt from my drawer, and after I changed, she tucked me into bed like a child.

"You good? You're not going to puke on me, are you? Do you need a bucket or anything?"

"Only for my tears."

She grinned. "Do you think your tears would be extra salty from all the margaritas?"

"No, because I was drinking lemon drops."

"Shit, that's right." She chuckled. "That was sugar around the rim, not salt."

"Can I ask you something, Mags?"

"Anything."

"Do you think Max is in love with his ex?"

Maggie's face scrunched up. "Where did that come from? You've never even mentioned an ex of his. Did he have a serious relationship recently?"

"No, not recently. He dated a woman for eighteen months, a couple of years back. But I've been trying to figure out why he wouldn't give me a reason he didn't want to try. The only thing that makes sense is that he didn't want to hurt me. Sort of like you not telling me about him showing up at the office yesterday. When you care about someone, you don't want to hurt them unnecessarily. So maybe he's in love with someone else."

Maggie frowned. "I'm not sure why he won't be with you. But I do know one thing. He lost the best thing he's ever had."

My eyes welled up. "Thanks, Maggie."

—Twenty-Eight—

Max

Ten years ago

"You boys have got to be kidding me." My mother walked into the doctor's office, took one look at me holding bloody tissues to my nose, and shook her head.

I pointed to Austin. "He started it."

Austin looked at Mom with sick-kid puppy-dog eyes. "I don't have the energy to start a fight."

"Oh, honey." Mom rubbed Austin's back. "Are you feeling okay?"

"I'm the one with the bloody nose!"

Austin grinned at me from behind my mother's back. *Such a dick.*

Dr. Wallace walked into the office, carrying a chart. "Sorry to keep you all waiting."

Mom took the seat between Austin and me. We'd flown out to California a few days ago for a second opinion on Austin's aneurysm. I'd tagged along to keep Austin company, even though Mom had taken over managing things after I'd finally got him to tell her what was going on.

"Thank you for seeing us on such short notice, Dr. Wallace," Mom said.

"Of course." He sat down behind his desk. "Why don't we get right into it, since you've come all this way, and I've already kept you waiting. I reviewed the files your doctor in Boston sent over, along with the scan taken last month and the one you took just this morning." Dr. Wallace looked directly at my brother. "I'm afraid I agree with Dr. Jasper's findings, son. That aneurysm should come out."

My brother frowned. "What happens if I don't want to have surgery?"

Dr. Wallace opened his drawer and took out what looked like a straw with something dangling from it. He smiled. "Excuse the low-tech demonstration. I find the minute I take out an iPad and start showing actual anatomy, patients get overwhelmed. Sometimes old-school simplicity works best. I get these straws from McDonald's. They're nice and thick, so it's easy to thread my balloon through." He held the straw horizontally, with a small piece of red latex dangling from a tear in the middle. He pointed to it. "This is the artery leading up to your heart." He pointed to the latex peeking out. "This is an aneurysm." He held one end of the straw closed and brought the other end to his mouth. "My breath is our blood flowing." When he blew into the straw, the small piece of balloon sticking out of the slit began to grow. He pinched off the air when it was the size of a raisin. "This is normal blood flowing through. But here's what happens when you start moving around and raise your blood pressure." He blew into the straw with more pressure, and the balloon grew to the size of a golf ball. "Eventually, this balloon gets stretched too thin, and it can pop. Then you're left with nothing plugging the hole, and blood leaks into the surrounding space of your heart chambers. I'm not trying to scare you, but if it bursts on its own, it's messy, and your chances are not nearly as good as if we remove it cleanly."

"Will it definitely burst?"

"That we can't say for sure. Some people walk around their entire life not ever knowing they even have an aneurysm. Much of it depends on the size and how fast it's growing. If yours was small, I might advise you to wait. But yours is not. It's very large. And in the month since you had that initial scan, it's gotten bigger, son."

Austin looked at Mom. "How big was Dad's?"

She frowned. "I don't know."

He looked at the doctor again. "How long is the recovery?"

"You'd be in the hospital a few days. Most people can resume regular activities within four to six weeks, but it takes two to three months to fully recover."

Austin took a deep breath. "What are the risks?"

"The biggest ones are bleeding and infection. There's always a small risk when you go under anesthesia, but for someone in good health and your age, the risk is pretty minimal these days. We do a lot of these surgeries."

My brother looked over at me. "What would you do?"

"I already told you. I'd do it. You don't want it to get even bigger and have it burst during the surgery like Dad's did. And you're already struggling to get around. Do you want to live like that?"

"No, but I do want to *live*."

I shook my head. "You know my stance. If you can't live like you want, you're already dying."

Austin looked at me a long time before nodding and turning back to the doctor. "How soon can you do it?"

Dr. Wallace smiled. "Let me get with the scheduling nurse and see when the next available date is."

"Thank you very much, Dr. Wallace," Mom said.

He nodded. "Oh, one other thing. I'm not sure if Dr. Jasper spoke to you about this, but Max and any other children should also be scanned."

"Scanned for abdominal aortic aneurysms?"

Dr. Wallace nodded. "Aneurysms in general. Your husband had one, and now Austin. When two or more first-degree relatives have them, we recommend the immediate family members—parents and children—be tested. There's an increased risk of other members having what we call familial aneurysms."

Twenty-Nine

Max

"I bought tickets to that charity hockey exhibition game you're playing in next week," Mom said. "I thought I'd fly down the day before and stay a few days so I can see your new place."

"I told you they gave me tickets for free. It just slipped my mind to forward you the email."

"It's for charity. I wanted to pay for them."

I nodded and poked at the pot roast she made every time I visited. It was usually my favorite.

"Are you okay, Max?"

"Yeah, I'm fine."

My mother leveled me with what my brothers and I had called the *mom eyes* growing up. Those things were better than truth serum. None of us had any idea how she did it, but with one look, she pulled whatever was lurking inside us out. It was like she knew the truth, and she just waited patiently for us to spill it.

I sighed and dragged a hand through my hair. "I miss Georgia."

Mom patted my hand. "What happened? I thought you two were doing so well and had something special."

I shrugged. "We did."

"So why are you missing her? Get on a plane and go visit. Practice doesn't start for a while yet, right?"

"Yeah. But she doesn't want to see me."

"Did you two have a falling out or something?"

I shook my head. "It's nothing like that."

"Then what is it?"

I frowned and looked up at my mother. "I don't want her to get hurt. If...you know."

Understanding dawned on her face. "Oh, no, Max. Have you discussed things with her?"

I didn't even have to answer. I just looked at my mom, and she shut her eyes.

"Max." She shook her head. "Why didn't you tell her?"

"Because Georgia is as loyal and pigheaded as they come. She'd be adamant that it didn't matter. But it would...*if*."

"So you made the choice for her?"

"It was for her own good."

"*Bullshit*."

I blinked a few times. My mother did *not* curse.

"I stood by your decision to not have the surgery because it's your body and your choice. I stood by your decision to keep playing hockey—even though it's the dumbest thing you could possibly do because you get whacked in the head a hundred times a season and that could easily cause a rupture and kill you—because hockey has been the love of your life since you could talk. But I will not sit here and accept that you are going to walk away from a woman you care about out of some false sense of chivalry to protect her. Do you love Georgia?"

I nodded and hung my head.

"Then how can you have no regard for her needs? There were two people in your relationship, yet you're acting like you're the only one."

"I'm trying to do the right thing, Ma. I want what's best for her."

She sat back down and took a deep breath. "I understand that your intentions were honorable, but you don't get to decide what's best for anyone but *you*. Don't you think I wanted to decide you couldn't play hockey because it was too risky? What if I'd gone to your team and told them about your condition? They'd have disqualified you from playing. You know they would—"

"That's different."

"Why?"

"Because what I'm doing is only hurting myself."

My mother stared at me. "Really? So if you drop dead on the ice after a stick to the head, the only one who would be hurt is you?"

I sighed. My head had been so screwed up since leaving New York. I'd lost Georgia and then Otto died—right when he'd finally decided to leave work and spend time with his family. I couldn't help but think he never got the chance because he waited too long, and I was essentially doing the same damn thing. Never once, since Austin died, had I questioned whether I was making the right decision. Until recently.

I spoke quietly. "Maybe I should just have the surgery."

Tears filled my mother's eyes. "Are you serious?"

I nodded. "I've been thinking about it a lot lately. Even when I retire someday, there's still going to be that unknown hanging over my head. And it's...gotten bigger."

My mother's eyes widened. "Oh my God, Max. How do you know?"

"I had another scan a month or so ago when I was out in California. I went to the same doctor who did Austin's surgery and all of our scans."

"That's your first visit to a doctor for it since your diagnosis?"

I nodded again.

"Are you having symptoms?"

I shook my head. "I just thought... I don't know what I thought. Maybe I was hoping it had disappeared or something. But I wanted to know."

My mother smiled sadly. "You wanted to know because of Georgia."

"Maybe. I guess. Probably." I paused, feeling tangled in my thoughts. "I feel like a coward. I made Austin have the surgery, but I'm too chicken shit to go under the knife myself."

My mother shook her head. "What are you talking about? You made Austin do it?"

"When he was diagnosed, Austin asked me what I would do if I were in his place." I swallowed and tasted salt in my throat. "I said I'd have the surgery. And I promised him he wouldn't die."

Mom studied my face. "Oh my God. And you've been carrying that with you all these years? Why didn't you say anything?"

"What am I gonna say? Hey, Ma, Austin is dead because of me?"

"Your brother was very intelligent, and he was also twenty-one years old when he had his surgery. He made the decision on his own. I know because he struggled to make it, and we talked about it a lot. He asked his doctor the same question he asked you, and his own doctor said he would have it done if it were him in the same predicament."

"But he trusted me."

"Honey, Austin's death is not your fault. You do know that, right?"

When I didn't respond, my mother reached across and took my hand. "Austin was out of breath from walking. He decided to have the surgery because he didn't feel like he could live a full life the way he was. I know you two were close, but he did *not* make that decision because of anything you said. And no one could have predicted that he would have a rare reaction to anesthesia the first time he went under."

I shook my head. "I might not have symptoms like Austin did, but losing Georgia makes me feel like I can't have a full life anymore."

"Tell me what the doctor said this time."

"Mostly the same as he said ten years ago. Any surgery has risk, but the risk of death is pretty minimal because it's a routine surgery these days, and the likelihood of me having a reaction like Austin is rare because I've been under anesthesia with no issues before. The risk for me is that my aneurysm is in the area of the brain that controls motor skills, so if any bleeding occurs, I could have some strength and coordination issues."

"Last time they said that would be temporary."

I nodded. "Yeah, they said therapy should be able to build it back if it happens. But let's face it, I'm twenty-nine. The likelihood of making it back to where I am today in hockey after that happening isn't great. The difference in speed and agility between me and the next guy who wants my job isn't that big."

"What about the risk of rupturing?"

"It's increased because it's grown, but I'm still only considered a moderate risk."

"Moderate for normal people whose blood pressure isn't being pushed at practice every day, and for people not getting their head bashed around with a stick."

I didn't answer, because of course she was right. I'd always known I had an elevated risk of rupture because of my job. But hockey was my life, so I'd never questioned my decision. I would've risked everything to play. Only lately, hockey wasn't feeling like the most important thing in the world anymore.

I shook my head. "I don't know what to do. I can't build something with Georgia knowing I'm putting myself at risk every day. I won't do that to her. But if I have the surgery, I might not ever play professional hockey again."

My mom frowned. "Sounds like you have a serious choice to make. Which one matters more to you?"

• • •

For the next few days I wandered. I'd shipped my car from New York to LA, and it hadn't arrived yet. So I rented a Jeep, and my dogs and I drove along the coast looking for something. What? I didn't know. Perhaps I was looking for a solution, some sort of a sign about what I should do. Nothing had jumped out at me as of yet.

Each day I ventured out without any plans and just drove until I saw something that interested me. So far I'd been to Malibu, Sequoia National Park, and the Santa Monica Pier. I couldn't help but think that if Georgia and I lived out here together, we'd visit some of those places on our next staycation.

This morning I'd headed south. I hadn't been sure what city I was going to, but when I saw signs for Rosie's Dog Beach, I figured that was one sign I couldn't ignore.

So the boys and I spent the afternoon walking along the water, where they were allowed to roam off leash. There'd been a shopping area not too far from there, so after we were done, I stopped to see if I could find some waters for the dogs and something to eat for me.

A half block from where I parked, I found a chicken place that fit the bill with outdoor seating, so I grabbed a table. But as we got up to leave after our meal, I looked two stores down and did a double take.

Eternity Roses.

Seriously?

What were the chances that I'd walk straight into one of Georgia's boutiques? I walked over and stared at the window for a while, looking at the displays, yet not really seeing them, before wandering inside.

"Is it okay if I bring my dogs in?"

The girl behind the counter smiled. "Only if I get to play with them."

"Deal."

She came out from behind the counter, and frick and frack practically attacked her. Four licked her face, and not to be outdone, Fred ran in rapid circles, chasing his own tail.

The clerk laughed. "Oh my gosh, they're so cute."

"Thank you."

"Is there something I can help you with?"

I didn't want to explain why I'd come in, so I figured maybe I'd send my mom some flowers for listening to my sorry ass the other day. "I'm just going to look around, if that's okay. I'd like to send my mom some flowers, but I'm not sure what yet."

"Sure. Take your time. I'll happily occupy these guys while you browse." She pointed to a wall with glass shelves and different arrangements on display. "Those are all stock pieces that can be made in any colors you want. But if you had something specific in mind, we can also make a custom arrangement. They just take two to three days more. Is this for a specific reason, like a birthday or get well?"

"More of a thanks-for-putting-up-with-me gift."

She smiled. "Those are always fun. There's also an iPad at the front counter that can give you some ideas of things people have custom ordered and a fun database of messages that has everything from poetry to sweet to funny."

I remembered Georgia saying she used to enjoy writing those messages when she first started out, so after taking a quick look around, I was drawn to the iPad.

Scrolling down to the suggestions marked *Just because*, I double-clicked and started to read. Some were funny, some were dirty, and some were just corny. I chuckled when I got to one written by Maggie P.:

Best friends are like peeing in your pants.
Everyone sees it, but only you feel the warmth.

That had to be the Maggie I knew. After a while, I stopped reading the messages and just scrolled the names to see who had written them. I guess I was hoping to find one written by Georgia. I didn't, but when I got to the very bottom of hundreds of messages and saw one by F. Scott Fitzgerald, I remembered Georgia had said she'd kept his books annotated near the register because his quotes simplified love for her.

It was
always
you.
-F. Scott Fitzgerald

I read that a dozen times, over and over. I wasn't sure if it was the glaring sign I'd been looking for, but it sure as hell was the simple truth. *It was always Georgia.* And in the end, *whenever* that day might come, I didn't want to look back with regret. Maybe those four simple words were a sign after all.

So when I got back in the car to head home, I decided to take Georgia's advice. I picked up my cell and scrolled through my contacts until I got to one of the last ones, and then I pressed *Call.*

"Hi. This is Max Yearwood. I'd like to make an appointment with Dr. Wallace."

• • •

A few days later, the charity hockey game arrived. I'd used it as an excuse to get my brothers to fly out, and since my mom had arrived yesterday, we were all under one roof. That rarely happened, except at Christmas. The exhibition game wasn't until seven, and I'd planned to tell everyone my news over breakfast, but I'd woken up with a splitting headache again. The last few days had been stressful, and my brain was taking it out on me. So I took a few Motrin and put my announcement off until lunch.

When the sandwiches and salads I'd ordered came, everyone gathered together around the kitchen island.

"So..." I cleared my throat. "I wanted to talk to you guys while you were here."

"You're coming out, aren't you?" my brother Will said, leaning back in his seat. "I knew it."

"What? No."

"If you're gambling again, you're going to be the only one going *into* the hockey game bruised up," Tate said.

"You better not be caught up in some harassment shit," Ethan said.

"Sex tape." My brother Lucas nodded. "It's definitely a sex tape. I really don't want to see your junk flashed all over the news, dude."

I shook my head. "What the hell is wrong with all of you?"

"I know I dropped Will on his head once," my mom said. "But the rest of you have no excuse. Let your brother talk."

I chuckled. "Thanks, Mom."

The room grew quiet, and all eyes turned to me. *Damn. This isn't as easy to say as I thought it would be.*

I took a deep breath. "I'm having surgery next Tuesday."

My mother was more in the loop than the others, so she understood before I explained anything else. She walked over and patted my hand.

"What kind of surgery?" Will asked. "Penile enhancement?"

"No, dipshit. The kind they can't perform on you since you lack the organ. Brain surgery. I decided to have the aneurysm removed. It's grown, and I think it's time."

"Oh, shit," Tate said. "You okay?"

I nodded. "I'm fine."

"Does your new team know?" Ethan asked.

"Not yet. I'm telling my agent tomorrow morning. I figured he'd have some advice about the best way to handle it."

"What's the doctor have to say?" Tate asked.

"Who's doing it?" Will asked.

"How long is the recovery?" Ethan chimed in.

Over the next hour, we ate lunch and I filled them in on everything the doctor had said and answered all their questions. Once everyone seemed satisfied, I excused myself and went to the bathroom in my bedroom to get some more Motrin. Then I stood out on the balcony to get some quiet fresh air.

My brother Tate followed me out and watched me take the pills.

"What are those?"

"Motrin. I can't get this headache to go away the last few days."

He nodded. "Stress will do that to you."

I finished off a bottle of water. "I need a favor from you," I said.

"Name it."

"If something goes wrong, and I don't...you know. I need you to promise me you'll go tell Georgia in person before word gets out on the news."

"Nothing is going to go wrong. But yeah, of course. You have my word."

I took a deep breath and nodded. "Thanks."

"What about when everything goes right? Where does this leave you two? You finally going to pull your head out of your ass and try to get your girl back?"

I smiled. "Try? You mean try to *stop* me."

Tate laid a hand on my shoulder. "You know when you know it's real?"

"When?"

"When the thought of being without her doesn't scare you half as much as brain surgery."

Thirty

Georgia

I opened the front door of my apartment at 6 AM, and Maggie rushed in. "Did you see the news this morning?"

She had on pajama pants with big red hearts and a T-shirt that said *V is for Valentine*, but the word *Valentine* was crossed out and underneath it was the word *Vodka*. Her hair was piled on top of her head, and what looked like yesterday's mascara was smeared beneath her eyes.

"No, why?" I asked. "And did you ride the subway like that? You look a little nutty."

She took out her phone. "Max was injured last night."

My heart stopped. "What? What are you talking about?"

She typed something into her cell and handed it to me. A news segment showed a hockey rink with a bunch of players down on one knee while paramedics worked on a player splayed out on the ice.

"During tonight's Hockey for Alzheimer's charity event," the reporter said, "Max Yearwood, the newest member of the LA Blades, took a spill. He went down during the second period while attempting a slap shot. No contact was made, and as far as we can see, the incident was not due to an injury. He was transported to Cedars Sinai where he is reportedly in stable, but serious condition. No word yet on what caused the All Star to lose consciousness."

"Oh my God. Stable but serious? What does that mean?"

"I Googled it on the way over. It said it means he's probably in the ICU for a condition, but his vitals are stable."

I felt frantic. "ICU? What could have happened?"

"I have no idea. But you have that meeting downtown with the bank this morning, and I was afraid you'd hear about it on your way and get upset. So I came over to tell you."

I sat, holding Maggie's phone out to her. "What do I do? His family all lives out of state. What if he's alone? Should I go there?"

"I'm not sure. I mean, you're not together anymore. So technically, he's not your responsibility. And the news could be blowing it out of proportion. He could've just passed out from being dehydrated or who knows—hurt his ankle, and that caused him to fall and hit his head."

"Yeah, I guess…" My chest felt tight, like it was hard to breathe. "Maybe I should at least call him."

"It's 3AM in California."

"Shoot." I sighed. "That's right. Well, my meeting is at eight, so maybe I'll just go to that, and then by the time I'm done, it will probably be ten, which is seven there, and I'll call and see what's going on."

"Okay."

"Can I see your phone again? I want to watch the video once more."

This time, I zoomed in on Max lying on the ice and ignored the reporter talking. He wasn't moving. He just laid there, completely still, while people worked on him. It left me with an even worse feeling than before. We might not be a couple anymore, but I'd never forgive myself if something happened. It was my fault he was even out in California this early.

• • •

"Damn it." I grumbled to myself as I climbed the stairs from the subway.

Max wasn't answering his phone. I'd called him the minute I walked out of my meeting, which was twenty minutes ago. Both times it rang and rang, only to eventually go to voicemail. I hadn't left a message the first time, but now I thought I should.

"Hi, Max. It's Georgia. I saw on the news this morning that you passed out on the ice or something. They said you were in serious but stable condition. I just want to check in on you. Would you please give me a call back or shoot me a text when you can?" I paused. "I hope you're okay."

It was a two-block walk to my office. I'd had a knot in my stomach since early this morning, and Max not answering only made it worse. I navigated the busy sidewalk in a daze, not remembering the walk from the subway when I arrived. The thirty-second elevator ride clenched my stomach with anxiety. There was no service in here, and I didn't want to miss Max if he called back. As soon as the doors opened, I rushed out and frantically checked my phone—which was exactly where my nose was still buried when I passed through reception without looking up.

"Georgia?"

The voice was familiar, but I couldn't place it until I turned around. "Tate?"

At first, I was relieved to see Max's brother. He'd be able to give me information about what happened and how Max was. But that relief faded when I realized what Tate looked like. His usual neatly groomed hair stuck up all over the place, the sides puffing out in a way that made me think he'd spent hours pulling it, yanking on the strands. Dark circles lined his eyes, and his tanned skin was now a gray, sallow color. I felt sick.

"Can we talk?"

"Is he okay? Is Max okay?"

Tate frowned. He glanced over at the receptionist, who was staring at us. "Do you have an office or somewhere we can speak in private?"

My response was delayed, but eventually I nodded. It took every ounce of focus I had to put one foot in front of the other and lead him to my office. Once we were inside, he shut the door behind us, and I immediately turned around.

"Is Max okay?"

"Can we sit, please?"

I shook my head. "You're freaking me out, Tate. Is Max okay?"

He blew out a jagged breath and shook his head. "He's in surgery right now. But things don't look so great."

The room started to spin and I thought I might pass out. Tate had been right. I needed to sit. With my hand clutching my stomach, I grabbed one of the guest chairs in front of my desk. "What happened?"

"He had an aneurysm. It ruptured."

I covered my mouth. "Oh my God. An aneurysm like Austin. And your dad."

Tate nodded and took the seat across from me. "Yeah. Aneurysms can run in families. After we found out Austin had an abdominal aortic aneurysm, our doctor suggested we all get scans. Max was the only other one of us who had one."

"When you found out Austin had one, you all got scans? So Max has known about his for *ten years*?"

Tate nodded.

"His is in his brain. It's in an area that controls motor skills, so if he removed it, there was a chance he could suffer some damage...and not play hockey again." Tate shook his head. "The screwed-up thing is, he'd avoided going to a doctor or getting a scan for the last decade. Then a month ago, he finally decided to go for a new scan. Last week he set an appointment to have the surgery. He was going to have it removed on Tuesday. But it ruptured while he was playing last night. He'd been getting headaches the last few days, but he chalked them up to stressing over the surgery. Turns out, it was leaking, and the headaches were warnings."

"Can they fix it with the surgery?"

"They're trying. The first twenty-four hours are the most critical. The doctors said since it ruptured, the chance of him not making it through this is forty percent, and if he does, there's a sixty-five percent chance he'll have some damage—that could range from impaired motor skills to... worse."

I stood. "Are you going there? I want to go."

"I actually took the redeye this morning to come talk to you. But I'm going right back to the airport after this."

"You came all this way just to tell me?"

Tate nodded. "I made a promise to my brother when he decided to have the surgery—that I'd come tell you in person if things didn't go well. You're the reason he decided to have the surgery at all."

"Me? But we're not together anymore."

"I know. Having the surgery meant potentially losing something he loved—playing hockey. Every time he skated onto the ice, his blood pressure rose, and it increased the risk of rupture. He didn't want to drag you into something that had so much unknown. But then he found something he loved more than hockey—*you*. And he was willing to take the risk so he wouldn't lose you."

Tears slid down my cheeks. "We need to go. I want to be there when he gets out of surgery."

Tate nodded.

On our way to the airport, my admin found us the next flight we could get and booked us tickets, even though it was going to be tight. Once we cleared security, we ran through the airport, trying to make it before the doors closed. I don't think either of us breathed until we were on the plane. Since we'd booked last minute, Tate and I weren't seated together. I was about ten rows behind him, but the alone time allowed me a chance to try to absorb everything he'd said.

How had I not put the clues together? I'd found an appointment card for a neurologist when we were out in California, for God's sake. And Max never could give me a reason he didn't want to try to make things work. It all made sense now; he didn't want to hurt me if he was going to continue playing hockey and put himself at risk. I should've realized he was trying to protect me. The man was headstrong and stubborn, but also noble and beautiful. I couldn't wait to tell him I loved him almost as much as I couldn't wait to yell at him for what he'd done.

I just hoped I got the chance to do both.

• • •

Max's mother's face stopped me in my tracks as we entered the ICU.

"Georgia?" Tate only noticed I wasn't next to him anymore, not that his mother stood outside a closed curtain looking pale as a ghost. "What's the matter?"

I shook my head rapidly, but couldn't form words.

He took my hand. "It's okay. He made it through. We have to do this one step at a time."

Tate traced my line of sight, and his face fell when he saw his mother. "Shit." He raked a hand through his hair. "Give me a minute."

I waited in the middle of the ICU while Tate walked over to his mother. The minute she saw him, she threw her arms around his shoulders and started sobbing.

Silent tears rolled down my face. *He can't... He just can't.*

Tate pulled back from the embrace and spoke to her. He looked over at me once as his mother wiped her eyes, and he held up one finger before slipping behind the curtain. When he came back out, he looked as pale as his mother. I watched him swallow before he walked back over. I don't think I moved a single muscle as I waited.

He blew out two puffed cheeks full of air. "They had to put him into a medically induced coma. His brain is swelling, which is common after the surgery he just had, but they weren't able to stop it any other way. They basically had to shut off his brain to give it time to heal." Tate scoffed. "Makes sense, I guess. The only way we could ever get him to stop fighting for what he wanted was to knock him out."

"How long will they keep him out?"

"They don't know."

I took a deep breath and wiped my tears. "Can I see him?"

"He doesn't look good, Georgia. His face is swollen, and he's hooked up to a million machines. Of course you can go in, but you might need to prepare yourself."

I stared at the drawn curtains surrounding the man I loved. "How do I do that?"

Tate frowned. "I wish I knew."

We walked over to his mom. She smiled and wrapped me in her arms. "Thank you for coming."

"Of course."

She looked me in the eyes. "He loves you very much."

I smiled sadly. "The feeling is mutual."

Tate stood next to me. "Do you want me to go in with you?"

I shook my head. "No, I just need a minute."

"Take all the time you need, sweetheart." His mother rubbed my back.

After a few deep breaths, I nodded and walked behind the curtain.

My heart stopped. Tate had warned me, but nothing could have prepared me for this moment.

Max didn't look like Max. If there hadn't been a curtain around him, I could have passed right by, still looking for the strong, beautiful man I knew. His skin was gray, and his face was so swollen. Tubes and wires were connected all over him, and bandaging wrapped around the top of his head from his eyebrows up. But his lack of expression scared me the most. I hadn't realized just how much Max's personality lit his face until now. Whether it was a smile, a smirk, or a frown, he was so animated and expressive. Now he looked...

I couldn't even let myself think it.

I had to pull myself together and be his strength until he was ready to fight on his own. So I stepped forward to the bed and took his hand.

"Hey. It's Georgia. You're going to be okay, Max. You're the strongest person I've ever met, and we can do this together." I took a deep breath and squeezed his hand. "I love you, Max. I love you more than anything, and I never got the chance to tell you that. So I need you to get better so I can look in your eyes and make sure you know it." I shook my head. "I also need to yell at you for hiding all of this from me. Just because you had a little brain surgery doesn't mean I'm letting you off the hook. I'm sure you know that."

The curtain rustled behind me. Tate stepped inside. "Just checking to see if you're okay."

I nodded and looked back over at Max. "I am. We're both going to be okay."

For the next twelve hours, Max's family and I stayed by his side. Doctors came and went, nurses adjusted monitors and hung new bags of medicine, but Max stayed the same. He didn't get better or worse. The doctors said they didn't anticipate any improvement in the short term. They just needed time for him to rest and heal. At midnight, Max's brothers got everyone together, and we made a schedule for the next twenty-four hours so someone would be by his side at all times, but each of us could get some sleep. Tate, Max's mom, and I were all going back to Max's house for a few hours.

But as we walked out of the ICU, I remembered something. "Can you just give me one minute?"

"Of course."

Max's brother Will was sitting by his side when I walked back behind the curtain.

"Do you want me to give you a minute?" he asked.

I shook my head and dug into my purse. "No, I just forgot to leave this." Pulling out Yoda, I set it on the tray next to his bed.

"Is that one of his?"

I nodded. "Yeah, he gave it to me the night we met."

Will chuckled. "If I had any doubt about you being the one, that just sealed the deal. He knew the day he met you."

I smiled. "I did, too. It just took me a while to admit it to myself."

"I'll keep my eye on the little guy. Go get some sleep."

"Goodnight, Will. Goodnight, Max."

Thirty-One

Max

She was snoring.

The first thing I saw when I opened my eyes was Georgia. Her head was in the crook of my shoulder in a hospital bed, and her body was curled up in a ball beside me. And she was damn snoring.

I smiled. *That might be my new favorite sound ever.*

I looked around the dark room, confused. I didn't remember how I got here, though somehow I *did* know where I was. Bits and pieces came back to me.

I remembered sitting on the bench, lacing up before the charity hockey game.

I remembered people talking to me while I slept. I could hear them, but they sounded very distant, like they were cutting through a thick wall of fog.

I remembered beeping. And someone washing my face. And being wheeled somewhere. And the nurses and Georgia laughing while they...did something. And the number ninety-six. What was ninety-six?

My throat was dry, and my neck hurt, but I didn't want to move and wake Georgia. And I was so damn tired.

So, so tired. I think I might've fallen back asleep for a little while, because when I woke up, Georgia wasn't snoring anymore. She was staring up at me. Our eyes met, and hers grew wide.

She jolted upright. "Holy shit! Max?"

It was hard to talk because my throat was so dry. "You were snoring."

"Are you joking? You've been in a coma for weeks and the first thing you say when you wake up is *I was snoring*?"

I smiled. "I think you left some drool, too."

Georgia covered her mouth and started to cry. "Oh my God, Max. I thought I was going to lose you."

"Shhh... Come here."

"I think I should go get the nurse. Or the doctor. Or both."

"In a minute. Just lie back down with me first."

She kept shaking her head and crying. "You're really awake. I can't believe you're awake. I'm afraid to lie down because what if I'm dreaming, and I go back to sleep and this isn't real when I wake up?"

"Stop overanalyzing."

"Are you in pain?"

"I feel like someone beat the crap out of me. But that's not new."

She snuggled back into the crook of my arm. "I'm so mad at you. You should've told me, Max."

"I'm sorry. I was trying to do the right thing. I'll make it up to you."

"Oh, you will alright. For the next forty or fifty years."

I smiled. "Your version of punishment is my version of heaven, sweetheart."

"Do you know how long you were out?"

I shook my head but remembered those numbers again. "Was it ninety-six days?"

"Ninety-six? No. You were out for eighteen days. Why would you think ninety-six?"

I shrugged. "I remember hearing that number."

Georgia's brows drew together before recognition dawned on her face. "Ninety-six?" She pointed over to the window. "You must've heard us talking about those."

I turned toward the window and squinted. The entire sill was jam-packed with action figures. "What are all those?"

"They're all ninety-six original *Star Wars* action figures. The one in the front is the Yoda you gave me the night we met. But all the others your teammates and friends sent you. Some of your doctors brought them, too." She shook her head. "I can't believe you heard us talking about those, that you remember the conversation. What else do you remember?"

I told her the jumbled bits that had come back to me.

"Wow. That's amazing. And I can't believe you're awake, Max. I would love nothing more than to lie down and snuggle with you, but I really think I should get the nurse to make sure you're okay. And I need to call your mom. She's been so worried. We all have."

I nodded. "Okay, but come here first. Bring your face closer to me."

Georgia leaned so we were nose to nose. My arms felt like they weighed three-hundred pounds, but I managed to lift one to her cheek. Her eyes glistened with happiness. "I love you, too, sweetheart."

She clutched her chest. "You heard me tell you that?"

"Of course. That's what kept me fighting."

• • •

Eight days later, I finally left the hospital. It took another week to get my family to go back home. I felt bad that they'd all been away from their lives for a month, but I also couldn't wait to be alone with Georgia.

My walking wasn't so great yet. It was going to take me a long time to build up my strength, so I stayed on the couch while Georgia walked the last guest out. When she came back, the house was quiet. She walked over to me.

"You hear that?" I said.

Georgia looked around. "No, what?"

I yanked her arm. "The sound of you moaning."

She giggled. "I don't think I was moaning."

"I guess it was just a premonition." I fingered the button of her jeans. "Why do you have so many damn clothes on?"

"Umm… Maybe because your brother just walked out the door two seconds ago?"

I unbuttoned her pants. "I hope you locked the damn thing."

"You're not supposed to do anything strenuous for four to six weeks."

"That's four to six weeks post-surgery. It's been more than thirty days. We're in that window."

Georgia bit her lip. "I don't want you to get hurt."

"I won't. You know why?"

"Why?"

"Because you're going to do all the work. Ride me, sweetheart."

I saw that familiar fire ignite in her eyes. "Okay, but you really need to let me do all the work. You can't top from the bottom, Max."

I made an innocent face and wrapped my hand around her throat like I knew she liked. "Who, me?"

We shed our clothes in a frenzy. Georgia first, and then she helped me undress. I could've managed myself, but I loved seeing her on her knees on the floor in front of me, yanking at my pants. Her fingernails scraped my thighs as she pulled off my boxers, and then she climbed on top and straddled me. I felt the wet heat of her pussy up against the bottom of my shaft.

"I want you," I groaned. "I fucking *need* you."

"I need you, too."

Georgia put her hands on my shoulders and lifted to her knees. I reached between us, fisted my cock, and dragged the head across her wet opening. She smiled, leaning in to kiss me as she lowered herself. It took every shred of willpower I had not to buck my hips and take over. The urge to fuck her into oblivion had my arms shaking.

She noticed. "Are you okay?"

"Never better, sweetheart."

She took a minute to steady herself and then began to rock back and forth, penetrating so damn deep. It felt like heaven and hell all rolled into one. This woman was the love of my life, and it was torture to hold back.

She arched her back, grabbing hold of my knees behind her, and gyrated her hips. When she moaned my name, I lost it. I fucking lost it. Screw taking it easy. If I was going to die, I wanted to die exactly as I was—with myself planted to the root inside the woman I planned to spend the rest of my life with. So I started thrusting, meeting her every rock with a roll and falling into the rhythm that was only ours.

"Max..." she yelled.

"Right there with you, baby."

We chased the edge together. Nothing had ever felt so good. So right. So real. Georgia squeezed me harder, her fingers digging into my hair as she spoke my name over and over. Then her eyes rolled back in her head, and I watched the orgasm pull her under. When her body started to go slack, I thrust up one last time and let go.

After, we were both panting. It might've only lasted a couple of minutes, but it was the best damn orgasm of my life. Georgia slumped into my lap, and I stroked her hair.

"Are you okay? Any pain?" she whispered.

I kissed the top of her head. "I'm good. I promise."

She sighed. "You know, I'm still mad at you."

"If that's how you show me mad, I'll be sure to piss you off plenty."

She slapped my shoulder. "You dumped me. And broke my heart."

"I know. And I promise I'm going to spend every day making it up to you."

My brother had told Georgia that right before everything happened, I'd made the decision to have surgery. But I realized she probably didn't know how I'd come to that decision.

"Did Tate tell you about my trip down to Long Beach?"

She looked up with her little nose wrinkled. "Long Beach? No. But that's where my boutique is."

"I know. When I first got out here, I was really struggling. It didn't feel like I'd made the right decision, but I couldn't risk you getting hurt. So I started taking long drives to think and clear my head. One day I wound up in Long Beach. I took the dogs for a walk on the beach, stopped to get them some water, and I walked straight into your store."

"Really?"

"Yep. So I went inside and looked around. The lady working there showed me the arrangements and mentioned that you had a database of suggested notes for cards. I remembered you'd said you used to suggest quotations for people who weren't good with messages."

"That's right. I had a few F. Scott Fitzgerald books in my first store, and I'd tabbed them and annotated quotes I loved."

I nodded. "I'd been driving all over, trying to figure out what to do. Turned out, the answer was in one of those quotes you picked out years ago."

"It was?"

"Yep. *It was always you.*"

Her eyes watered as she smiled. "It was always you, too."

Epilogue

Georgia

Two years later

Tonight was bittersweet.

I stood at the window in the owner's skybox, looking down at the ice. Max's entire family was all here, too, milling around somewhere behind me. I would rather have been down below, but Celia and Miles Gibson had insisted they host everyone for the big night, and I just couldn't say no. Technically, Miles was Max's boss, but Celia and I had also become good friends. They frequently invited me to watch the games up here with them, but ever since Max had skated back out onto the ice, I'd felt the need to be closer to the rink.

It had been a tough couple of years for Max, with lots of ups and downs. After his surgery, it took almost a full year for him to get back to where he needed to be to play hockey again. And even after countless hours of physical therapy and training to regain his strength, Max would be the first to tell you that while he might be fit to lace up, he wasn't the player he'd been before. The ruptured aneurysm had caused some long-term issues, the worst being tissue and nerve damage in his neck that made the recovery time after each game longer and longer.

Which was why tonight was his last game. At the ripe old age of thirty-one, Pretty Boy Yearwood was retiring. It had been his choice, not at the team's insistence, and that's how he wanted to go out—on his own terms.

Though, he wasn't actually going too far. During the year Max couldn't play, he'd still gone to every practice and every game. He'd become sort of an unofficial assistant coach for the team, and during that time, the head coach had recognized that Max had skills that were valuable on and off the ice. So while Max was retiring from playing today, as of September, he'd be the strength and conditioning coach for the Blades. His job would be to develop athletes to the pinnacle of their performance—something he knew better than anyone. The best part of the change was that he only had to work at practices, so he wouldn't have the crazy travel schedule of a player anymore.

As for me, I still had my office in New York, though I mostly worked remotely from California these days. I had since the day I'd flown out to be with Max after his surgery. At first, it was because he had needed me during his recovery, but over time, I'd fallen a little in love with California. New York would always have a piece of my heart, but I loved the laid-back atmosphere out here so much. Almost losing Max had taught me a lot about priorities. Turns out, my schedule wasn't too busy for a relationship after all, but my relationship needed to be the first thing I scheduled, rather than the last.

The final buzzer sounded, and my eyes welled up. Since the team hadn't been in playoff contention, the win tonight didn't change their season—though I'm sure it helped keep spirits high. All of Max's teammates gathered around him, jumping and celebrating the end of a decade-long career. Normally fans rushed to get out of the arena as soon as a game ended, but no one left their seat tonight. They waited for Max to lift his stick over his head and take one final lap. When he did, the place erupted in a standing ovation.

I couldn't stop crying as I watched. The Jumbotron zoomed in on his smiling face while he skated and waved, and when he got to the section below where I was seated, he looked up and winked, flashing the dimples that still made my knees weak. Things had really come full circle—from the night we'd met and I'd seen his face light up that screen, to today as his career ended and the beginning of whatever would come next for us started. *Best blind date ever.*

Max's brother Tate walked up next to me and put his arm around my shoulder.

"Stop worrying. He's happy," he said. "Those first few months when things were iffy about whether he'd be able to come back, I wasn't sure how he would survive without being able to play. But now he's made peace with it—and so much of that is because of you, Georgia. You made him realize what's important, and he's really looking forward to getting Austin's life-size Lincoln Logs business off the ground. He told me you're going to help. Hell, if you're half as successful with that as you are with your roses, you're going to make Austin proud."

I wiped my tears. "My makeup is already going to be a mess. Don't make it worse, Tate."

He smiled and squeezed my shoulder. A minute later, Maggie stood on my other side. She was now dating one of Max's teammates. They'd met at a barbeque at our house last summer and had been inseparable since. It had worked out great for me because it meant she spent a lot of time out in California, and we traveled to games together sometimes, too.

"How you holding up?" she asked.

I sighed. "Exactly how you'd expect."

My best friend smiled. "You want to walk down to the ice with me? Celia said Miles is going to say a few words. You should be there when Max comes off."

I nodded. "Yeah, let's do that."

Maggie and I flashed our all-access passes and made our way down to the ice to stand near the rink exit. The players were still celebrating when team owner Miles Gibson walked out onto the ice. He had a microphone in his hand, and he motioned for everyone to quiet down while waving Max over to the center of the arena.

"Good evening, everyone. I don't think I have to tell you that tonight was this guy's last game as a player. Max Yearwood is leaving the ice after a ten-year career with six-hundred-and-seventy-two goals. That puts him in the top fifteen all-time scorers, rivaling players who've had careers twice as long."

A woman in the stands screamed, "I love you, Pretty Boy!"

That started a gaggle of laughter and a myriad of others professing their love. Max shook his head, looking down and rubbing the back of his neck as if he was embarrassed. But I knew his ego had enjoyed every moment of tonight.

Eventually, Miles got control of the crowd again. "Jeez, and they say men are bad." He chuckled. "But on that note, I just wanted to thank Max for his dedication to the team. Though he's only been with us a couple of years, he's become a big part of the Blades family. And we're delighted to announce that while you might not be seeing this man on the ice next year, you will be seeing him on the sidelines. Max Yearwood leaves us as a player today, but he joins us as a coach next season."

The crowd went crazy again. Miles let it go on for a minute and then quieted everyone once more. "Since it seems like people are not as interested in me as they are the man standing next to me, I'm going to turn the mic over to the man of the hour. Ladies and gentlemen, I give you Max Yearwood."

Oh wow. I had no idea Max was going to make a speech, and I didn't think he did either. If he'd been aware, he hadn't mentioned it. Lord knows, I would've been freaking out being put on the spot like that. Public speaking was the one thing I still hadn't tackled from my summer to-do list I'd given Max.

Though this situation didn't seem to bother Max. He took the mic and waved to the crowd like the natural showman he was. "Thank you so much," he said, running a hand through his hair. "Jeez, I thought this would be easier. But it's hard to say goodbye to something that has been your entire life since you were four." He looked around the arena. "I still remember the first hockey game I ever went to. I'm one of six boys, and my dad usually took the older kids to games, but it was my birthday—the big four. So instead, he brought me and my next-oldest brother, Austin." Max paused and took a deep breath. He looked down at the ice for a few seconds, probably thinking about how they weren't both here anymore. When he looked up, he swallowed and pointed up to the top row of the arena. "We sat in the next-to-last row. I remember sitting on the edge of my seat the entire game and being mesmerized by how fast the players could skate. I told my dad that very day that I wanted to be a hockey player." Max patted his chest. "My dad tapped me here and said, 'Okay. But this is what makes a hockey player, son. Anyone can skate.' Twenty-seven years have gone by since that day, and those are still probably the truest words I've ever heard about this sport. Hockey is all about heart."

He paused and took another deep breath, again patting his chest. "That heart got me back here this year. But this heart also knows it's time to go. So today I want to say thank you for all of the years you've given me. All of you have become my family—which makes it only fitting that I close out my career on the ice by giving you a piece of my heart."

He turned to face the side of the rink where I stood and smiled. "Could someone please help my girl come out here? She's not so good on the ice, either on skates or in those sexy shoes she's wearing tonight."

My eyes widened. But before I could panic too much, one of Max's teammates had already opened the gate to the ice, and two others skated over and offered me their hands. I turned to Maggie, freaking out and looking for help, but she only smiled.

"Go get your man, my friend."

The next thing I knew, I was walking across the ice, escorted by two large men on skates. In the center of the arena, they handed me off to Max and skated away.

Max took one look at my face and smiled. "You're freaking out right now?"

I nodded, which only made him laugh.

I gazed up at the stands, at all of the eyes watching me, and the rumbling voices all seemed to stop at the same time. The arena grew quiet enough to hear a pin drop. I wasn't sure if I was imagining it or not, but when I turned back to Max I realized what had silenced everyone. Max had knelt down on one knee.

Oh my God. My trembling hand flew up to cover my mouth.

Max brought the other one to his lips and kissed it. "Georgia Margaret Delaney, I have been crazy about you since the night I crashed your blind date."

I shook my head. "That's because you *are* crazy."

Max squeezed my hand. "The only thing that makes leaving hockey bearable is knowing what's waiting for me on the other side. You have given me so much more than I ever thought possible. You give me strength and the courage to change—not just with my career but as a man. I want to grow old with you, Georgia."

He picked up something next to him on the ice, a black velvet ring box and...a Yoda. Max had a pretty big collection of them now, especially after his hospital stay, but the one in his hand had a small chip on its ear. It looked like the one I'd carried with me every day since we met. Max noticed me staring at it.

"Yeah, he's yours. I borrowed him from your purse last night when you weren't looking. I figured I needed every bit of luck I could get." He winked. "You don't need the luck. You already have me."

Max cupped my cheek, and I noticed his hand was shaking. For all his boisterous confidence and cocky pride, my big, tough guy was nervous. My heart melted a little bit more. He took another deep breath and blew it out with a smile before opening the ring box. Inside was a sparkling, emerald-cut diamond.

"Georgia, you are the reason for the smile on my face every morning and every night. Today I'm asking you to put it there forever. Will you, sweetheart? Will you marry me and make me the happiest guy in the world?"

I leaned in and cupped his cheeks in my hands, pressing my forehead to his. "Yes! Yes, I'll marry you."

Max crushed his lips to mine. Somewhere in the distant background, I heard the roar of the crowd.

When our kiss broke, he whispered, "I love you, babe. We've come a long way from my summer proposal to the real thing, haven't we?"

"We sure have."

"I'm *really* freaking relieved this was a decision you didn't need to debate forever."

I smiled. "I only need to debate things that are uncertain. When it comes to you, the only question I have about our life together is, how soon can we start?"

Acknowledgements

To you—the *readers*. Thank you so much for sticking with me on this journey. I hope Max and Georgia's story allowed you to escape for a short while, and you'll come back soon to see who you might meet next!

To Penelope – Writing can be a lonely profession, but not when you have a friend who is with you every step of the way. Thank you for always taking the ride with me.

To Cheri – Thank you for your friendship and support. I hope 2022 gets us back on the road!

To Julie – Thank you for your friendship and wisdom.

To Luna –So much has changed over the years, but I can always count on your friendship and encouragement. Thank you for always being there, often at 5AM.

To my amazing Facebook reader group, Vi's Violets – more than 22,000 smart women (and a few awesome men) who love to talk books together in one place? I'm one lucky girl! Each and every one of you is a gift. Thank you for all of your support.

To Sommer –Thank you for figuring out what I want, often before I do.

To my agent and friend, Kimberly Brower – Thank you for being there always. Every year brings a unique opportunity from you. I can't wait to see what you dream up next!

To Jessica, Elaine and Julia – Thank you for smoothing out the all the rough edges and making me shine!

To Kylie and Jo at Give Me Books – I don't even remember how I managed before you, and I hope I never have to figure it out! Thank you for everything you do.

To all of the bloggers – Thank you for inspiring readers to take a chance on me and for always showing up.

Much love
Vi

Other Books

The Invitation
Inappropriate
We Shouldn't
The Spark
The Rivals
The Naked Truth
All Grown Up
Sex, Not Love
Beautiful Mistake
Egomaniac
Bossman
The Baller
Left Behind (A Young Adult Novel)
Beat
Throb
Worth the Fight
Worth the Chance
Worth Forgiving
Belong to You
Made for You
First Thing I See
Well Played (Co-written with Penelope Ward)
Cocky Bastard (Co-written with Penelope Ward)
Playboy Pilot (Co-written with Penelope Ward)
Mister Moneybags (Co-written with Penelope Ward)
British Bedmate (Co-written with Penelope Ward)
Park Avenue Player (Co-written with Penelope Ward)
Stuck-Up Suit (Co-written with Penelope Ward)
Rebel Heir (Co-written with Penelope Ward)

Rebel Heart (Co-written with Penelope Ward)
Hate Notes (Co-written with Penelope Ward)
Dirty Letters (Co-written with Penelope Ward)
My Favorite Souvenir (Co-written with Penelope Ward)
Happily Letter After (Co-written with Penelope Ward)

About the Author

Vi Keeland is a #1 *New York Times*, #1 *Wall Street Journal*, and *USA Today* Bestselling author. With millions of books sold, her titles have appeared in over a hundred Bestseller lists and are currently translated in twenty-five languages. She resides in New York with her husband and their three children where she is living out her own happily ever after with the boy she met at age six.

Printed in the USA
CPSIA information can be obtained
at www.ICGtesting.com
LVHW040008120424
777190LV00032B/470

9 781951 045630